Destroyer

Book Three of the Expansion Wars Trilogy

Joshua Dalzelle

©2017

Print Edition

This is a work of fiction. Any similarities to real persons, events, or places are purely coincidental; any references to actual places, people, or brands are fictitious. All rights reserved.

*****

Edited by Monique Happy Editorial Services

www.moniquehappy.com

Prologue

"The provisioning ship is early."

"It might not be a Logistics Command or Merchant Marine ship ... it could be some asshole from Fleet coming out for another surprise inspection that will slow us down for at least a month."

"An odd sentiment coming from a Starfleet captain."

"My rank is just a formality, Mr. Seifert," Captain Ella Marcum said. "I'm no more a Fleet officer than you are."

"Of course," Seifert agreed amicably though his tone indicated he believed otherwise. Ella didn't bother pursuing it. Her last name, while opening doors for her, was often a hindrance. People just assumed because her father was the CENTCOM Chief of Staff that she was a banner-waving, mindless *patriot*. The truth was that she was only interested in her research, and if the United Terran Federation military wanted to pay for it, she'd accept a commission from Fleet Research and Science Division and worry about looking like a hypocrite *after* she'd accomplished her goals.

Her father was a soon-to-be-extinct species. Centuries of peace shattered because idiots like him and that half-wit Earther starship captain couldn't ask questions before opening fire. This latest tousle with yet another alien species would likely be found out to be another tragic misunderstanding ... but at least something positive might come of it. Maybe the elected leadership might begin to realize that tighter oversight on the fleet was necessary.

The Phage War, the Darshik conflict, the splintering off of the Eastern Star Alliance ... they were all incidents that Ella knew could have been prevented if cooler, more rational people had been in key positions at the time. She knew for a fact that Jackson Wolfe had fired first on a Phage ship before even a cursory attempt at communication by someone qualified could be made. Celesta Wright and Ella's own father had dragged them into a conflict between the Darshik and the Ushin without fully understanding the dynamics. The needless death by the hands of a few trigger-happy officers was simply unacceptable.

"They're not responding to the standard com laser request," Seifert said. "Shall I switch over to RF coms?"

"Maintain com silence," Ella said after a moment. "They know the approach and they'll be within range of the visual docking beacons soon enough."

"Captain, the procedure states that we must have confirmed identification of any inbound ship before allowing it to dock."

"Spare me the lecture about tedious, paranoid Fleet procedure, Mr. Seifert." Ella sighed. This was why she hated bridge watch with a passion. Seifert was nice enough and he'd proven himself useful to her as a young, virile male on a station awash with pudgy, middle-aged academics ... but the poor bastard was a slave to doctrine.

"This facility's very existence is highly classified, much less its exact location. If we have a ship on direct approach it stands to reason they're authorized to be here. We'll follow procedure and maintain our own com silence and when they're within range we'll try the com laser again and attempt visual recognition of the ship type."

"Aye aye, ma'am," Seifert said, squirming with discomfort.

The Feynman Research Outpost had been in heliocentric orbit within an unpopulated star system for the better part of thirty years. They were tasked with pushing the boundaries of what humans knew of gravity manipulation. Much of Terran technology was based on found or recovered alien artifacts, at least the major advances like faster than light travel, and until recently had been a fairly stale field of study. Small advances were made as more powerful reactors were developed and more efficient field generators were designed, but there had been no major breakthroughs until the Phage War.

Now, after being exposed to the Vruahn and their mastery of gravimetric forces, money and resources had been poured into the facility. The researchers at Feynman had quietly provided the Tsuyo Corporation the data and practical engineering necessary to implement the first reactionless drive, a system the all-powerful company then perfected and was now installing into a whole new generation of Terran starships.

Since then, the scientists at Feynman had moved on and were pursuing a weapon the Vruahn had exposed them to: a deployable gravity bomb. The term was a complete misnomer, but the short of it was that Fleet had become obsessed with the small munitions that had so effectively nullified the Phage's own reactionless drives, leaving them as easy prey for Terran missiles. The human scientists understood the base principles involved; however, they simply had no means to power such a device once it was disconnected from a starship's powerplant.

"These thermal signatures are all wrong," Seifert said with a frown. "This doesn't match up to any known ship class. I recommend we set Defense Condition Bravo, ma'am."

"I think you're being just a little over-dramatic, *Lieutenant*," Ella said, pronouncing his rank as if it were an insult. "Calm yourself and allow them to—" Alarms began blaring and cut off the rest of Ella's admonishment. She'd seen this particular alert before during the readiness drills she hated so much, but had never expected to have it go off for a real-world contingency. The klaxons and flashing red lights meant only one thing: imminent attack.

"Is it the ESA?" she shouted.

"No!" Seifert said, frozen in horror over his console. "The computer is saying it's a match for a Darshik cruiser!"

"Impossible," Ella breathed. "Nobody knows where we are."

Before Seifert could answer her, the alarms cut out suddenly and the overhead lights began to flicker. On all the terminals there were warnings flashing about the loss of main power and the status of the backup systems as they came online. Already she could feel that the station's gravity was reducing under the emergency power system, and the bank of terminals that controlled the station's defensive systems winked out completely.

"What was that?" she asked as the deck shuddered and loud clangs rang through the hull.

"Another ship we didn't see has just clamped onto our docking arm," Seifert said. "We're being boarded."

"Quick! Fire the drone!" Ella hissed.

"Only you can—"

"Right," she said, yanking out the key she wore around her neck on bridge watches. She ran to a small control panel near the hatch and lifted a protective cover so she could cram the key into the slot, her shaking hands making it necessary to try more than once. As soon as the key was turned, a large illuminated red button popped up from another access panel with the word *LAUNCH* flashing in white letters. Ella smacked the button and breathed a sigh of relief as she heard the point-to-point emergency com drone blast free from its cradle that was only one deck above the bridge. The drone was updated in real-time with backups of all research data as well as archives of the station's internal com system and telemetry feeds. It would make a direct-line flight back to CENTCOM HQ in the DeLonges System.

She switched the key back the opposite direction and grabbed the corded microphone for the station's PA system.

"This is Captain Ella Marcum. We're being boarded by hostile forces. I've unlocked all small arms caches on every deck … defend yourself as best you can."

"Shouldn't we be getting to the lifeboats, ma'am?" Seifert asked as she tossed the microphone back onto the console.

"There's nowhere to go, Lieutenant," she said. "Grab a weapon and get ready."

Chapter 1

"Attention to orders!"

The sound of hundreds of boot heels slamming together echoed through the chamber.

"Effective immediately, Senior Captain Celesta Wright is promoted to the rank of Rear Admiral. Her selfless dedication and sacrifice to Starfleet, the United Terran Federation, and humanity as a whole is well-documented. Her heroism in the Phage War along with her quick thinking and decisive actions in the Battle for Juwel ensured the planet was not lost to the Darshik.

"Admiral Wright will immediately assume the post of Chief of Operations, Seventh Fleet.

"At ease."

There was the rustle of clothing as everyone in the cargo bay relaxed from attention, most adopting a loose parade rest. The ceremony was as Celesta had wanted it; with only the people who had actually served with her and without the unnecessary pomp that she found so grating about most Fleet ceremonies.

"Admiral?"

"Thank you, Admiral Pitt," she said, the microphone hidden under the shirt collar of her dress blacks amplifying her voice.

"I will keep my remarks brief so that we aren't standing in this cold cargo bay any longer than we have to." There was a dutiful spat of laughter from the crowd as she collected her thoughts. "As the old guard moves on and the leadership from the Phage War retires, it will be up to many of you to shape the future of Starfleet in such uncertain times.

"We're in the midst of great political upheaval, divisions between the enclaves that may be irrevocable, and a new enemy at the gate. But amidst this darkness there are some points of light ... Starfleet has been reinvigorated and given new purpose, something that was sorely lacking in the previous centuries. Advances are coming so quickly that new generations of starships are being designed before the previous even enters service. We will prevail. While the odds may seem long right now, have faith in your officers and in each other. I am honored to be given the opportunity to serve and help continue the work of transforming the Mighty Seventh—Black Fleet—into the Federation's premier fighting force. Let's get to work."

With a nod she stepped away from the edge of the stage to a round of enthusiastic applause that went on even after she'd walked off the back of the platform and made her way to the hatchway. She'd taken the posting as Seventh Fleet's Chief of Operations under protest. The *Icarus*, a *Starwolf*-class destroyer and her first command, was being decommissioned after the last depot-level inspection showed that she had far too much structural damage from her many battles to safely be put back into active service.

Celesta naturally assumed that she'd be given command of a newer class of destroyer or even moved up into one of the latest boomers that were being put through their paces in final flight testing. But while she sat in limbo on the New Sierra Platform, the new official headquarters of the Federation Starfleet, waiting for the *Icarus* to be fully decommissioned, the leadership structure of the organization was turned upside down.

President Augustus Wellington, not a particularly healthy man when he assumed office, died unexpectedly from a massive heart attack just a month prior and the procedure for succession within the newly minted Federation was a bit muddy. It was assumed that the only recently appointed Vice President Nelson would step in, but more than a few PMs saw the sloppily worded order of succession as an opportunity. From what Celesta had been able to see in the media, however, Nelson was moving quickly to solidify support and cement his position as Chief Executive, even going so far as to begin making his own appointments.

Wellington's death was only unexpected because even for someone who enjoyed excess as much as Wellington had, modern medicine had been able to all but eliminate heart disease. Suspicions of foul play weren't being seriously entertained, but it was still a hot topic of discussion down on the surface of New Sierra, the Federation's capital world. While the news personalities in the capital city ran with stories of intrigue surrounding the former President's death, Vice President Nelson was quietly using the emergency powers granted him in the Federation's charter to shuffle people around in key positions within the military. Some of those who were asked to leave came as a surprise to everyone.

"Short and to the point. I'd have expected nothing else." Celesta turned at the familiar voice to see a well-groomed, middle-aged man leaning against the bulkhead in a civilian suit that looked brand new.

"Admiral Marcum," she said with a polite nod.

"It's just Joseph Marcum now," the former CENTCOM Chief of Staff said. "My *retirement* was made official as of 0500 this morning. I'm here on a day pass so that I can clean my office out and say goodbye. Do you have a minute?" When Celesta hesitated, he raised his hands in a placating gesture and stepped in closer to her.

"I understand that you may be one of those celebrating my ouster," he went on. "But I think that I have some useful advice that a newly promoted admiral might need ... especially one that has spent most of her career as a warrior and not a politician."

"Very well, Admiral," Celesta said, refusing to call the man by his first name. It was partially out of respect for the rank he once held but also for the officer she had once thought him to be. Her mentor, legendary starship captain Jackson Wolfe, thought her to be laughably naïve when it came to the trust she put in flag officers. Now that she was one, and he was not, she wondered if his hard, fast rule regarding the admiralty applied to her.

"My old office should give us a place to have a chat without being overheard," Marcum said. "And congratulations, Admiral. Despite the recent friction between us, I want you to know I consider you to be the best starship captain I had under my command ... and that includes the other guy." Celesta could only shake her head at the reference to Captain Wolfe. If ever there was someone Marcum would have wanted to see booted out of the Fleet before his own *retirement* it would have been the maverick from Earth that had been a perpetual thorn in his side.

****

"So what will happen to you now that Wellington is gone?" Celesta asked.

"That's a really good question," Pike said, pulling his shirt all the way on and standing up from the bed.

The pair had been circling each other for years, neither willing to sacrifice any aspect of their careers for a relationship or openly admit to the other how they really felt. With Celesta being stuck on the New Sierra Platform for months while the *Icarus* was dismantled and Pike hovering around after his boss's demise, there had been little for either to do but spend time with each other. Celesta had to admit privately that it may have been a mistake to keep things on hold for as long as they did.

"I'm still assigned to the office of the Presidency, not the person holding it," Pike continued. "I'd imagine I'll be given the choice of retiring, continuing on under President Nelson, or going back to CIS. They're down to only a handful of agents right now so the last option is the most likely."

"Weren't there more than a few connected people waiting to nail you to a wall once Wellington was no longer protecting you?" Celesta asked, reaching for the Fleet issue workout gear she used as sleepwear.

"You paid attention to my whining," Pike said, placing both hands over his heart and fluttering his eyes. "This really is—"

"Don't ruin things with that mouth of yours," Celesta warned. "And answer the question."

"The person that most wanted my head on a platter was none other than Fleet Admiral Joseph Marcum," Pike said as he rummaged around in the small alcove that served as a kitchen in Celesta's temporary billeting. "We may need to go to the mess deck … there's nothing in here but some questionable-looking crackers and what appears to be a sort of fruit paste. Do they stock guest billeting with expired shit they pull out of lifeboats?"

"So now that Marcum has been retired you're sure there's nobody else waiting to take out their frustrations with Wellington on you?"

"Nobody that has the juice to touch a full agent," Pike said. "But to be honest ... I've been doing this a long time and retiring on a full colonel's pension has a certain appeal right about now."

Celesta didn't comment on what might have changed to make the squirrely CIS agent consider retiring when just a year ago he said he'd work until he died or they forced him out. She was afraid the answer would be that the time they'd spent together on the Platform had completely readjusted his life's priorities. While that would be flattering, it also carried a level of responsibility she wasn't sure she wanted to take on.

"Let me clean up and put on some utilities; then we can head down to the flag officer's mess," she said.

"Want me to sneak down there so you can just happen to bump into me?" Pike asked seriously.

"Not this time," she said. "While it made sense to be discreet before, there's no longer the risk of a conflict of interest, or the appearance of one. Just toss on some civvies and give me about ten minutes."

****

"Jillian!"

Jillian Wolfe turned around to see a longtime friend she hadn't seen in years jogging up the corridor towards her.

"Commander Michael Barrett," she said, smiling warmly and embracing her former brother-in-arms from their days serving on the *Blue Jacket*, an antique *Raptor*-class destroyer where they had both served under a then-obscure Captain Jackson Wolfe. They'd also both served aboard the *Ares*, Wolfe's second command and a ship that was a major player during the Phage War.

"It's actually *Captain* Barrett now." He beamed. "My promotion was made official last week and I'm to be given command of the *Aludra Star* now that Captain Wolfe has been put back on a destroyer where he belongs. What brings you to New Sierra?"

"I was giving a presentation to the CENTCOM Fleet Acquisition Office about the training programs we've developed for the Gen IV starships," Jillian said. "I made sure to coordinate my trip with Celesta's promotion ceremony."

"Seems strange … she's not that old and she's a rear admiral while your husband is still a senior captain," Barrett said as he fell in beside his friend. "That probably came out wrong."

"I know what you meant," Jillian laughed. "Celesta had a lot of time in grade and CENTCOM is taking advantage of all the confusion within the civilian leadership to get her confirmation rammed through Parliament before someone realizes that she's being promoted above a few dozen qualified senior officers.

"As for Jackson … well, you know him as well as anybody. He's taken on this last mission to serve out the remainder of the extension Marcum forced on him, but he wants to be retired before he wants a star on his collar."

"How is he doing?"

"I couldn't tell you," Jillian said. "I know the *Nemesis* has passed her last set of flight qualification tests in record time, but during the next few months of crew training, communication will be few and far between."

"Did he tell you he stole an officer right out from under me?" Barrett asked. "Lieutenant Idris Accari was promoted to Lieutenant Commander ahead of the rest of his class thanks to having enough time in service from when he was an enlisted spacer. Captain Wolfe grabbed him before the *Icarus* even made port ... I was hoping to put him on the bridge with me aboard the *Star*."

"He did mention something about that." Jillian had stopped in front of a bank of lifts. "So will you be shipping out soon too?"

"No ... I'm working with Fleet R&D to try and use ships like the *Aludra Star* as more than just cargo haulers to deploy drop shuttles onto the surface," Barrett said. "The broad strokes are that we want to make the *Vega*-class assault carriers more versatile than just moving personnel and material to a planet's surface."

"Intriguing," Jillian said. "If you're going to be around for a bit, we should try to get all the old *Blue Jacket* crew together one night. Maybe even Agent Pike." She was moving to call for a lift car and Barrett took the hint.

"Of course," he said. "I'll try to organize something."

As he turned to walk away, he saw a young ensign scurrying down a side corridor and could only chuckle. When the hell had he become the "old man"? Hell, even Jillian Davis—Jillian *Wolfe*, that is—was heading up a major training program for CENTCOM. Celesta Wright was a damn admiral, he was sitting in the command seat of his own starship ... the young officer he'd just seen hardly looked old enough to be a first year cadet.

His next thought was far less jovial. When he was a fresh-faced lieutenant junior grade serving aboard the *Blue Jacket,* there had always been many layers of officers over him, a security blanket that, despite his fears, someone above him knew exactly what to do. Now *they* were the ones in charge and he didn't feel like they'd learned nearly enough to be relied upon to do the right thing. It was a sobering thought, but one that only made him that much more determined to do it right and not make any foolish mistakes that led to lost lives and ships.

Chapter 2

"Goddamnit! Cut power! Heave to and let her drift!"

"Zero thrust, aye!"

"That's part of the problem right there," Captain Jackson Wolfe said, straining to get himself under control. "*Nemesis* doesn't *use* thrust."

"Yes, sir," the helmsman said emotionlessly, but Jackson saw his shoulders bunch up. He regretted the loss of composure, but he had to snap his crew out of this inexplicable lethargy and fast.

"This is the fourth miss in a row," Jackson said, forcing a calm tone as he stood up and smoothed out his uniform. "These target drones don't have half the capability of the ship we'll be facing, yet we can't seem to knock one down once we get in close. Our kill ratio in simulations was eight-two percent. What the hell is the problem?"

When nobody answered, he continued. "If anybody has something, speak up. This ship is slated to be fully activated within the next two months and we're being tasked with a seek and destroy mission against one of the sneakiest, toughest targets the Fleet has ever seen. Not to belabor the point, but *this* isn't good enough. That Darshik ace will not hold still for us like the target drones that we've not been able to hit."

The *TFS Nemesis* had just entered active service six months prior and the accelerated training schedule his crew had endured was nothing short of brutal. His first and second watch bridge crews were stellar performers with the new ship, so he was now running the backups through a grueling set of live fire exercises before they were ordered to begin their mission. At first he thought it was just a bad case of nerves from having him on the bridge with them, but after repeated failures he suspected that they just didn't have enough reps to be proficient.

"Nav, are we heading towards anything?"

"Negative, Captain," the specialist third class at Navigation said. "The sky is completely clear, no course corrections needed."

"Take a break, everyone," Jackson said. "Safe all weapons and call up second watch. Tell your backshops to stand down and we'll come back at this tomorrow."

The crew quietly climbed up from their stations and, looking completely dejected, filed off the bridge as their relief watch came in. None of them met Jackson's eye as they walked out.

"A word in private, Captain," Lieutenant Commander Idris Accari said quietly. He'd been on the bridge as an observer as per Jackson's request.

The young officer had been an enlisted navigation specialist aboard the *Ares*, Jackson's second command, and had been recognized as having the raw talent and potential to make an outstanding officer. After he'd served with distinction aboard the *Icarus* as Celesta Wright's OPS officer, Jackson had swooped in and snatched him to be his tactical officer when he'd learned the older ship was being decommissioned. Other than the well-earned reputation of not being able to keep it in his pants, Accari had been a near-model young Fleet officer. Jackson was happy to see that his instincts had been proven correct when he recommended him for an Officer Candidate Training slot.

"This is private enough," Jackson said. "What's on your mind?"

"Captain, I—"

"I know you feel personally responsible for the backups since you've been acting CO during their training sessions," Jackson said. "This isn't a misplaced apology for the performance I just saw, is it?"

"Not exactly, sir." Accari didn't wilt under Jackson's intense stare. "I do think an explanation is at least in order, however."

"Go on."

"This backup crew never trained in scenarios where so much of the automation was disabled," Accari pressed ahead. "That's not an excuse for how poorly this run went, but I think that perhaps more of the blame should be shifted to me since I performed all their training scenarios with all the ship's avionics working perfectly."

"Then what we have here is a learning experience for everyone," Jackson said. "You made a critical error in their training when you didn't take into account that any time we have to dig that deeply into the crew roster for replacements, it's almost guaranteed the ship has taken some significant damage and the automation will almost certainly not be fully functional. They need to learn the hard way just like you did way back when you were a navigation specialist. They've also just learned that I will not pull punches with them like their training instructors did in the simulators on Arcadia … time to find out who can hack it and who needs to be replaced."

"Yes, sir," Accari said.

"You're still responsible for them, Lieutenant Commander," Jackson said. "My advice to you would be to address them sooner than later and make sure they know that everything we do on this bridge is life and death. You know that better than most officers in the fleet. Our live fire trials are over in the next fifteen hours and we'll be given our orders, so the next time one of them has to sit in a seat up here it may very well be the real thing." He patted Accari on the shoulder as members of second watch filtered onto the bridge, including his brand new XO, Commander Chambliss.

Jasper Chambliss was from a planet called Hermes in the New America enclave. He'd served as the Flight OPS department head on Jackson's previous command, the *Aludra Star*, and had also been the skipper on a light frigate as a young lieutenant before moving up into the larger mainline ships. Chambliss had proven to be a highly effective officer during the campaign to free the planet Juwel from the Darshik, so when he asked if he could transfer, Jackson had jumped at the chance. Chambliss was put on the short list of XO candidates during the first stages of crew training and Jackson quickly made his choice to make the move permanent.

"I have the bridge, Captain," Chambliss said after checking the ship's log and taking status off the main display.

"Very good, Commander," Jackson said. "Training schedule for the watch is at your discretion. Simulator mode only ... I expect orders declaring us to be fully activated soon and then we'll be leaving directly from here."

"Understood, sir," Chambliss said. "Enjoy your evening."

Jackson walked quickly through the hatch before Accari could open up with another volley of *explaining*. If it were any other officer he would use the term *excuses,* but he knew that Accari's main concern was that Jackson not have a bad opinion of the junior officers he'd been in charge of. If they all learned something from the experience—other than to assume that their CO was a complete and unreasonable asshole—then it wasn't time wasted.

"To the officer's mess, Captain?"

"Sergeant Barton." Jackson nodded to his Marine escort. "Yes ... I'm having dinner with your boss this evening."

"Put in a good word for me, sir."

"Why would I lie to the man, Sergeant?" Jackson asked with a smile the Marine couldn't see.

Sergeant Willard "Willy" Barton had been a member of the expeditionary force that had been first sent to counter the Darshik troops landed on Juwel. Those Marines had been stranded and cut-off without most of their equipment and no relief as the Darshik blockade kept the Federation Starfleet at bay. It wasn't until Captain Wolfe had run the picket line and successfully deployed the drop shuttles from his assault carrier that the tide of battle had turned for the beleaguered Marines. Once they'd rotated back from the front, Barton, along with many of his fellow Marines from the Juwel campaign, had requested reassignment to Fleet detachments and service aboard starships ... specifically, they wanted to fly with the captain that had hauled their asses out of the fire.

While it wouldn't be a request normally taken seriously by CENTCOM, the Marine Corps handled its own assignments and the general in charge of Fleet

Operations just happened to be Brigadier General Javier Ortiz, once Detachment Commander Major Ortiz that had served aboard both the *Blue Jacket* and the *Ares* with Captain Wolfe. When the general had heard of the number of transfer requests coming in for shipboard duty from a Marine frontline combat unit, he looked into it personally and, in a moment of nostalgic weakness, had granted most of them, assuming the Marine in question was qualified for detachment duty.

General Ortiz had screened the officers carefully, still carrying the shame of the attempted mutiny on the *TCS Blue Jacket* that some of his men had been a part of. It was one of the main reasons he granted so many transfer requests amid the strident protests of the expeditionary force commanders; he knew that any man requesting a transfer blindly based solely on the commanding officer of that ship would be loyal to that captain and watch his back.

When Jackson entered the officer's mess, Sergeant Barton discreetly took his post by the hatch and stood at a loose parade rest, scanning the room. The young NCO took his job very seriously, and while Jackson would have normally scoffed at his paranoia and dismissed him back to the detachment once the ship was underway, the Central Intelligence Service had already caught three Eastern Star Alliance infiltrators aboard Fleet facilities. A few had been interrogated vigorously enough that they'd admitted they were to look for targets of opportunity as well as gather intel. Jackson knew that his name had been thoroughly demonized within the ESA as the man that caused the Phage War. An operative could make a real name for himself in the old Asianic Union political circles by killing the captain that fired the first shots.

"Sit down, Major," Jackson said as Major Lucas Baer climbed to his feet and stood at attention when he approached the table. "There's a standing order aboard to not render honors on the mess deck ... no point in making people jump up and down while they're eating."

"Yes, sir," Baer said, sliding back into his seat. "This is my first detachment duty aboard a Fleet ship and it takes some getting used to."

"And each ship is different depending on her CO's preferences," Jackson said. "So this is your first cruise?"

"No, sir," Baer said, politely putting his dinnerware down until his captain had fully settled into his seat. "I flew two short cruises on Merchant Marine ships during the war until I transferred to an infantry unit. I have to say ... if I had known what food was like on a mainline warship I'd have requested detachment duty much sooner."

"The perks of rank, Major," Jackson laughed. "Your grunts don't have it quite so good. How is the training going?"

"Very good, sir. My Marines will be more than ready to repel boarders should the occasion arise. We're staying out of the crew's way as much as possible, training in critical areas like Engineering during night hours when nothing more than monitoring is going on."

"Excellent," Jackson said absently. "I also want you to add a new regime to your training: I want your people ready to board a Darshik ship if necessary."

"Sir?" Baer stopped eating and leaned back.

"I know that's not in our doctrine, but we have a valid translation matrix thanks to the Ushin, a ship that's capable of running down and grappling a cruiser, and the area to use as holding cells," Jackson explained. "This likely won't ever come up, but this mission will be full of first times for all of us, I think. Just flying around blindly trying to bump into something so elusive as this Darshik ace isn't much of a plan ... we'll need intel and I'd prefer to be ready to execute a raid on one of their ships should the opportunity present itself."

"We have detailed information on their ships' interiors thanks to the mostly intact hulks left in the DeLonges System," Baer said thoughtfully. "We'd need a place to train, of course."

"Cargo Bay Four will be empty for the foreseeable future," Jackson said. "Use that space and tell Engineering I authorized any fabrication needed to create a proper training environment."

"I'd need a simulated airlock and then the rest could just be mocked up using stacked cargo containers ... the more I think about it, the less difficult this seems, sir," Baer said.

"Like I said: It probably won't come up," Jackson said, now attacking his dinner in earnest. "But if we happen to disable one of their cruisers it's an opportunity I'd rather not pass up."

"I'll get right on it, Captain."

****

"*Sir, com drone just entered the system ... official order packet has come through as well as a priority message for you.*"

"Send it to the terminal in my office," Jackson said. He didn't recognize the voice of the relief com officer over the intercom.

"*Aye, sir.*"

Within seconds, his terminal beeped to let him know that he needed to enter his credentials to access classified information stored on the secure servers. Recently Fleet had cracked down on the handling of classified material in the wake of so many ESA spies being routed out of key positions within the organization.

It depressed him that in the midst of a war with the Darshik they still had to worry about sabotage from within by another human faction, but it didn't surprise him. What *did* surprise him was that as far as CIS could tell, the ESA hadn't suffered a single attack at the hand of the Darshik. Given how intertwined ESA and Federation space was, that seemed almost statistically impossible given the systems that had been hit near the border.

"Where the hell is it?" Jackson grumbled to himself as he navigated down through the multiple layers of security to finally get at the folder containing his new orders and personal communiques that had been flagged as sensitive. When he saw that his orders had been dated three weeks prior by Seventh Fleet's newly minted Chief of Operations, Admiral Celesta Wright, a wide smile split his face. He was enormously proud of her accomplishments and was happy to see she'd developed into a finer Starfleet officer than he would ever be. She was both a skilled warfighter and set the right kind of example for the younger officers coming up behind her. The memory of a too-young commander being forced onto the bridge of the *Blue Jacket* against both their wills was a stark contrast to the polished, confident flag officer she was today.

His smile faded, however, when he saw that there was a flash intel brief in the folder also and it was signed by someone who was notorious for bringing trouble into Jackson's life.

"Fucking Pike," he muttered, opening the brief.

"*Captain,*" Pike's voice came through the speakers when Jackson selected the file. The accompanying image wasn't of the agent's face, but of what could only be a deep space facility. It was one that Jackson had never seen before. "*This is semi-off the record, but I just wanted to give you a heads up before it filters down through the official channels. This is the Feynman Research Outpost, or what's left of it. It's a deep space research station that's been instrumental in most of the advances we've made in gravimetric field generation and control.*

"*The first Prowler on the scene was able to confirm that the station had been hit with multiple strikes from a Darshik plasma lance. This probably happened to cover the fact that the station had been boarded. They were able to fire off their emergency com drone that had copies of all the logs and research, so CIS was able to confirm that a Darshik ship had snuck up on the facility and grappled onto one of the cargo airlocks.*"

The imagery shifted to the high-resolution shots taken by the station's cameras of a ship latched onto one of the docking outriggers. There could be no mistaking the ship's origin.

"*As you can likely tell, it is indeed our elusive ace that we tangled with in the Juwel System, and he's made some upgrades since then. I'm including the location of Feynman along with a more detailed analysis of what they did there. You didn't hear this from me ... but we've learned that the gravimetric subluminal drive that ship is using was likely adapted from the RDS pod* the Icarus *had to jettison in Darshik space. Who knows what they could have gotten their hands on if the outpost workers weren't able to purge the computers and destroy their research in time.*

"*One other note of interest: The newly retired Fleet Admiral Joseph Marcum's daughter, Ella Marcum, was a researcher aboard the station. She's also one of thirty-five people who are still officially listed as missing in action since their bodies were never recovered ... not even when the residuals were tested for DNA after the initial fight near the airlock.*

"*The very existence of this station is a highly guarded secret, but I feel like you need the information sooner than later considering what's in the orders Celesta just sent you. Good luck, Captain. Pike out.*"

"Damn," Jackson whispered as he flicked through the pictures of the gutted research station. It wasn't pretty and it looked like the Darshik raiders knew exactly what they were after. A path of destruction could be drawn from the docking arm all the way down to the main research areas. The bridge and crew quarters were largely left alone until the enemy ship speared the structure with those damned plasma lances.

Forcing himself to set aside the horrific imagery of the station, he opened up the official copy of the *Nemesis's* orders and verified their receipt. He then authorized the com section to transmit the "receive acknowledgement" to the com drone that was circling back around the system, waiting for their reply so it could transition back to the nearest platform in the Arcadia System. The newer drones were capable of much more than pre-programmed point-to-point flights between platforms and could be dispatched from ships or to uninhabited systems to relay com traffic.

Their orders were short and to the point: The *TFS Nemesis*, Captain Jackson Wolfe commanding, was tasked with locating and destroying the Darshik warship known by CENTCOM codename *Specter*. Captain Wolfe was authorized to use any and all means at his disposal to accomplish the mission up to and including commandeering local Fleet assets when necessary during the pursuit. The *Nemesis* had nine months to complete her mission.

The last line of his orders was the one he was waiting for: *As of receipt of transmission, the TFS Nemesis is fully activated and considered a man of war in the United Terran Federation Starfleet and shall operate within the boundaries of the United Terran Armed Forces charter.*

"Time to go hunting," Jackson said with a grim smile. Even during the Phage war he'd never felt a hatred for an enemy like he did for this *Specter*. Now, with a destroyer under him, he was ready to exact some long overdue payback.

Chapter 3

"Let's make this quick!" Jackson said as he walked into the command deck wardroom, silencing all of the extraneous conversation. All of his senior staff and department heads were already seated and waiting for him.

"As of 1145 ship's time, the *Nemesis* is fully activated and we've been given our first mission. You all know what that tasking is, so we'll not belabor that now ... all mission details will be disseminated through the normal channels once we're underway. When you're called, I want a simple go, no-go, and then we're heading for the first jump point.

"Engineering?"

"Go."

"Operations?"

"Go."

"Tactical?"

"Go."

"Navcom?"

"Go."

"Crew Support Systems?"

"Go."

"Marine Detachment?"

"Go, sir."

"And, finally, XO?"

"The *Nemesis* and her crew are ready, Captain," Chambliss said.

"Okay, then. We're steaming for the Columbiana jump point with the ultimate destination of the Cassandra System," Jackson said. "It's an uninhabited system with the only thing of interest being the former Feynman Research Outpost, now a derelict hulk thanks to our Darshik friend.

"It's not likely we'll intercept it anywhere near there at this point, but it's a place to start and it's a short flight. All concerns and questions at this point need to be routed through OPS or the XO, but I'd ask you to hold off until you get your specific mission briefs. Any immediately pressing issues?"

Nobody raised a hand or spoke up. His crew was made up of seasoned combat veterans, so if he had to say what the mood of the room was it would have to be bored, although there were a few eager smiles among the group.

"First watch will report to the bridge immediately," he said. "I want to be under power and heading to the jump point within the next ninety minutes. Dismissed."

"With all due respect, might I ask why we're heading to the Cassandra System, Captain?" Chambliss asked once everyone had filed out. "From what I can tell from the brief you sent me, the Darshik have already hit it … we're not really equipped for the type of forensic investigation that could give us a next destination."

"First off, never hesitate to question me about an order I've given you're not clear on, Commander," Jackson said. "I do applaud your choice of timing and discretion, however. As this isn't an emergency, it's best that the crew doesn't see us potentially disagreeing on a course of action.

"You're absolutely correct; I don't expect that we'll find anything there since the *Nemesis* isn't equipped for that sort of work, and it's unlikely that the Specter will still be sticking around. However, there's an off chance it *could* be … its motivations are largely a mystery and it might have intentionally attacked a remote station with the hopes of drawing more Terran ships out into the open. But the main reason is that instead of waiting for a com drone we'll be right there within radio range if the CIS teams that *are* qualified to investigate the scene find anything. We'll be able to act on it immediately rather than wait weeks for a drone to come into the DeLonges or Columbiana systems."

"Very good, sir," Chambliss said, nodding thoughtfully. "And being underway keeps the crew active and alert."

"Also true." Jackson patted his XO on the shoulder while simultaneously steering him towards the hatchway. Getting a new Executive Officer was always a strange dance, but at least this time Jackson was familiar with Chambliss and respected him. His last XO, Commander Simmons, had remained aboard the *Aludra Star* to help bring Captain Barrett up to speed and maintain continuity aboard that ship. That was the hell of the way Fleet handled personnel: Just about the time a captain and executive officer had gelled as a team and were kicking ass, Fleet Operations would split them up to spread around the experienced officers. He was always guarded during the first few missions with a new one, but he had high hopes for Jasper Chambliss.

By the time Jackson strode onto the bridge, his Marine escort taking position just inside the hatchway while two more stood outside as sentries, first watch was in their seats and the air hummed with activity.

"Nav!"

"Course and velocity plotted for the Columbiana jump point, sir," a chief with salt and pepper hair sitting at the nav station answered.

"Helm!"

"New course entered and ready, Captain," the helmsman said. "Main engines are ready. Engineering has cleared the *Nemesis* for maneuvering."

"Very well," Jackson said. "Proceed onto new course, all ahead one-half."

"Ahead one-half, aye!"

The *Nemesis* was the first ship to enter active service with an integrated reactionless drive system. All the gravimetric field generators were buried within the main hull of the starship and she didn't carry the normal, massive magneto plasma drive pods like other ships in the fleet. Instead, smaller, less powerful plasma engines were fitted to extendable pylons in case of emergencies. After four months' training on the *TFS Endurance*, the *Nemesis's* sister ship, and then another two breaking in his own ship, Jackson had become comfortable with the system.

Some of the older spacers weren't thrilled with the new drive and claimed it would leave them stranded, but after pushing two identical ships to their limits over the six months of testing, Jackson had every confidence that Starfleet had provided him a reliable ship. It also seemed that some of his complaints about the *Starwolf*-class ships had been taken seriously as the *Nemesis's* armor was significantly beefed up, close to four meters of alloy over critical areas, and all of it was removable off the inner hull in segments for replacement.

His first ship, the *Raptor*-class destroyer, *Blue Jacket*, had been made of three-meter-thick alloy, but the hull had been one monolithic piece with openings cut into it for hatches and access points. While incredibly strong, it also meant that if the hull was compromised there was no practical way to repair it. From what he could see of the *Nemesis's* design, the engineers had made her able to take a hard hit and survive as well as able to be repaired and go right back at it.

"OPS, is that com drone still in the system?" Jackson asked.

"Yes, sir," the lieutenant at the OPS stations reported. "It's making its final course correction before heading for the DeLonges jump point."

"Send one more message addressed to Seventh Fleet Operations letting them know we're underway and on mission," Jackson said. "Put nothing in there regarding course or destination."

"Aye aye, sir," she said. Her name was Ayko Hori and, like him, she was from Earth. Her obvious Japanese ancestry made people assume she was from one of the two planets within New America that the bulk of Japanese colonists had flocked to centuries ago, and it was something she bristled at each time it was casually mentioned. Unlike Jackson, who had always downplayed his heritage, Ayko was defiantly proud of being from Earth.

She was also strikingly beautiful, something that caused him some concern as he saw his tactical officer continually stealing glances at her. Jackson knew that Accari was a consummate professional … but he also had a certain reputation among the female officers. While there was no actual Fleet regulation concerning relationships among crewmates, some captains imposed "hands-off" policies to varying degrees, mostly among bridge crews that would serve on the same watch together. The last thing a CO wanted was a lovers' quarrel disrupting the operations of their ship. Jackson had yet to implement anything like that himself because it had never been a problem, but he made a mental note to have Commander Chambliss keep an eye on it. He felt he was too close to Accari personally to be objective and it was the XO's job anyway.

The *Nemesis* swung smoothly onto her new course and surged ahead; the only way the crew could tell she was accelerating was by watching their instruments. Jackson was among the captains that would sorely miss the old plasma thrust engines, but he couldn't argue with progress when it put a weapon like the *Nemesis* into his hands to hunt that alien bastard down.

"*Nemesis* is at transition plus ten," the helmsman called out as the destroyer shot past and settled down at ten percent over her transition velocity. It was the velocity buffer Jackson had decreed to be their standard for normal warp transitions.

"OPS, deploy the warp drive and charge transition capacitors," Jackson ordered. "How long until we hit the jump point?"

"Seventy-eight hours, sir," Nav said.

"Coms, tell Engineering I want a full diagnostic done on the warp drive before we get there," Jackson said. "They're clear to take the RDS offline as they need to when it's time to test the field emitters."

"Aye, sir."

"OPS, set us back to normal watch schedule and let second watch know that they're going to be coming back on duty shortly." Jackson stood up. "XO, you have the bridge."

"I have the bridge, aye," Chambliss said and stood as well while Jackson walked off the bridge.

"So the hunt begins, eh Captain?" Barton said as he fell in behind Jackson.

"That it does, Sergeant," Jackson said with a tight smile.

****

"Admiral, come in."

"You asked to see me, sir?" Celesta said, walking into the expansive office with a large, curved window that looked down onto New Sierra.

"Have a seat." Fleet Admiral Pitt gestured to a large chair in the small lounge area. "Can I get you something to drink? It's after 1800 station time so I'm having a snort. Bourbon okay? It's not the stuff Wolfe gets, but it's not bad."

"That'll be fine, Admiral," Celesta said. Once Pitt had poured them both a drink and sat across from her, she decided to cut to the chase. "Can I assume this afterhours meeting and expensive liquor is because you're about to tell me something I don't want to hear?"

"Direct." Pitt nodded in approval. "Admirable, but you'll need to temper that if you expect to navigate these political waters as a flag officer."

"I have no—"

"Spare me." Pitt waved her off. "You took the promotion because you're as ambitious now as you were when that idiot Winters put you on Jackson Wolfe's bridge. You're likely already picking out the new furniture for this office." Celesta said nothing as she had to concede that Pitt made a valid point. He'd just been promoted to CENTCOM Chief of Fleet Operations and answered directly to the Chief of Staff and the President himself.

"And while you still have that rebellious spark all Black Fleet destroyer captains have ... we have a problem to discuss, and it can't be something that ever leaves this office or we'll *both* burn for it."

"Oh, shit," Celesta said wearily. "What now?"

"Have you met the new President yet?"

"No," Celesta said, now dreading where the conversation was going. She knew President Nelson by reputation only, but what she knew made her leery of how he would perform as a Commander in Chief.

"I just came back up from the surface," Pitt said, leaning back and rubbing his temple. "It was an exhausting day of briefings trying to get the new CIC spun up and aware of all Fleet operations. He became particularly concerned by what he called an overly aggressive misstep by Black Fleet in initiating a seek-and-destroy mission on a single Darshik ship."

"You mean the *Nemesis's* mission to eliminate the specialized Darshik cruiser that's taken out nearly half a dozen Terran starships single-handedly?"

"Yes," Pitt said. "President Nelson feels that a more diplomatic approach might be in order considering that we now know we're dealing with an ideological offshoot of Ushin society. He thinks that we should be offering limited support with the goal of allowing them to sort it all out themselves and thus keeping the Federation out of either side."

"That's ... naïve," Celesta said, groping for a polite word given they were discussing the current sitting President. "The Ushin have already shown that they're incapable of dealing with the problem themselves. I can understand not wanting to get the Federation involved in what is essentially an internal Ushin matter, but we're already well past that. The Darshik know where we are and we've already engaged them in battle."

"Agreed, but he was adamant that we limit combat operations to the direct defense of Terran-held systems and concentrate specifically on those with populated worlds," Pitt said.

"This still works," Celesta said with a shrug. "Wolfe's mission could be seen as—"

"Our new President isn't *that* naïve," Pitt interrupted again. "He specifically wants the *Nemesis* to stand down ... his words. He feels like the risk is minimal to ignore the problem of a single ship for the time being while the Ushin work to resolve issues with the Darshik. Once that happens, the problem of the Specter takes care of itself."

"And what is it that you think?" Celesta asked after a long, uncomfortable moment. "We don't even know what the Darshik's leadership structure is, but I have to think that even if a diplomatic resolution between the two were achieved, this Specter would simply go rogue."

"I think you're well aware of my opinion on this type of appeasement strategy," Pitt said. "But what we think is irrelevant. The new CIC has given us a direction he expects to be implemented. Since all Black Fleet orders originate from your office, I thought you should at least get a heads up before I have to officially order you to stand down the *Nemesis* mission."

"So that's really the *only* reason I'm sitting here?"

"Tell me something, Celesta ... how do you think Jackson Wolfe will react to being told to abort his hunt and bring his ship back to port?" Pitt asked with a perfectly straight face.

"I think we understand each other, Admiral," Celesta said.

"I'm sure I have no idea what you mean, Admiral Wright," Pitt said.

Chapter 4

"Transition complete."

"Position confirmed, sir. We've arrived in the Cassandra System just under thirty-eight thousand kilometers off our targeted jump point."

"OPS, let Engineering know I'd like to tighten that up significantly by our next warp flight," Jackson said. "Coms?"

"Fleet beacons coming through loud and clear, Captain," Lieutenant Demaryius Makers reported from the com station. "Three CIS Prowlers, a com carrier, two frigates from Fleet Research and Science, and six contacts that aren't specified by class."

"Very good." Jackson slipped his restraints off and stood up. "OPS, stand down collision alert and activate our own beacon. Let's not have any misunderstandings between us and any tactical assets that may be lurking in this system."

"Aye aye, sir."

The new warp drive that had been fitted to the *Valkyrie*-class starships used the latest and greatest in gravimetric field generators, and the emitters didn't need to be extended out away from the ship in order to form the fore and aft distortion rings. The system was much more efficient and provided a higher stable warp factor than the previous generations of FTL drives, but the tradeoff was that transitions back to normal space could sometimes be a bit on the bumpy side.

After exhaustive testing, Tsuyo Corporation's scientists discovered that the issue stemmed from the way the distortion rings collapsed with the new style of emitters. There was no real danger to the ship or crew, nor was there any available solution. Anxious to get the new ship into service, Fleet R&S deemed the new warp drive safe and modified the standard operating procedure to include mandatory crew restraints during transitions. Since Jackson wasn't qualified to dispute the findings regarding the drive's safety, he could only accept the conclusions and order that a collision alert be sounded ten minutes prior to transition to allow the crew time to get into restraints.

"Engineering has cleared the *Nemesis* for maneuvering, sir," Lieutenant Hori said. "Commander Walsh also asked me to tell you—and I'm quoting—he'll bet you a case of proper whiskey that the *Nemesis* will be within ten thousand kilometers of her target next transition."

"Coms, please send an open-channel message to the fleet identifying us and asking them where we'll be permitted to fly," Jackson ordered, deciding to ignore the semi-inappropriate message from his colorful new Chief Engineer. While the man had come with mixed recommendations, the issue was moot: He was one of only three engineers of sufficient rank that was qualified on the *Valkyrie*-class. Skilled or not, the man's lack of decorum when communicating to the bridge—especially via a junior officer—grated on Jackson's nerves.

"I don't want us bumbling down into the investigation area."

"Aye, sir."

"Helm, let's clear the jump point," Jackson said. "All ahead one-third, take us down outside the orbit of the tenth planet."

"All ahead one-third, aye," the helmsman said. "Coming about forty degrees to starboard, twelve degrees declination."

"Nav, verify our flightpath is clear," Jackson said.

"Nav radar is active, clearing the flightpath now, sir," the chief said.

Without having anything particular to do at that moment, Lieutenant Commander Accari took it upon himself to bring up the *Nemesis's* passive tactical sensor array and began scanning the area where the station wreckage was, forwarding the data stream to the OPS officer so she could decide what to put up on the main display. Jackson appreciated the initiative and watched as the long-range optics began to "stare" at the same spot in space, allowing the limited light to filter in so the computers could begin building a complete picture of the devastation.

Even the grainy, computer-enhanced images were enough to set the crew's blood to boiling. The hull was peppered with gaping holes from where Darshik plasma lances had pierced the station at what appeared to be at least half a dozen places. At such a close range, the weapon was able to completely punch through the thinly armored research platform and the humans aboard it wouldn't have stood a chance.

Jackson's thoughts briefly flitted to Admiral Marcum's daughter and what the man must be going through. The two of them were only barely civil with each other, certainly not friends, but as a father himself Jackson could sympathize with Marcum's difficult situation he found himself in. It must be even more frustrating since he'd just been removed from a position where he had had the power to take action after his daughter had been killed ... or at least Jackson assumed she was dead. They'd yet to recover more than a few of the bodies and the Darshik had never showed any interest before in taking prisoners.

"Message coming in from one of the Prowlers, Captain," Lieutenant Makers said. "From the time stamp it seems it was sent thirty seconds after our beacon signal would have reached the salvage fleet."

"Send it to my station," Jackson said and pressed the button on his armrest to activate the holographic monitor that would project from above his headrest. It would follow his head movements and obey hand signals to move out of the way if needed.

TFS Nemesis,

Welcome to the Cassandra System, Captain Wolfe. Please remain outside the orbit of the seventh planet to ensure your RDS fields do not interfere with the recovery operation. I am assuming you are here in connection to your track and kill mission ... there are some developments on that front that I think we need to discuss over a secure channel. I will send further details shortly.

Agent Uba

"Why does that name sound familiar?" Jackson mused aloud.

"Sir?" Commander Chambliss asked.

"There's a full agent aboard one of those Prowlers ... goes by the name of Uba," Jackson said. "It's ringing a bell in my head for some reason."

"Agent Uba was the CIS asset on scene when the *Icarus* first encountered the Darshik in the Xi'an System, sir," Accari offered over his shoulder.

"Nobody likes an eavesdropper, Lieutenant Commander," Chambliss said. "But thank you for the insight. What can you tell us about him?"

"We've just exhausted all I know about the man, sir," Accari said.

"I remember now," Jackson said, manipulating the holographic display so he could access his private files on the secure servers. "I read his report on the Xi'an incident. I was forwarded a copy as a courtesy since the Darshik felt the need to heap further insult upon injury by blowing up the *Ares* as a declaration of war."

"Accari? You were there for that incident aboard the *Icarus* ... anything to add?" Chambliss asked.

"Nothing that isn't likely in the official record, sir," Accari said. "I was serving as the OPS officer aboard the *Icarus,* and as far as any of us know the Darshik we're after wasn't in the system at the time. Agent Uba remained aboard the CIS Prowler during the engagement and did not directly involve himself."

"Coms, send a message back to the Prowler asking if Agent Uba would be willing to rendezvous with the *Nemesis* so we can meet in person," Jackson said.

"Sending message now, sir."

"Why have them come to us?" Chambliss asked, leaning in and speaking just above a whisper.

"I've had more than a few dealings with agents," Jackson said. "I'd rather not do this over a com channel that can be intercepted or recorded. If he's wanting to talk about *developments,* we can be assured that it isn't anything good and possibly not anything legal."

"Understood, sir," Chambliss said, although Jackson noted the man looked startled at that last part.

"No response from Agent Uba, but the Prowler is sending us course data," Lieutenant Makers said after half an hour had passed.

"Its navigation beacon just changed too, sir," Lieutenant Hori said. "It's now squawking rendezvous data along with the normal ident broadcast."

"Nav!"

"Aye, sir, plotting course now," the nav operator called out. "Estimated time to contact taking into account the Prowler's course change … thirty-nine hours."

"Helm, all ahead full when you get the new course," Jackson said. "Nav, you're responsible for any course updates so make sure you're getting tracking information from OPS on the Prowler."

"Aye, sir."

"Engines answering all ahead full, aye!"

"Commander Chambliss, you have the bridge." Jackson stood and pulled his coffee mug free of its magnetic holder. "Maintain normal watches and alert posture … I think we're relatively safe given all the CIS assets scanning the system. Take the time to conduct any training you feel might be helpful."

"I have the bridge, aye," Commander Chambliss said, also standing and walking among the bridge stations.

Jackson left the bridge intent on making another round of impromptu visits—he avoided the word *inspection*—of the lower decks before tackling the growing pile of reports that needed to be signed off on as part of the routine business of running a starship. As new as the crew and ship were to him, and they to each other, he wanted to make his presence felt as much as possible. When the shit inevitably hit the fan and the *Nemesis* was tested in combat, he wanted the crew to have a firm idea of who was running the show when orders started flowing down from the bridge.

Being below deck in combat could be a terrifying thing. Unless you were in the CIC you often didn't have any idea what was happening. The ship would begin taking fire and you had to have faith in your captain and that he was doing his job so you could keep doing yours. Early in his career, right after receiving command of the *Blue Jacket*, Jackson had largely ignored anything that didn't happen on the bridge or in Engineering, an oversight that had wrought terrible consequences when some of his crew mutinied and seized control of the ship in the middle of battle. It wasn't something he was proud of, but tried to learn from.

"Any particular destination, Captain?" his Marine escort asked. He recognized him as one of Barton's friends: Sergeant Castillo. He was another of the expeditionary Marines that had been on Juwel that requested to serve aboard his next ship.

"No place in particular, Sergeant," Jackson said. "Just wanting to meet as much as the crew in person as possible before we're all too busy for such things."

"Understood, sir."

****

"Prowler is coming up off the port flank, ten thousand meters and holding there," Lieutenant Hori said.

"We're received a message via the short-range com laser," Lieutenant Makers said. "Agent Uba is coming over via one of the tenders and requests we throttle back our main drive to make the approach easier."

"Acknowledge the request, Coms," Jackson said. "Helm, main drive to standby ... reactive attitude jets only to maintain course."

"RDS to standby, aye," the helmsman said. "Bringing the auxiliary maneuvering system online."

"Coms, inform Flight OPS to open the hangar bay and prepare to receive a standard fleet tender and inform Major Baer we have an inbound ship with visitors," Jackson ordered.

After the Prowler had come fully alongside the *Nemesis* and stabilized its course and speed, Jackson saw a bubble-canopied tender zip out of the CIS ship's tiny hangar bay. A CIS Prowler wasn't a large ship, quite a bit smaller than a frigate and dwarfed by the new *Valkyrie*-class destroyer. It was designed for stealthy interdictions and intelligence gathering, not combat. The crew complement was only sixty-two people, whereas the *Nemesis* carried a complement of over two thousand spacers and Marines.

"Flight OPS is ready to accept the incoming tender and Major Baer reports he already has sentries posted at the airlock," Makers said.

"Commander Chambliss, you have the bridge," Jackson said. "I'm going down to meet our guest and escort him up to the observation lounge."

"I have the bridge, aye."

The *Valkyrie*-class ship continued the trend among the later classes of Terran starships of moving the bridge down off the top of the superstructure to protect it. They all utilized large, semi-domed main displays and there was no logical reason to perch the ship's command center atop a tower, if there even ever was a good reason other than nostalgia for waterborne naval vessels. The *Nemesis* had a truncated superstructure that housed a pair of tender berths, officer's mess, and bridge crew life boats. It also had an observation lounge that doubled as a meeting room that gave three-hundred-and-sixty-degree views of the ship's dorsal surface.

Jackson took the lift outside the bridge hatchway down to a cross-corridor that linked both the starboard and port main access tubes. Each tube was an arching tunnel fifteen meters wide that ran three-quarters of the length of the ship. When they weren't being used to move bulky parts and equipment, they were a quick way to traverse the ship without having to climb through dozens of compartments. Since he was going aft, Jackson jogged across to the port tube before turning aft, his Marine escort trailing silently behind him.

"I didn't expect such a large welcoming party," a man whose ethnic ancestry was impossible to determine said with a sardonic smile. "How are you, Captain Wolfe? It's a pleasure to finally meet you in person."

"Just SOP, Agent Uba," Jackson said, shaking the proffered hand. "Besides the Darshik, the damned ESA have made certain we need to take internal security seriously, even while underway."

"Understood," Uba said.

"If you'll follow me, we can go to the upper observation lounge. It's a secure room since I'm assuming what you're about to tell me isn't for everyone's ears," Jackson said, gesturing towards the open pressure hatch leading out of the airlock bay.

"You would be correct, Captain. You may also gather your senior staff, if you wish. It might save time if I just briefed everyone at once."

"Very well," Jackson said, pulling his personal comlink and pressing the hotkey that would open a channel with the *Nemesis's* OPS officer. He gave a vague order on the personnel he wanted to meet them in the lounge and left it up to Commander Chambliss to work out the details. He, the agent, and his Marine escort made the trip back to a lift that ran all the way to the command deck in silence. The ball of ice in Jackson's gut was now starting to spin the closer they got to the lounge. A full agent sure as shit didn't make the trip all the way over to tell him he was being promoted or had won the Columbiana cash lottery.

****

"Grab a seat and we'll get started," Jackson said as Commander Chambliss and Lieutenant Commander Accari walked into the observation lounge. Major Baer and Lieutenant Commander Hawkins, the CIC department head, were already there.

"This is Agent Uba—as in an actual CIS agent—and he's here to brief us quickly on a topic I've yet to be privy to."

"As you likely saw, we brought a full com carrier with us on this recovery operation," Uba began without greeting. "It's helped to keep me in the loop on all my backchannel sources of information within CENTCOM and the United Terran Federation government. I received word from an associate that Admiral Wright was called to Fleet Admiral Pitt's office recently and told to draft stand down orders for the *Nemesis*."

"They think we need more training or shakedown time?" Commander Chambliss asked.

"No ... your mission is being scrubbed," Uba said. "The civilian government is now reconsidering the wisdom of a prolonged hot war with a species of indeterminate strength while Starfleet is just now getting back on solid footing.

"You'll likely receive official orders the next time this ship flies through an established system. I was sent a heads up on the off-chance you came out here first to try and pick up the Specter's trail. From what I understand, Starfleet is being tasked with pulling back and assuming a completely defensive posture while the Ushin and Darshik work things out."

"I'm still not sure I understand why all the special effort to tell us," Jackson said. "You could have included this in your initial message about navigation hazards ... or not at all and just let us find out once we flew out of here. What's really going on?"

"There are ears everywhere, Captain," Uba said, looking as if he was struggling to figure out how to say what he wanted without exposing himself. "Certain parties that frequent the upper decks of the New Sierra

Platform thought you might appreciate a warning that along with the order to abort your current mission it's entirely likely you'll be recalled to DeLonges or Arcadia."

"Ah," Jackson said, now understanding. "And these parties would prefer that the *Nemesis* was either still flying between Terran and Darshik space or perhaps even just ignoring our orders altogether and continuing on with the original mission. Am I close?"

"I couldn't say, Captain," Uba said. "I was simply asked to pass on a message, and now I have."

"Is there anything else that we should know?" Jackson said, raising a hand to quiet his crew as they reacted to the news of being pulled off mission.

"Logistical support is also being pulled back," Uba said. "The normal combat patrols we've been operating will be reduced in favor of reconnaissance routes. Unofficially, the thought is that even if a few colonies fell before the Ushin could negotiate a peace it would save lives in the long run."

"Is there anything to indicate that the Ushin are even willing, or capable, of negotiating an end to hostilities?" Major Baer spoke up. "From everything I've seen, the whole reason we were dragged into this conflict was because the Ushin are all but powerless to stop Darshik aggression."

"That's the flip side of the coin," Uba said. "It's also entirely possible the Darshik will complete their conquest of the Ushin and then—"

"And then they'll be able to fully concentrate on us," Jackson interrupted. "The Darshik aren't going to be satisfied with just suppressing or eliminating the Ushin worlds. I would have thought the invasion of Juwel would drive that point home."

"The last thing I have—and the main reason for all the secrecy—is that sometime within the next ten months, an Ushin delegation is supposed to be coming to DeLonges," Uba said. "It's there that they will be told the Federation is withdrawing its support, but the negotiations could go the other way. The Ushin may convince the government to continue on with the Darshik campaign."

"That *is* something," Jackson said. "If word of that got out, you could potentially be fighting off the Darshik *and* the ESA."

"The ESA?" Chambliss asked.

"They're all cleared, there just wasn't a need-to-know before," Jackson said at Uba's unspoken question.

"The ESA's intelligence gathering has been far more effective than we would like to admit," the agent said. "Through various counter-intelligence operations we've learned that they know about our reciprocal agreement with the Ushin to trade planets and technology for military assistance. It makes them very nervous as they were already at a technological disadvantage thanks to the Federation retaining New America and Britannia during the restructuring."

"Not to mention a fully intact Tsuyo Corporation," Chambliss said with a nod. "That makes sense."

"That's pretty much all I have for you, Captain," Uba finished. "This was just a friendly heads up and a favor to someone on the off-chance you brought the *Nemesis* out here first. I know I don't need to, but I'm going to remind all of you anyway: Some of the things discussed in here are classified at the absolute highest levels. If there's a leak we *will* know where it came from. Any questions for me before I get back to the excitement of watching Fleet techs comb through the charred wreckage of that station?"

"No word either way on Dr. Ella Marcum?" Jackson asked. "We'll likely be heading back to New Sierra, so if there's news I'd like to give it to her father in person."

"Nothing," Uba shook his head. "All the MIAs are *really* missing. Even some of the crew we couldn't locate bodies for left enough biomaterial for identification. Nothing on Dr. Marcum or her associates. Don't read too much into that, though ... highly unlikely the Darshik decided to start taking prisoners all of a sudden."

"This particular Darshik isn't like the rest, but point taken," Jackson said. "I think that will be all, Agent Uba. Thank you ... the Marine escort standing by the lifts can take you back to the hangar bay."

Knowing a dismissal when he heard one, the CIS agent nodded to the room and walked out, closing the hatch behind him.

"So what do we do with this information?" Chambliss asked. The other officers were looking at Jackson with a sort of eagerness that bothered him.

"Nothing to do with it," he said firmly. "As soon as possible, we'll swing back around and fly back to the Columbiana System where I assume our new orders will find us."

He was well-aware of his reputation and thought he understood what the crew wanted of him ... and it sent a wave of anger through him, making his ears burn. Despite what was said of him, he was *not* some loose cannon that gave the finger to orders and regs whenever it pleased him. When he ignored orders to pursue the first Phage Super Alpha, the circumstances were entirely different than the ones he found himself in now: They had already made contact, established hostile intent, and saw a clear and imminent danger to Terran-held worlds.

The second time he had blatantly ignored orders had been to pull his destroyer, the *Ares*, out of formation because Admiral Marcum refused to budge when new evidence was presented that showed they were about to toss a lot of lives and ships away for nothing. He'd gambled that he was right and in the end he'd been vindicated when the *Ares* had found the Phage core mind and managed to destroy it.

Of the two incidents he felt completely vindicated in the former, but acknowledged that he'd been in the wrong during the latter despite the outcome. While he shouldn't be surprised by it, he despised the *rogue* label that had been applied to him ever since, almost as much as the bigoted *Earther* slur that had followed him most of his career. Every decision he made had been him doing his very best to do the right thing. Sometimes what was right didn't necessarily align with what was correct.

"We need a chance to regroup and look at this mission more objectively," he insisted. "Former President Wellington put this together, rushed us through space trials and crew quals, and gave us the near impossible task of tracking down a single ship that doesn't want to be found. These decisions were made in the wake of a planetary invasion ... maybe it's better that cooler heads take their time to revise the strategy. I want to end this more than anyone, and I still think cutting the head off the snake will take the fight out of the Darshik fleet ... but this mad rush is a recipe for disaster. Everyone but Commander Chambliss is dismissed."

"Did you really mean what you just said, sir?" Chambliss said as the last grumbling officer walked out and clanged the hatch shut behind them.

"Fuck no!" Jackson swore and pushed his chair back violently, causing Chambliss to nearly jump out of his skin. "If anything I want to fly this ship into Darshik space and begin blowing up the strategic targets Celesta Wright mapped out and wait for that son of a bitch to come to me. But ... the younger officers can't think like that."

"I understand and agree completely, sir," Chambliss said. "But what happens if we get ordered to dock back at New Sierra ... we'll be completely out of the fight when this asshole strikes again and I think we both know it's just a matter of time."

"That's a good point," Jackson said, rubbing his chin. "If we stay underway, at least we'll be in position to do something if CENTCOM changes our orders." He turned away, looking out over the hull gleaming under the floodlights they illuminated the ship with while she was running in uncontested, friendly space.

"Maybe we should take advantage of the com carrier in this system to get word back to Admiral Wright about our intentions, sir," Chambliss said. "If she's in the loop, maybe she can preemptively craft our new orders to ensure we're not sidelined."

"You're a devious man, Mr. Chambliss." Jackson turned and smiled. "I like the way you think."

Chapter 5

The Forge was an ancient construct. It had been bought and sold a few dozen times and refitted countless more over its two-hundred-and-seventy-year history. Currently it was serving as a feeder production facility for the Tsuyo-Barclays and HEI Ironworks shipyards that were further down near the planet of Columbiana, the seat of power for the New America enclave in the system of the same name.

Starship production had been ramping up as quickly as capability allowed since the middle of the Phage War and hadn't slowed a bit since the Darshik arrived on the scene. The Forge was tasked with laying out the hulls for six different classes of Federation military and merchant starships. Once the hulls were completed, inspected, and tested, they were moved out to a staging area in orbit over the largest moon of the sixth planet. From there the hulls were towed down to one of the two massive shipyard complexes as needed so the ship could be completed and turned over to Starfleet.

It was nice, dull work … and that's just the way Der Kabalari liked it. He was a retired shuttle pilot that had survived the Battle of Nuovo Patria on one of the Fourth Fleet destroyers that had been in the thick of it. After the largest battle in human history, and now that he was a civilian, he appreciated the monotony of his new career. The work of a tug driver was easy enough for a former combat pilot and the pay was sufficient that, when combined with his military pension, allowed him to afford a small place planetside that had its own yard and—no bullshit—real grass.

"Which one is this guy?" Der asked over the open channel.

"*How the hell would I know? What hull are you in front of?*"

"It's one of those new Orbital Authority ships … the ones that look like the old *Starwolf*-class," Der said.

"*I don't even know what that means. Just read me the damn number from the ident tag!*"

"No need to be a prick about it," Der mumbled without keying the mic. He activated the tug's scanner that fired a low-power IR laser, automatically finding the identification tag, and displayed the hull's info on his multifunction display.

"Alpha alpha seven eight—no, three—one niner."

"*So that was alpha alpha seven THREE one nine?*"

"That's what I said," Der said shortly. He hated the little bastard they'd put in charge of depot movements. The lady that ran the Forge's docking control was nice enough and had been prior service so they got along well, but anytime he had to come get a hull to pull down to one of the yards it was always a chore.

Once he pulled the hull out of its orbit he would bring it around and accelerate it along the course Depot Control gave him and then let it go. It would drift through the system and then be grappled down closer to the yards by another group of tugs. It saved them the time and fuel of dragging it the whole way down there.

"*Go ahead and grapple on and then stand by for your move ticket. It shouldn't be mo*—." The little bastard's voice cut off mid-sentence. It stopped the exact instant a flash behind him lit up the whole cockpit. He hit the jets and spun the tug around just in time to see the last wisps of flames disappear about where the Forge was supposed to be. He looked down and saw that he had no status coming from the facility, not even the navigation beacon.

"Forge Control, Tug Delta-Two, how copy?" he said over the open channel. He repeated his call twice more on the local emergency frequency before he saw other flashes, this time closer. He spun about and saw that all the gleaming hulls lined up were taking hits. The high-speed chunks of alloy from what used to be the Forge were exploding into brilliant sparks as they hit the thick armor. It didn't take a genius to figure out what had happened: The Forge had exploded somehow. He slammed the controls down to send the tug shooting backwards between the two hulls lined up on either side of him, intent on getting behind them and out of the way of the incoming debris. One hit from even a smaller chunk at that speed and he'd be a dead man.

"Mayday, mayday, mayday," he called over the system-wide emergency frequency. "This is Tug Delta-Two in orbit around Varanda Moon ... The Forge has exploded, repeat, the Forge has exploded. No idea on damage, no idea on survi—what the fuck is that?!"

The strangest ship he'd ever seen glided so close to his position that it was actually visible to the naked eye. The front half of the ship was angular and swooped down to a sharp point, but the back half was a strange mishmash of framing spars, drive components, and weapon placements that looked like they were attached as an afterthought. He'd heard all the rumors among the active Fleet crews rotating through the shipyards and had no doubt that this was the same

Darshik ship that Captain Celesta Wright had tangled with over Juwel. What the fuck was it doing so deep in Terran space?

As the tug's multi-spectral optics automatically focused on the only moving object near him—other than the debris still pelting the hulls around him—he could make out a bit of hull damage that had been hastily repaired and the signature hash marks down the prow.

"*Tug Delta-Two ... we have the explosion near your location on sensors*," a call came over the system-wide channel twenty minutes after he'd made his mayday call. "*Please verify that the Forge has suffered catastrophic failure.*"

Der began to sweat profusely. It wasn't some system failure; it was an enemy ship that took out the Forge. They needed to be alerted ... but as soon as he transmitted again he would give away his position and the son of a bitch was sitting *right there*.

"Thought I'd left all this shit behind," he sighed. "It's just not fair ... finally get my house and now I'm going to die in this piece of shit tug." He flicked the switch on the throttle for his mic.

"This is Tug Delta-Two ... Darshik ships have taken out the Forge," he said. "Repeat, Darshik warships are *in the Columbiana System!*" He let go of the switch, wanting to minimize his transmit time, but the Darshik warship was already turning towards him and angling closer to the formation of hulls.

He knew he couldn't outrun the big bastard with his little tug, but he'd be damned if he just sat like a bug waiting to be stepped on. Der spun the tug around and zipped behind the second row of hulls, dropping down and behind them to race back the way he hoped the Darshik wouldn't expect: away from Columbiana. The tugs they used out here had miniature fusion powerplants that fed the ionic jets for normal flight and the larger MPD engines for when they needed to break a heavy load out of orbit. Der reached over and flipped the covered switch up to begin generating plasma in the MPD chambers, doubting he had enough time for it to make a difference.

****

"Are we hearing this right?"

"Yes, sir. Apparently the Darshik have just taken out the Forge."

"Coms! Are we getting any orders from Columbiana Orbital Control or the Fleet office to move for intercept?" Captain Michael Barrett said, not getting up from his seat on the bridge of the *Aludra Star*. The ship was in the system preparing for his proof of concept demonstration for Starfleet when they began receiving calls over the emergency channel about exploding orbital facilities and Darshik warships.

"Negative, sir," his coms officer said.

"Sound general quarters! Set condition 2SS!" Barrett barked, startling the crew. "This is *not* a drill. Tactical, I want live munitions loaded ASAP and I want the *Star* ready to fly and fight within the next hour. Move it, people!"

"Engineering is bringing the reactors to combat levels!"

"Munitions backshop is removing the hard safeties from all missiles, laser batteries are charging!"

The calls from Coms and OPS came fast and furious as the crew responded quickly to his orders. Most of the crew was still the same group that had been battle-hardened under Jackson Wolfe during the battle for Juwel. Now it was up to him to earn their trust the same way Wolfe did, but so far he was more than impressed with how they responded to unexpected situations.

"Coms! Get ahold of *somebody* on Columbiana and find out who the hell is coordinating the defense of the system, please," Barrett said.

"There seems to be a lot of confusion, sir, but it looks like the Fourth Fleet ships in the system are now all flying towards Columbiana to form a picket line," the com officer said.

"And the two irreplaceable shipyards that are orbiting the fourth planet?" Barrett asked, incredulous that all Fleet assets would pull back and leave the facilities unprotected. From a strictly strategic standpoint, they were easily the most vital thing in the system, the lives on the capital planet notwithstanding.

"Fourth Fleet Command is saying they don't have the assets to protect both and that the capital is the priority," the OPS officer said. "General orders are coming over the Link now ... they also have no confirmation that any Darshik are actually in the system, much less a location or potential target."

"Oh for ... the shipyards are the next target," Barrett said, forcing himself to remain calm, cool, and professional ... the man in charge with all the answers. "That's the only logical place to strike next after hitting the Forge. Is Fourth Fleet Command ordering us into their defensive picket line?"

"No, Captain," the com officer spoke up. "First and Seventh Fleet ships are not being ordered anywhere at this time."

"OPS! Plot me a course that takes us out past the Tsuyo-Barclays complex," Barrett ordered. "Tactical, full active sensors and begin sweeping for returns that are consistent with what we have for Darshik ships in the database, including the Specter that the *Icarus* ran into. Helm, once you get your course you are cleared to engage the main engines: all ahead flank."

"All ahead flank aye!" the helmswoman said.

"Coms, tell Flight OPS I want the launch bays closed and secured as quickly as they can manage it. Suspend recovery operations for now and order the sleds we still have out there to loiter," Barrett said.

"Aye, sir."

Moments later, harsh booms reverberated through the hull as the massive armored doors slammed shut over the shuttle launch bays. Adrenaline spiked through Barrett at the realization that he was about to take a starship into combat as its captain for the very first time ... and his assault carrier was vastly overmatched when compared to the Specter. The *Aludra Star* surged ahead on the power of her magnetoplasma main engines on an arcing course that would pull them up out of Columbiana's orbit and off towards the vulnerable shipyards.

"Coms, try to get in touch with someone on both shipyard complexes and warn them we believe they're at risk for imminent attack and give them our ETA," Barrett said. "OPS?"

"ETA ... seventeen hours including our decel burn," the OPS officer said.

"Also make sure they're aware this particular ship is very stealthy and can perform much more accurate intrasystem warp hops than a standard Darshik cruiser," Barrett finished his order.

"Aye, sir," the coms officer said. "Getting the contact channel information for both complexes now."

Seventeen hours ... by the time they got there it was possible two of the most important Federation shipyards would be tumbling from the sky. Barrett had heard of the attack on a highly secret research station out in the middle of nowhere and now they were looking at an attack on critical infrastructure and military production capability. Where were these assholes getting such accurate intel about Terran vulnerabilities?

"Fourth Fleet Command is sending us a message asking if we're leaving the system, Captain. How should I respond?"

"The truth, Ensign," Barrett said. "Tell them we're moving to defend the two shipyards higher up the well. We'd be of minimal use in orbit over Columbiana."

"Aye, sir," Ensign Wu said and slipped her headset back on.

"Do the shipyards have any defensive capability?" the XO, Commander Simmons asked. He'd remained aboard the *Star* when Barrett had been named as her replacement CO. Jackson Wolfe had spoken highly of him and Barrett trusted his former captain implicitly when it came to judgment of other officers.

"Minimal," Barrett replied. "This system is Fourth Fleet's home base so normally there would be a large concentration of warships loitering in the orbits between third and fourth planets, but Starfleet is spread so thin that anything in the area will either be unarmed or not even spaceworthy ... certainly nothing that could put up a meaningful defense."

"Yes, sir," Simmons said. The commander seemed neither fearful nor anxious about the coming engagement. Instead, he projected the calm aura of a professional that was both confident and competent. He knew better than Barrett how overmatched the *Star* was, but nothing about his demeanor would suggest that he had any doubts about his CO's decision to rush into battle.

"It's too bad we aren't carrying live munitions on the sleds during these final stages of testing your new tactics, Captain," Simmons went on softly. "The bastard may see the *Star* coming and recognize her."

"And then step right into a trap when its overconfidence brings it close to finish us off," Barrett finished for him with a nod. "It's too bad the sleds are loaded with dummy munitions. Otherwise this would be a hell of a proof of concept for CENTCOM."

"Yes, sir," Simmons said with a smile before raising his voice. "Tactical, please put weapon statuses on the main display as munitions gets our missiles ready to fly."

"Aye, sir."

"XO, let's go ahead and start rotating people out so that everyone is fresh and ready when we get within the operations area," Barrett said.

"Yes, sir," Simmons said. "I was about to ask if you'd like us to go to split shifts."

"I'll leave the details to you, Commander," Barrett said. "In the meantime, you have the bridge. I'll relieve you in five hours so you can grab some rack time. I'll need you here when we're closing in on the shipyards."

"I have the bridge, aye."

Barrett nodded to his XO and walked quickly off the bridge and towards his quarters. He was immensely thankful that Simmons was enough of a professional that there had been no friction when Barrett was promoted over him and given command of the ship he'd served on for years. In their initial discussions, Simmons freely admitted that he had aspirations of command one day, but that he understood Barrett's service record meant that CENTCOM was going to be looking to put him in command of his own ship soon and the *Aludra Star*'s seat happened to open up first.

Their shared connection of having both served under Jackson Wolfe had helped smooth over most of the awkwardness when two strangers are thrown into such a close working relationship. Simmons had been enthusiastic and helpful when it came to working out the details of Barrett's revised tactics for the *Vega*-class assault carriers and had largely resisted the usual "Well this is how we used to do things ..." mantra that came when an outsider began making radical changes.

When Barrett got to his quarters, he set an alarm to wake him in four hours and then flopped back on his rack without even taking his boots off. He was careful to temper his impatience at his ship's more modest speed after years of being used to the *Icarus*'s capabilities. It was tempting to push the engines even harder and run her up past flank and into emergency power, but he'd see a minimal gain and risk damaging his ship before she even made it into battle. Part of him had been hoping that when his single little assault carrier had sped off to protect the shipyards that Fourth Fleet Command would redeploy some of their *Intrepid*-class destroyers, but so far the Link data showed all Fourth Fleet ships maintaining tight formations around Columbiana.

He'd been involved in nearly every major incident since the first Phage unit showed up in Terran space, but always as a background player. There would be no hiding behind the experience and boldness of Wolfe or Wright this time. He was surprised to learn that with that realization came a feeling of calm. He'd made his decision, the crew and ship were ready ... it was time to prove that he deserved to sit in that seat.

****

"Contact! The HEI Ironworks complex is reporting sporadic radar returns that are consistent with the profile we sent them."

"How long until we're within detection range for our own tracking radar?" Barrett asked.

"Still another five hours, sir," Lieutenant Dole spoke up from OPS. He was another holdover on the *Aludra Star* from the Juwel campaign and, as Wolfe had indicated might be the case, Barrett was less than impressed with his initiative. To be fair though, the man had never failed to provide what was asked of him.

"OPS, how much more aggressive can our decel burn be?" Barrett asked.

"Even under full emergency power we're over four hours from the HEI shipyard," Dole said. The *Star* was already rumbling and groaning as the mains roared at full reverse to slow their mad dash.

"Give me a projected course correction for intercept based on the last position provided by the shipyard's radar operators," Barrett said. "Assume that we'll be entering the engagement under acceleration and no longer braking."

"That cuts us down to just under two hours assuming we're back under full power within the next ten minutes," Dole said. "We'll be carrying so much velocity that we won't be able to do much more than overshoot the engagement area and come onto a course that will allow us to slow and sling around the sixth planet ... that means we can't make it back to the shipyards for another forty-two hours, give or take."

"Helm, all ahead flank," Barrett said, making his decision in an instant.

"Sir?" Simmons asked.

"This gives us our best shot at actually getting there in time," Barrett explained, making sure his voice was loud enough for the entire bridge crew to hear. "The *Star* would be hard-pressed to stand toe to toe with this enemy ship as you all are well aware, and if we continue to decel so that we're able to maneuver over the fourth planet we'll likely be too late to do any good."

"Yes, sir," Simmons said. "Coms, relay our new plans to Fourth Fleet Command."

"And tell them we highly recommend they sent a destroyer or three out here as fast as they can fly," Barrett added. "Tactical, when we cross the fifteen-million-kilometer threshold I want four hornets fired directly at where our updated data has the target. Full burns on first and second stages and then detonate the warheads once they're within four million kilometers."

"Programming now, sir," Lieutenant Commander Adler said from the tactical station. She went about the task without question and with a proficiency Barrett wasn't used to seeing from her.

As Celesta Wright's former tactical officer, Adler had been given the option of transferring over to the *Star* with Barrett when it was decided the *Icarus* was to be decommissioned, or she could put her name back into the pool and take her chances on a new assignment. Barrett had been completely surprised when she'd asked to serve under him given the fact there was little love lost between them. The promotion board had apparently been very frank with her when she was passed over for full commander, and when she reported to the *Star* the newly promoted captain saw a genuine effort on her part to step up her performance.

"When you have that program locked in, I want two Shrikes prepped for a snap launch that will take them on a course tangential to our own by two degrees to port," Barrett went on. "Utilize as much momentum from the launchers as possible and keep the first stage burns minimal ... coordinate with CIC and the munitions backshop for any help you may need on that. Set both missiles for silent running; no telemetry stream back to us. We'll just have to hope they make it to where we want them to be."

"Aye, sir," Adler said and immediately pulled her headset all the way on and reached for her com panel.

"The Hornets are to be a distraction," Barrett explained to his XO, who was patiently waiting until he'd finished giving orders. "They'll fly out at full burn with active sensors and then blow up in a big light show at the end. We'll try to sneak around a pair of Shrikes ahead and to the outside of our orbital insertion vector and then when our radar gets a positive lock we'll—hopefully—have two weapons in the area that have a chance at making a hit."

"Sound strategy, Captain," Simmons said.

"It's a desperate gamble," Barrett admitted with a barely perceptible shrug. "But with the sleds currently in the launch bay just training models with dummy ballast loaded on them, we're limited in what we can do. Our laser batteries are able to do significant damage, but we don't have the engine power to get in close and then escape before it can turn its plasma lance on us." Barrett sighed and rubbed at his scalp.

"To be honest, XO, I'm just trying to chase this bastard away from the shipyards. In past engagements it's shown itself to be very hesitant to risk taking a direct hit, and I'm betting that a close call with a pair of Shrikes will send it slinking off until Fourth Fleet decides to redeploy into an actual defensive grid."

"Understood, sir," Simmons said. "And I stand by my previous statement: It's a sound strategy."

"Hornets and Shrikes prepped to fire, sir," Adler said.

"Fire," Barrett ordered. "OPS?"

"One hour and fifty-six minutes, sir."

"Coms, let the HEI shipyard know that we're inbound with weapons hot," Barrett said. "I'd appreciate it if they would include all their high-res radar data on the Link."

"Aye, sir."

The bridge was almost peaceful with the steady, soft hiss of the environmental ducts and the gentle rocking from the engines straining at full power. Barrett looked around and saw that his crew looked alert, but relaxed, and had to keep reminding himself that they were all battle-hardened spacers. The moment wasn't like how he'd imagined it would be, this first time into battle as the master of a starship. He assumed he'd feel like a fraud or that the crew would sense his own fear and it would shake their confidence, but instead he felt … ready. It wasn't that he was at all eager to pit his assault carrier against the specialized Darshik cruiser, but he was confident that his strategy would allow for the best odds of protecting vital Federation assets as well as keeping his crew and ship from harm.

The *Star* would be screaming by the fourth planet at nearly nine percent the speed of light, far too fast for the Darshik to intercept and employ their preferred close-in weapon. If the Shrikes he would fire shortly did the trick of forcing the Specter to turn and run or warp-hop further out into the system, he could consider the engagement a wild success. Barrett had to keep reminding himself, however, that this was no ordinary ship commander he was facing and every time this ship appeared in Terran space it had some new tactical capability added to it.

"HEI complex Link data coming in now, Captain," Dole reported. "CIC is adding to our own sensor feed and accounting for propagation lag … here it comes." The lieutenant gestured to the main display where more detail was being added to the tactical overlay of the system. A bright red, flashing reticle icon flying near the outer edge of the station's defensive range came through with all the associated sensor data. Barrett could see right away something was wrong.

"Shit," he said. "Look at its relative velocity."

"It's just enough to keep up with the shipyard's orbital velocity," Adler said. "Virtually motionless, sitting just outside their missile range."

"Right on both counts, Lieutenant Commander," Barrett agreed.

"HEI's Complex Operations Control reported the enemy has fired seven low-power particle beam barrages at them over the last fourteen hours," Ensign Wu spoke up. "I'm sorry, sir, it's like pulling teeth trying to get all the information from them in a concise way."

"Don't apologize for something that isn't your fault, Ensign," Barrett told her. "Was there any damage from the weapons fire?"

"Negative, sir," Wu said. "The impact caused some bright sparks and scorched off the outer hull coating but no actual damage."

"Just enough to keep their attention—"

"Tactical!" Barrett cut off his XO. "Spit two Shrikes out the aft tubes … no targeting data and no first stage burn."

"Firing Shrikes from tubes four and six, aye," Adler said. "Missiles away and standing by for target package … tubes four and six reloading with the last of the Shrikes for the rear launchers. Do you want me to have Munitions transfer two more from the forward magazine?"

"Not at this time," Barrett said. "We may need them for the forward tubes shortly. Adler, be ready to *quickly* turn those Shrikes loose. Let them auto-target on any Darshik return they get. We probably won't have time to feed them a full targeting package.

"Look alive, everyone! The Specter is just pacing the station outside their maximum effective range and we're the only ship so far coming to the defense. We're probably being baited in, so keep a sharp eye on our six and make sure you're ready to react instantly."

"They've used this tactic before," Simmons said as he rolled his shoulders and massaged his neck. "They'd try to keep us focused on the obvious attack while their cruisers would—"

"Possible contact, quartering in off the aft-starboard quadrant," Adler said calmly. "Intermittent returns but CIC puts the range at one hundred and sixty-four thousand kilometers."

"Do they have a profile for the ship?" Barrett asked.

"The computer is matching it to the Specter with a probability of eighty-seven percent," Adler answered.

"This ... isn't good," Simmons said. "*Two* Specters?"

"One ship trying to stay hidden, one sitting as obvious bait," Barrett mused. "We're only seeing what they want us to see right now. Tactical, fire the two lead Shrikes at the target over the HEI complex. Let's shake things up a bit and see what sort of reaction we get. OPS, back Tactical up and monitor the trailing ship."

"Sending targeting data and fire authorization to deployed Shrikes now," Adler said. "First stage will fire again in four minutes."

Barrett thought hard on the position he found himself in. The ship over the fourth planet was obviously meant to be seen and fired at, but was the ship behind him *really* meant to stay hidden? Or were they allowing gaps in their countermeasures to try and continue herding him along? He had the two ship busters he'd deployed earlier streaking towards the first ship and he had two more that had been spit out of the aft tubes that were just trailing along behind them, slowly increasing the gap as the *Star* continued on under power. He had weapons coverage fore and aft of the *Star*, but he still felt like he was missing the big picture.

"Sir! Message coming in from Fourth Fleet Command," Ensign Wu said. "They're sending three *Intrepid*-class destroyers to our aid."

"Excellent news," Barrett said. "They could ignore a single panicked tug pilot but not hard sensor data broadcast over the Link."

"At maximum performance the destroyers can be here in nine hours, sir," Lieutenant Dole said. "The telemetry over the Link shows them running at full emergency power."

"Helm! Hard to port!" Barrett barked. "Everything she's got! Tactical, keep a sharp eye on our trailer."

"Hard to port, aye!"

The *Aludra Star* groaned as the g-load increased and she ponderously began to push onto the new course. After a few moments the deck really began to vibrate and the crew was shaken in their seats as the main engines struggled to overcome their inertia.

"Contact over the HEI shipyards has disappeared," Dole said, raising his voice over the rattling of the ship. "Transition flash is consistent with an intrasystem hop."

"Did the computer categorize the flash to a specific ship type?" Barrett asked.

"It most closely matches a standard Darshik cruiser."

"That ship was the decoy," Barrett announced to the crew. "We will now assume that the real Specter is still tailing us. Tactical, have the Shrikes we fired at that decoy come about and burn their second stages ... put them in high orbit over the fourth planet."

"Safing warheads and sending course corrections now, sir," Adler said. "No further contact from the pursuing ship."

"Helm! Zero thrust ... steady as she bears," Barrett ordered. "OPS, begin plotting reciprocal courses to get us back to that planet, back to Columbiana, or on an intercept to get behind the destroyer screen coming to meet us."

"Engines answering zero thrust, aye," the helmsman said. "The *Star* is now ballistic."

"Tactical, safe the Shrikes we had flying along behind us," Barrett said. "Put them in orbit as well if you can. Fleet can't afford to waste any right now, so we can't just blow them."

"Aye, sir."

"This is strange," Simmons remarked. "They had the upper hand ... why all the theatrics and then just cut and run when we fire a few missiles from long range?"

"That's a good question, XO," Barrett said. "Coms, find out from—"

"Distress call coming in from ... the Carsten Deep Space Observatory," Ensign Wu said. "It's on the other side of the system in a heliocentric orbit past the eighth planet."

"I've never heard of it and I'm from this system," Simmons said.

"What's the nature of their distress, Ensign," Barrett asked.

"They say they're under attack by a single ship of unknown origin," Wu said. "The signal terminated mid-sentence on the second call."

"Son of a bitch," Barrett said, leaning back. "That was the objective. The Forge and the two shipyards were just to focus and get us moving on the wrong thing. They had to be believable so they picked critical infrastructure targets. For us to get the distress signal now means they must have attacked that station as soon as they knew most of the Fleet ships were heading to the planet."

"So they could then go and attack an observatory, sir?" Adler asked, genuinely confused.

"Have you ever heard of a crewed observatory, Lieutenant Commander?" Barrett asked. "They're either all automated or ship-based. It's almost guaranteed that the Carsten Observatory was the cover story for another highly secret research lab ... and that makes it at least the second one the Darshik have hit within the last seven months."

"Orders, sir?" Simmons asked.

"Take us back to Columbiana," Barrett said, standing up. "It would take us days to get back around the system and Fourth Fleet has much more capable ships to attempt an intercept. You have the bridge, Commander. Stand down from general quarters and let Fourth Fleet Command know that we have four Shrikes that will need to be retrieved."

"I'll take care of it, Captain," Simmons said.

Chapter 6

"How long do you think they'll keep us out here?"

"Until the Ushin delegation is gone," Jackson answered, trying to not become annoyed at the question he'd heard at least three dozen times by as many officers since they'd arrived.

The *Nemesis* had flown hard all the way back to the DeLonges System only to find that a six-ship Ushin delegation was already in orbit over one of New Sierra's moons while a pack of Terran warships, including the first operational *Juggernaut*-class battleship, shadowed them.

As soon as New Sierra Orbital Control had received the *Nemesis's* beacon they'd sent orders telling the destroyer to get into formation with the other Seventh Fleet ships flying in high orbit over the smallest of the two gas giants in the system. They'd been there for seven days now, trailing along behind one of Black Fleet's last true fleet carriers, now relegated mostly to post-battle recover efforts. They'd been overflown nearly two dozen times since entering the formation as all the commanders of Seventh Fleet ships wanted to see the new *Valkyrie*-class up close and render honors to their most infamous shipmaster.

In the downtime, Jackson had decided to reinstate the tradition of Captain's Mess in order to get a better feel for his new crew under nonworking conditions. After hosting officers and enlisted spacers from Engineering the previous evening, Jackson was now comfortably lounging with his senior staff and bridge crew, collars on their dress blacks open and more than a few empty bottles of expensive wine sitting on the white tablecloth.

"I wonder if our mission was so well-known that it'd be considered provocative for us to enter orbit over the capital," Accari said.

"I doubt it, Idris," Commander Chambliss said. Jackson noticed his XO used first names with his subordinates during occasions like a formal mess. He didn't disapprove of the familiarity, it was just wasn't his style.

"Fourth Fleet has assumed security of the inner system along with the few Orbital Authority ships actually in service," Chambliss went on. "I doubt any more thought was given to it other than a controller on duty saw a Black Fleet transponder and directed us into the formation the other Black Fleet ships were already in."

"Maybe," Accari said. The young officer had inadvertently cultivated a few back-channel sources of intel and Fleet scuttlebutt due to his popularity with the ladies. Being privy to the machinations of the upper tiers of CENTCOM caused him to look for conspiracies and deeper meaning in even the most mundane orders that came down.

The conversation lulled as people leaned back and enjoyed the last of their drinks while an instrumental style of music from Earth played softly over the speakers. For a brief moment Jackson could imagine he wasn't in the military and the men and women sitting around the table were just his friends, not his subordinates and certainly not people he might have to order to actions that could lead to their deaths.

"*Captain, we have an unidentified ship approaching off our starboard flank requesting permission to dock*," the second watch com officer's voice came over the intercom harshly.

"Interesting," Jackson said, pulling his collar right and refastening it. "I'm on my way."

"Sir?" Chambliss asked.

"I have my suspicions as to who this is," Jackson said. "Enjoy the rest of your evening; you're all still off-duty until first watch."

Jackson stepped out of the hatchway and was unsurprised to see that Sergeant Barton was standing at parade rest along with the two regular Marine sentries. He nodded to his personal escort and pointed so that Barton would know he was indeed moving to the lifts and not just down the shallow set of steps to the head.

"Emergency, Captain?" Barton asked.

"Not yet, Sergeant," Jackson said. "But the night is young and the person I suspect is coming to see us rarely brings me good news."

Barton's brow furrowed, but he remained silent. The lift quickly descended from the observation lounge near the top of the superstructure down to the secure command deck. The system required that Jackson enter a pass code before the doors would open for him.

"Report!" Jackson said as he walked onto the bridge.

"Sensor data of the ship is on the main display, sir, and the credentials match with a generic—"

"CIS code," Jackson finished for the lieutenant commander from CIC that was manning the bridge. "I'm quite familiar with the ship, Lieutenant Commander. Coms, tell them they're clear to begin docking maneuvers and let Flight OPS know that we have visitors."

"And Major Baer, sir?" the ensign at OPS asked.

"Negative, Ensign," Jackson said. "I'll have Sergeant Barton with me and that will be sufficient."

"Aye, sir."

"Friends of yours, Captain?" Barton asked once they were alone in another lift car.

"I suppose that technically he is," Jackson said. "At least I assume it's him given that only a few of those ships exist."

By the time they reached the starboard airlock the lights were cycling from amber to green, letting them know that the Broadhead II had made hard dock and the pressure was equalized. Jackson peered into the short tunnel of the airlock to make sure it was whom he assumed it to be and was surprised that Agent Pike wasn't alone.

"Shit," he muttered. "Barton, stand at attention and prepare to render honors to a flag officer."

"Sir?"

Jackson didn't bother explaining himself. He reached over and keyed in his command codes authorizing the main hatch to cycle. As soon as the hatch popped and began to swing open, Jackson stepped back and snapped to attention.

"Attention on deck!" he barked. Barton automatically slammed his heels together and, since he was armed, rendered a salute as Agent Pike walked through.

"For me?" he asked, putting both palms on his cheeks and feigning a surprised look.

"Get out of the way, you fucking idiot," a voice growled from behind him. "And stand at ease, Jackson … I'm a goddamn civilian now."

"At ease, Sergeant," Jackson said. "I'd heard you were retired now, Admiral. I still feel like you've earned that respect when stepping onto a Federation starship."

"An odd sentiment coming from you, all things between us considered," Joseph Marcum said, coming forward and extending his hand. "She's a beautiful ship, Captain. Is there a place we can talk in private and maybe find a bottle of something or other that's usually banned on Fleet starships?"

"My office, Admiral," Jackson said. "This way."

The motley procession wound its way through the ship until they ended up outside the hatchway of Jackson's office on the command deck. Barton automatically took his post and stood ramrod straight, staring straight ahead.

"Is there someplace he can go?" Marcum jerked a thumb towards Pike.

"*He*?" Pike protested mildly.

"Pike, if you go up to the observation lounge you'll likely catch my senior staff still in the middle of raiding the ship's wine stash," Jackson said. "Sergeant

Barton, please call ahead and let the sentries know that someone that looks like a homeless rambler will be attending Captain's Mess a bit late."

"Funny," Pike said sourly and walked off towards the bank of lifts. Jackson had no doubt the agent already knew how to get around in a starship whose design had just entered service.

"I'll admit, Captain, this is not the reception I expected to receive from you given the fact there aren't any stars on my collar anymore," Marcum said once the hatch sealed behind him. Jackson took his seat and exhaled loudly, looking up at the ceiling. "I half-expected you to cycle the airlock when you saw who it was and let the air out a bit for me and that unbelievably annoying CIS spook."

"Admiral ... I know there has been friction between us, but it was for legitimate reasons," Jackson said after a moment. "When I pulled the *Ares* out of formation and took her on my own in direct defiance of your explicit orders, I could have been rightly prosecuted. I know that political powers had also forced you to bring me back in what I can only assume was a PR stunt when the war took a bad turn.

"I still respect the job you did during the Phage War in spite of everything. All the minutia aside, I'm not sure anybody else could have wrangled the numbered fleets together and coordinated the later stages of the war the way you did. I don't dislike you personally, but I was often frustrated by what I assumed was your tendency to put political considerations above what was best for Starfleet."

"Fair enough," Marcum said, also taking a long moment before speaking. "I suppose when I take an honest look at why I've been so disgusted with you during your career is that part of me wished I had still been like you. I can't honestly say I'd have had the balls to take a single ship looking for that Phage core mind or transition an obsolete assault carrier deep into an enemy-held system without my escort ... but there was a time when I would have.

"Before I get into why I had that fucking lunatic Pike bring me out here as a last favor cashed in, I want you to know that it was never personal, even if I might have made it seem like it was. I respect you as an officer and as a man ... now before this gets too sappy and we start crying on each other's shoulders about our childhoods, how about you break out some of that sweet Kentucky bourbon I know you have in that desk and I'll tell you what's happening right now over the capital."

****

Admiral Wright was sitting in her office, preparing her notes for a presentation she was making to the Parliamentary Subcommittee on Fleet Readiness regarding the strength and availability of Black Fleet assets, when the door swung open with a bang.

"Do come in, Admiral." Celesta glared up at Admiral Pitt. Behind him she could see her admin staff fretting and looking in nervously after Pitt had apparently plowed through their protests to get to her office.

"Sorry," Pitt said absently before swinging the door shut. "Did Pike load this place up with all the usual anti-detection goodies?"

"I beg your pardon, sir?"

"You know ... all the CIS gadgets to make sure your office can't be monitored directly or remotely?" Pitt asked. "Yes or no, Wright."

"This office is secure," Celesta said evasively. "Can I assume there are some developments with our Ushin friends?"

"No ... well, probably," Pitt said with a shake of his head. "But I'm here about something else: The Columbiana System was attacked by the Specter. This is all very preliminary and highly classified but I have no doubt that it'll be coming your way."

"You're not kidding, are you?" Celesta sank back into her seat, her face ashen. Columbiana was the seat of power for the New America enclave and possibly the Federation's most important industrial base. "Losses?"

"The Forge was completely taken out," Pitt said. "It was that pre-process feeder—"

"I'm aware of what the Forge is—was—Admiral."

"And it likely would have gotten a free shot at the two shipyards there too if it wasn't for your protégé, Captain Barrett," Pitt finished.

"Barrett? Ah, yes ... the *Aludra Star* is there for the final testing of his new assault carrier tactical concept," Celesta said. "I don't suppose he got lucky and took out the Specter?"

"Didn't land a single shot," Pitt said. "But, I'm hearing that there's another highly classified after-action report that says Tsuyo had a secret research platform along the system boundary in Columbiana and that the shipyard attack was a diversion. The lab was hit while all the attention was on the other side of the system ... total loss."

"This is not a coincidence," Celesta said. "Two top secret research stations in a row that *I* didn't even know about? Where the hell is this thing getting its intel?"

"I couldn't even begin to guess," Pitt said. "That sort of information would likely be circulated outside of our circle. Fleet doesn't need to know—." He was cut off as both of their comlinks began chirping simultaneously.

"If you got the same message I did we've got about ten minutes to get down to Deck 32 for a briefing by the new CENTCOM Chief of Staff," Celesta said.

"I did," Pitt said. "We'll have to continue this later."

As Celesta walked beside Admiral Pitt, each of them trailed by their personal staff, she thought about what it meant that the Specter was changing tactics and hitting Fleet research outposts. The obvious answer was that it was after the newest Terran technology to either develop a defense or to integrate it into its own mishmash of dissimilar hardware, but that was unlikely for a few reasons. More realistically, Celesta thought that it was a tactic to deny the Federation any further major advances in ship design or weaponry.

These research stations were lightly guarded, isolated, and staffed almost entirely by civilians. They were soft targets that had major impacts when taken out. What worried her most was that there was no way in hell this ship was just finding these installations by bumbling around within Terran space. The only way to get that sort of detailed information was from the inside … she just hoped that it was effective espionage and that they hadn't been betrayed by their own. The fact the Specter was flying unimpeded through Federation space and popping up in systems it shouldn't even know existed was terrifying. Maybe they'd get lucky and the briefing she was being called to was to order the *Nemesis* mission reactivated.

****

"If everyone is here, we'll get started," Fleet Admiral Dax Longworth, CENTCOM Chief of Staff, said from the podium. "Marines, please close and lock the doors."

Admiral Longworth was a physically unimposing man. Short, bald, and with an odd stoop to his shoulders that gave him a timid, almost fearful appearance. He wasn't from the operational side of Starfleet so most of the flag officers in the room for the briefing that had come up the ranks serving aboard starships had never met or heard of him. He'd been in Logistics Command for most of his career where he'd served with distinction, but most of the officers in the room were highly skeptical that his experience over there would count for much when it came to managing the entire Federation military.

"I've been asked by the President himself to come up here and give you an update on what's happening with the Ushin delegation parked in this system," Longworth said once the doors had swung shut. "We have representatives from each numbered fleet here as well as Merchant Fleet and cleared civilian liaisons from firms that do business near the Frontier.

"To keep this short and sweet: The Darshik have surrendered. Not to us, but to the Ushin. As many of you might know, the Darshik are actually a politically ideological offshoot of Ushin society, but they're the same species. Things have gotten so bad on the Darshik planets from the constant state of war that the populations are starving, the economies are in ruin, and the regional governments are looking at a full rebellion if they don't do something.

"Two of the three planets sent emissaries to the Ushin and offered a complete and unconditional surrender in exchange for aid. The third planet is controlled by a warlord that is usually aboard a Darshik ship we've codenamed Specter. This planet has *not* surrendered, but they're in much the same poor shape as the other two and the citizens there are desperate for Ushin help.

"The President feels this is now a problem that will quickly solve itself without any need for an intervention by us. He is recommending to Parliament that we withdraw military support from the Ushin and begin anew with diplomatic efforts. Without the logistical support of his bases on the other two planets, we feel confident that the Specter poses no real risk to the Federation and that the resources it would take to hunt him down could be put to better use here."

"Apparently the Juwel fiasco took more out of them than we thought," Pitt whispered to Celesta as Longworth began taking questions from the attendees.

"This guy still has one powerful starship, his own fleet of cruisers, and who knows what else besides the single planet," Celesta said. "He's not going away quietly."

"No, he's not," Pitt agreed. "The question now becomes what horrific act of war will this asshole perpetrate next before leadership decides enough is enough."

Celesta didn't answer. A handful of warships bent on doing as much damage as possible, and apparently with detailed knowledge of Terran space, was not something that could just be ignored. There were far more sensitive targets than there were Fleet assets to protect them. She feared Pitt was right: It was just a matter of time before the next attack, and this time it might not be some lightly manned research outpost.

Chapter 7

The Tsuyo Corporation was an ancient entity, tracing its lineage directly back to a company of the same name on Earth that had first developed the warp drive and launched the very first interstellar exploration vehicles. It had been the only aerospace company that had remained after Earth's third great world war and had survived by combining the industrial might of a flagging United States and a resurgent Japan. Ironically, the world's two most tech-centric nations had produced something in their desperation that had ultimately doomed them both.

Once warp-drive-equipped starships began flying colonists to newly discovered planets, the top fifteen percent of every generation left an overcrowded, polluted, and war-ravaged Earth for a new life. Earth's economy collapsed and within the span of a couple of centuries the birthplace of humanity was little more than a slum. It took the next one hundred and fifty years for the remaining citizens to reorganize themselves and repair the damage centuries of conflict and industry had caused. While Earth was now a lush, beautiful planet once again with a thriving economy, her people had never forgotten the centuries of insult and neglect. Even now Earth remained independent, aligning with neither the United Terran Federation nor the Eastern Star Alliance.

Even though Tsuyo still maintained a strong presence on Earth, the fact that their machinery took humanity to the stars first meant the company had been able to establish certain controls on the technology to ensure their monopoly continued. Jillian Wolfe looked up in wonder as the speedy intrasystem yacht she was on dropped away from Tsuyo's newest pride and joy: the Amaterasu Habitat.

Amaterasu was the largest man-made structure in space by a factor of at least five, dwarfing the second largest, the New Sierra Platform. Whereas New Sierra was still mostly exposed structural spars and spindly docking arms from its previous life as a heavy construction shipyard, Amaterasu was a solid, gracefully arching structure that lived in harmony with the spherical planet it orbited. The planet was a barren, rocky world in the Kirin System, a star system owned wholly by the Tsuyo Corporation that had no habitable worlds but did have above average concentrations of iron and other crucial elements in its three asteroid belts and the two smallest rocky worlds. It was also used as a semi-secret proving ground for various Tsuyo starship designs.

"It's truly amazing, Mr. Hoshino," Jillian said as Amaterasu became smaller and less pronounced.

"Thank you, Mrs. Wolfe," the Tsuyo liaison said with a bow. "She is our pride and joy, a true testament to Tsuyo's technical prowess."

"You said something about this being just a stepping stone?" Jillian asked, feigning interest. To her, one orbital platform was much like any other even if it was enormous. She had been lassoed into a tour of the expansive facility while she was in the Kirin System surveying the outer asteroid belt as a possible training location. The small yacht she was in was a Fleet vessel that could comfortably fit its complement of twenty-two and had enough engine power to allow her to do a full survey of the system. What it didn't have was its own warp drive, so until the fleet carrier came back to pick them up, she was stuck playing host to a Tsuyo rep that seemed to have an unwholesome obsession with her husband.

"Oh yes!" Hoshino said enthusiastically. Jillian cringed inwardly. It had been a polite question, but she could see that she'd just opened yet another floodgate.

"Habitable planets are so statistically rare and terraforming has yet to prove a viable theory ... at least within one or two generations," he continued. "We think a more practical method of exploiting a g-type main sequence star's energy in the habitable band is to simply build our own habitats. Amaterasu is still just a proof of concept despite being home to over four hundred thousand people right now. Larger interlocking, independent structures anchored within the orbit of planets like the one below could provide for billions ... perhaps even trillions."

"You don't think it's risky putting that many people on a platform that could suffer catastrophic system failure at any time?" the yacht's first mate spoke up. "You couldn't evacuate most of them in time."

"Statistically, the risk is lower than putting a population on a geologically active world." Hoshino sniffed. "Our habitats have no volcanic or seismic activity, no weather that we don't generate ourselves, controlled radiation exposure, air that is filtered of pathogens we don't wish to be there. Believe me ... Amaterasu is safer than living on your home planet."

"Let's agree to disagree," the first mate said in a bored tone and turned back to his terminal monitor. He was one of the most arrogant lieutenants Jillian had ever been around. He'd started the flight in the Kirin System trying to proposition her until he realized who she was, then he realized her connections might be his ticket off the small runabout. He complained loudly and often about the injustice of someone as obviously skilled as him not being on the bridge of a mainline warship.

"We have a … this doesn't make any sense," the sensor operator said from his cramped station.

"What is it?" Jillian asked. She was an assimilated O-5, not technically a Fleet officer anymore, but the captain of the yacht had taken to giving her rotations on the bridge.

"The computer is telling me it's a transition flash, but it doesn't match anything in the database," the operator said. "It was small like a Prowler might make, but it wasn't uniform the way all Terran warp drive flashes are."

"Does it match any of the non-associated anomalies?" Jillian asked tensely. She was well-aware of the Darshik Specter and its unique warp transition. All Fleet ships had a database of "anomalies" to look out for, and she knew that the Specter had been added to the latest update. If it showed up, the computer would give the proper warnings.

"Negative, ma'am. It was too far within the system to be a warp flash from any known type of starship anyway," he said, turning away from his monitor to look at her.

"How close?" she asked.

"The computer calculates it to be—"

"Look!" the first mate shouted just as a brilliant flash lit up the entire bridge. It was so bright the forward windows dimmed automatically.

"No!!" Hoshino cried out once their eyes adjusted. Amaterasu was burning in space. The mammoth station had been pierced in multiple places and secondary explosions were tearing pieces off, some of them measuring kilometers across.

Jillian watched in horror as a white lance stabbed through the hull of Amaterasu and began to walk up slowly, disappearing after a few seconds. She knew a Darshik plasma lance when she saw one, but she'd never heard of one with that sort of destructive capability.

"Load all sensor data on a point-to-point com drone and fire it off, NOW!" she shouted to the sensor operator. "And shut down all active sensors, go silent."

"Destination for the com drone," he asked, his voice shaking.

"New Sierra Platform ... priority one-alpha-one," she said. "Pilot! We won't be able to outrun that ship ... is there anywhere to hide?"

"No, this planet has no moons and we're three-quarters of a billion kilometers from the asteroid field," the pilot said.

"Take us down!" Hoshino said, pointing at the planet wildly. "This ship can land and there's no atmosphere to speak of down there. Take us down and land in one of those impact craters. Shut the engines and the sensors off and try to hide."

"Do it!" Jillian barked. "And pick a crater near one of the poles ... Amaterasu isn't going to be able to stay in orbit much longer."

Even as she said it the lights on the station were winking out, and on the optical sensors they could see it was beginning to list and lose altitude. Without a heavy atmosphere to slow it down and burn it away the station would hit the planet with tremendous force. Jillian thought that could work in their favor as it would create a hell of a mess for someone to try and look through even with the most advanced sensors.

"Keep all passive sensors trained on Amaterasu," she said. "Try to get a look at the ship that hit her."

"All those people," the first mate whispered as the pilot swung the small ship away and down towards the planet, pushing the engines up.

"Why don't you go wake the captain up," Jillian told him. He appeared to be locked up and wasn't doing any good on the bridge. Since the yacht hadn't taken fire or performed any evasive maneuvers, the captain was likely still snoring in his rack, totally oblivious to the devastation right above them.

"I think I found a target," the pilot said. "Initial readings show we'll fit down in the depression easily and the surface looks solid enough so the landing gear won't sink."

"Good," Jillian said, her hands shaking after the massive adrenaline shock her system had just gone through. For the first time in a long time she felt genuinely afraid. The small yacht had no warp drive, no weapons, and there weren't any other Fleet vessels in the system that she knew of. There were a lot of Tsuyo research and construction vessels to support Amaterasu, but no warships. Hopefully they could hide on the surface and blend in while her com drone raced for New Sierra to at least let CENTCOM know that the Darshik were stepping up their game.

The yacht began to shake violently as it streaked down into the beginnings of the wispy atmosphere, warning alarms blaring and the computer spitting out a stream of warnings to reduce velocity. Without having to be told, the pilot ignored them and pushed the throttles on the mains up a tick further.

"Let's clean her up!" the pilot called out. "Prepare for atmospheric flight."

The small ship was designed to be flown safely within a planet's atmosphere and land, so at the pilot's request the flight engineer retracted all the protruding radomes and antennas into the hull to "clean up" the yacht's flight profile. Almost immediately the buffeting lessened dramatically as the now-slick craft pushed deeper into the atmosphere, its lifting body design actually starting to generate a little lift.

"Have we been spotted?" Jillian asked, looking up as Amaterasu could still be seen breaking apart through the dorsal observation portholes.

"We're blind until we can redeploy the sensors!" the flight engineer shouted over the sound of the slipstream screaming over the hull.

"Have you lost your fucking mind, Wolfe?" Captain Eckler thundered as he stumbled onto the bridge.

"Look!" Jillian pointed upwards. "A Darshik ship just took out that habitat. We have to hide!"

Eckler blinked a few times, apparently in a stupor, before nodding slowly and looking around his bridge.

"Report!" he finally choked out.

"We're making our way to this depression in the northern polar region, sir," the sensor operator spoke up, pointing at his display. "We'll land there and go dark … hope they don't see us."

"How long?"

"Coming about on our final turn now, Captain," the pilot said. "Flight, shut down internal gravity and stand by to fire retro thrusters."

"Gravity off, retro burn prepped," the flight engineer confirmed. "On your mark."

"Mark!" the pilot shouted, slapping the throttles back to idle and pitching their prow up a few degrees. The deck shook mightily as the ventral thrusters all fired, taking up the weight of the ship as it slowed well past the point of the lifting surfaces being effective.

"Stabilize!"

"We're stable, we're stable!" the flight engineer shouted. "Just get us down!"

"Drop landing gear and stand by for final decent," the pilot said, sweat running off his brow. The sturdy little craft was built to be able to fly and land within an atmosphere, but not at breakneck speeds and with a spooked crew running from an enemy warship in orbit.

"Gear down!"

"Here we go."

Jillian's stomach dropped as the port side dipped precariously, the thrusters still shaking the deck hard enough to cause her feet to go numb. Slowly the pilot leveled them, turned the ship to the orientation he wanted, and began reducing thrust to slowly settle them to the surface. At two-hundred-meters altitude Jillian could make out their target on the display, fed to the pilot through the ventral optical sensors.

"Ten meters!" the sensor operator called out. A few seconds later there was a jarring hit that almost knocked Jillian off her feet.

"We're down!" the pilot called out. "Shut down main engines and thrusters."

"Mains coming down, thrusters off," the flight engineer called out.

"Damage?" Captain Eckler called out in the eerie silence, his voice now too loud with the roar of engines and slipstream gone.

"No damage, no casualties reported."

"Redeploy our sensors and get eyes on what's left of Amaterasu and try to get a positive identification on the enemy ship," Eckler said before turning to Jillian. "Did you get one of our com drones off about the attack?"

"Yes, sir," Jillian said. "All the preliminary sensor data and the ship's log was sent to New Sierra."

"Outstanding, Commander," Eckler said, using her assimilated rank. He himself was a commander in rank but assumed the title of captain when he was aboard. "So CENTCOM will be aware of the situation and we still have one com drone left … assuming we're able to get back into space to use it."

"Sensors redeployed," the operator said. "We're on passives only. There are too many lifeboat signals to pick out how many survivors might have gotten off the station, but it looks like a lot."

"That's something at least," Hoshino said, the first time he'd spoken since they began their descent.

"Do you have family aboard Amaterasu, Mr. Hoshino?" Jillian asked.

"My wife and three children," the Tsuyo rep said in a flat voice, his eyes full and unfocused.

"Perhaps you'd like to return to your quarters for a bit," Eckler said gently. "We'll keep you in the loop, and if we start to get a better idea of the situation I'll let you know if we're in a position to take action."

Without any sort of acknowledgement, Hoshino turned and walked off the bridge. Jillian's heart broke for him and her thoughts went immediately to her twins. They were on Arcadia in the care of her parents and, she had assumed, completely safe from the Darshik. But if they could strike here, was there any place in the Federation that was really safe?

Her thoughts also were with her husband. He was in constant danger on his latest mission, and while the Federation all knew the implacable Captain Wolfe, she knew Jackson, a man with sometimes crippling self-doubt and someone who carried the guilt of thousands of deaths on his shoulders. She knew he was cunning and relentless, but this Specter—for she had no doubt who was commanding the Darshik ship—had just taken out hundreds of thousands of civilians for apparently no reason. Could Jackson go toe-to-toe with that sort of ruthless disregard for life? Or would his instincts to protect innocents at all costs compromise him and give this Specter the chance to take the *Nemesis* out?

****

"Captain Wolfe to the bridge. Captain Wolfe to the bridge."

The insistent calls from the computer over the intercom, along with his own comlink chirping in chorus, pulled Jackson out of the deep sleep he was in. It was the type of sleep he only enjoyed aboard a ship when it was either docked or in a formation with other ships like now.

"What the hell?" he grumbled and rolled off his rack, clearing his throat. "On my way."

The *Nemesis* had been sitting in orbit over the gas giant with the rest of the Black Fleet formation for so long he thought maybe CENTCOM had forgotten about them. Pike and Marcum had departed over a week ago and he'd heard through the command-level chatter in the system that the Ushin delegation was heading home at any time. If his mission to track and kill the Specter had truly been scuttled, he wished that they'd either give him a standard patrol route to serve out his time or, barring that, just release him outright and let him slink back into retirement.

He checked his prosthetic leg once more before sliding on his pants and pulling on his utility top. The new leg was much, much better than the previous model. Its tactile feedback was so good and the actuators so smooth and quiet that he was no longer actually aware that it wasn't his real leg. The Tsuyo doctors swore they were on the verge of a breakthrough that would allow them to regrow the leg, but with hardware this good, he wasn't in any hurry.

On his way out of his quarters he abstractly wondered why, with the technology available, cybernetic enhancements had never caught on. Maybe if they continued having to fight ground wars someone would think of enhancing their soldiers.

"What's the good word, Captain?"

"You ever sleep, Sergeant Barton?" Jackson asked. He'd grown to enjoy the fact that Barton seemed to know just how far to push the line of familiarity while not stepping over. It made having him as a near constant shadow much more tolerable.

"Sergeant Castillo and I have switched over to split sixes for your guard detail, sir," Barton said.

"Castillo? Who says I want that lunatic watching my back?" Jackson asked. Barton laughed good-naturedly and took his post just outside the bridge hatchway as the captain walked through.

"Report."

"Captain, we have a priority one alpha channel request coming in," the second watch com officer said. "CENTCOM is preparing to broadcast a command-level briefing to most ships in the system within the next two hours and we're one of them ... the confirmation codes have already come in from New Sierra."

"Send it to the observation lounge and have Commander Chambliss join me there ASAP," Jackson said.

"Aye, sir."

****

"This is a bit unusual," Chambliss remarked after Jackson had told him everything he knew. "Aren't these things normally pre-recorded and then sent as an encrypted data message?"

"Yes," Jackson said, eyeing Chambliss's sugary pastry with undisguised envy. One drawback of getting older was he couldn't eat whatever he wanted anymore with any expectation of his workout regimen keeping him trim.

"Maybe with so many ships in the system at one time they figured this was easier."

They finished their breakfast in silence while the large holographic screen that was projected over the end of the table showed the United Terran Federation Starfleet emblem along with the words "Stand By" crawling along the bottom. The new projectors on the *Valkyrie*-class were so good he could project a substantial-looking high-resolution screen anywhere he wanted it. Jackson caught the change in the screen out of his peripheral vision and looked up to see Admiral Pitt standing behind a lectern in a briefing room that was also packed with Fleet officers.

"Good morning, or whatever time it is for those of you on the two dozen ships this is being broadcast to," Pitt began. Jackson saw the drawn look on his face and knew something had happened, and he could take a pretty good guess at what had been the cause.

"We received an emergency point-to-point com drone ten hours ago that came in from the Kirin System, a system owned by the Tsuyo Corp with no habitable planets … but it did have a population of around four hundred and fifty thousand people. This broadcast has an accompanying data packet and in it are all the technical specifications of the Amaterasu Habitat Project.

"What we've been able to verify is that nearly three weeks ago Amaterasu was taken out by a Darshik warship in what's being considered the highest loss of civilian lives since the Phage took out Haven. We've dispatched emergency search and recovery vessels but they're some weeks out still.

"The reason for this initial briefing is to give you a heads up. The Ushin may have negotiated a tenuous peace with the Darshik, but it appears not everyone is abiding by the ceasefire. I've been authorized by the President via the CENTCOM Chief of Staff to tell everyone hearing my voice to consider themselves on alert. The rogue Darshik elements could strike here next, or the decision might be made to mobilize for a counterstrike. Either way, take stock of your ships, get your crews spun up, and call for provisioning if you need it. I *do not* want to hear about a starship delaying its departure if so ordered because it's waiting for consumables or munitions. Top off your air, water, and food and make sure your ships are fueled and ready to fight.

"That's all I have for you at this time. All commanders need to hang loose and be ready for specific instructions that we'll be sending out shortly."

In true Pitt style, the broadcast terminated without any extraneous words or unnecessary filler. Once he had said everything he had wanted to say, he killed the feed.

"Holy shit," Chambliss hissed. "There were hundreds of thousands of people on that habitat."

"You're familiar?" Jackson asked.

"Yes, sir," Chambliss said. "It was an ambitious project that really stretched what we thought was possible with self-sustaining orbital platforms."

"Why the hell would the Darshik hit something like that?" Jackson wondered. "It's an unnecessary provocation at a time they can least afford it."

"*Captain, we just received a message instructing us to maintain position and be ready to accept a VIP guest within the next twelve hours,*" the com officer's voice came over the intercom. Jackson did the math in his head and figured it must be one of the larger fleet shuttles coming from the New Sierra Platform.

"Acknowledged," Jackson said. "Please inform Major Baer and Flight OPS so they're ready."

"*Aye, sir.*"

Chapter 8

"Attention on deck!" The sound of boot heels snapping together echoed through the room.

"Permission to come aboard, Captain."

"Permission granted, Admiral," Jackson said. "Welcome aboard the *Nemesis*. By your order, Admiral?"

"At ease!" Admiral Pitt barked. Jackson nodded to Celesta Wright, standing just behind Pitt, and the pinched look on her face made his stomach clench. This wasn't a social visit.

"Honor guard, dismissed," Major Baer said, turning and motioning the ten Marines out of the airlock receiving area before assuming the position of parade rest.

"I hope you come in peace, sir," Jackson said with a laugh when he looked over Pitt's shoulder and saw who else had accompanied him.

"Captain Wolfe, I think you've already met Commander Essa." Pitt gestured for the man behind him to walk up. "I'm placing NOVA Team Blue on detached duty aboard the *Nemesis* under your command. Hopefully you won't need them, but they'll be here if you do."

"Is my mission back on, sir?" Jackson asked eagerly.

"We should talk in private." Pitt looked around. "Just the three of us, and then you can decide how to disseminate the information to your crew."

"Follow me, Admirals," Jackson said and walked off towards the lifts, Sergeant Castillo falling in right behind them.

They exchanged tense small talk on the way up to the superstructure. The observation lounge had been built as a multi-purpose area, but Jackson had taken to conducting any meeting there that involved more than two people. The space was nice, the view was much better, and the furniture far more comfortable than what was in his office. Not only that, but it seemed to put people more at ease to talk on neutral ground rather than his personal domain.

"Judging from Admiral Wright's face I have a feeling I'm not going to like what you're here to tell me," Jackson said once the hatch had closed and locked.

"You've already heard the vague brief regarding the Amaterasu attack," Pitt said. "I've come out here personally to let you know some things that I hope won't cloud your perspective, but I also don't believe in hiding information like this from my people. I'll leave it up to your good judgment to decide if you've been compromised.

"The com drone that came in with the sensor data of the attack was sent by your wife. She was aboard a small Fleet runabout in that system mapping out prospective training grounds and had just departed Amaterasu when the attack began."

Jackson felt like the room was spinning and he leaned forward onto a chair to keep himself from falling. What the hell was Jillian doing out in the Kiran System in a fucking yacht with no Fleet assets in the area?

"Captain, we have no reason to believe at this time the ship she was on was caught up in the attack," Celesta said. "The last part of the transmission she sent stated they weren't being actively targeted."

"I assume there's a reason you're telling me this while bringing NOVAs onto my ship at the same time?" Jackson asked.

"The attack has rattled people. Badly," Pitt said. "The President seemed content to allow an internal Ushin power struggle play out without interference, but now the Tsuyo Corporation board of directors is pissed. Rumor is they want this rogue Darshik Specter brought down ... and they've specifically requested you to do it. Off the record, I think we all know where the real power lies within the Federation. I'd expect your official orders to come through at any time."

"Sir, I—"

"In the meantime," Pitt cut him off, "I'm ordering the *Nemesis* to fly directly to the Kirin System for a fact-finding mission in relation to the latest attack. You will depart immediately, Captain."

"Thank you, sir," was all Jackson could manage to get out.

"Don't make me regret this, Wolfe." Pitt pointed his finger across the table at Jackson. "I want this ship repositioned so she's able to more quickly respond when those inevitable orders come through, but I am *not* authorizing you to go cowboy out there and resume actively hunting this bastard without express permission. The Kirin System is closer to the Juwel System than DeLonges is, and you'll need those jump points to cross over into Darshik space."

"The Ushin are officially accepting the Darshik's unconditional surrender, at least for two of their three planets," Celesta took up the briefing. "All active Darshik combat units are to be considered rogue and hostile. You are authorized to defend yourself and any Federation ship or system, but at this point you are not to pursue past our borders."

"Two of the three?" Jackson asked.

"The system where Admiral Wright took out that derelict Super Alpha is still declaring itself independent," Pitt said. "The Ushin politics are as murky as everything else we think we know about them, but it seems the commander of that unique warship has a complete stranglehold on that planet. They've fortified the system with a force of unknown strength … all we know is the Ushin don't feel they can safely approach the planet."

"So the war is over save for this one asshole still flying around blowing up every Terran orbital installation he can find," Jackson said.

"It's more than one ship but yes, that's the long and short of it," Celesta said. "There's more … the detailed analysis of the sensor data Jillian sent back shows a ship that isn't consistent with the original Specter. This ship looks bigger and more refined, whereas the other was a hodgepodge of borrowed technologies."

"And if they get a toehold somewhere else they can start producing these more powerful starships in greater numbers," Jackson said, his cheek twitching at the mention of Jillian being involved in the latest attack. "That also explains why Barrett reported that he saw the ship we fought over Juwel so recently in the Columbiana System," he continued. "The big dog got a new ship, so a subordinate must be flying the one Pike disabled."

"Our assumption as well," Pitt said. "That's everything we have, Wolfe ... get your ass out to Kirin and take a look around. This ship will easily overtake the recovery ships we've dispatched. Hell, she'll outrun the goddamn com drones, so make sure you remain there long enough for Admiral Wright to get your orders out to you."

"Aye aye, sir."

****

"Prepare the *Nemesis* for departure," Jackson said without preamble as he strode onto the bridge. "OPS, tell Engineering I want my ship ready to break orbit within the next twenty minutes. Coms! Message Fleet Control and let them know we're breaking out of formation and pushing for the Kirin jump point and we'll be at full power."

"Aye, sir!" Lieutenant Makers said enthusiastically.

"OPS, put me on the shipwide if you please," Jackson said as he slid into his seat.

"Go, sir."

"Attention crew ... we've just received orders to depart for the Kirin System as fast as the *Nemesis* can safely make it. More details will be forthcoming through your department heads, but just know that the ship may get her first real combat action sooner than later.

"The Darshik have attacked a Tsuyo orbital habitat and the civilian casualties are expected to be shockingly high ... likely in the hundreds of thousands. We're going there on a fact-finding mission as we're currently the fastest ship in the fleet, but we also need to be ready for anything. This is what we've been training for ... let's make sure that if given the chance we put an end to this bastard. That is all."

"Kirin System?" Commander Chambliss asked. "So our mission is back on?"

"Not entirely, XO," Jackson said. "I'll be giving a briefing to the senior staff as soon as we're transitioned out of this system to give you all the details, but for right now I want to be underway as quickly as we can manage it."

"Understood, sir."

The *Nemesis* thrummed with power as the crew readied her for departure. His crew dove into their tasks with an enthusiasm that was borne out of endlessly circling the same planet for the last five weeks. It didn't matter where they were going, all they had to hear was that it was someplace different.

Soon the *Nemesis* broke smoothly from orbit, her powerful main drive allowing the destroyer to accelerate away directly without having to bump up into a higher transfer orbit first. Once they were clear of all the Black Fleet formations, and the com section had fielded all the good luck calls from the other ships, Jackson ordered them to flank speed on an arcing course that would take them up the well and to the Kirin jump point. He had been overjoyed to find out that there was a direct warp lane between DeLonges and Kirin.

Even as the *Nemesis* screamed towards the jump point, Jackson couldn't help but think no matter how fast his ship was, he would be too late. He also had real concerns about his ability to command the mission should he find out that Jillian had been killed in the Kirin System by the Darshik ace he'd been pulled off the trail of earlier. The regulations were explicitly clear in situations where a commanding officer found himself to be emotionally compromised. If he felt that he was simply unable to detach his feelings from the task of command then it was up to him to step down. He looked over at Commander Chambliss, who was busy scheduling briefings so that the information he had been given by Pitt was able to be filtered down through the senior staff and department heads. Did he trust the man to command the ship in battle if he couldn't? Should he tell him of his predicament now so that Chambliss was able to keep an eye on him?

"Six hours to transition," Lieutenant Hori called out from the OPS station.

"Acknowledged," Jackson said, shaking his head. "Open the hatches over the warp emitters and charge the transition capacitor banks."

"Hatches opening up ... all four emitters deployed."

Jackson settled back for the last few hours until the *Nemesis* would cheat her way around relativity and outrun the light from DeLonges Prime to the Kirin System. His guts were twisted in knots at the prospect of what he might find there. The thought of losing Jillian was so horrifying his mind seemed to tiptoe around the issue, refusing to look at it head on. Instead he bathed in the righteous anger that came from the deaths of hundreds of thousands of innocents and let that burning sensation fill him. There would be no mercy once he caught up to this Specter. He'd hunted one alien invader across star systems before, and this time he wasn't bringing a ship that was decades out of date. He intended to give no quarter and would only be satisfied with the death of this Darshik rogue.

"Emergency power is stable!" Jillian called over her shoulder.

"Bringing the scrubbers back online," came the faint shout back.

The ship had landed safely but had been pummeled by debris raining down from the falling habitat. They'd had nine hull breaches so far and the last major impact had knocked their main power out. The chief engineer said the power junction was irreparably damaged and he had no choice but to shut their only fusion reactor down completely. Without main power there was zero chance of the ship taking off again, much less making it to orbit. The yacht had effectively just become an emergency shelter and they only had breathable air and heat for as long as the emergency power held out.

The com systems all still worked, but their passive sensors located on the dorsal surface hadn't survived the barrage of incoming debris. Their location hadn't been far enough north to completely miss the strikes as the station broke apart, but they were saved from the largest chunks that would have smashed the yacht flat. Those bigger pieces of structure had also kicked up a cloud of dust so heavy upon impact that most of the ship's optical sensors were now useless, and Captain Eckler had ordered them retracted to protect the sapphire lenses from the swirling grit.

They did have one wavelength that still gave them some detail: long-wave infrared. They had two imagers that could see in that part of the spectrum and look through the dust to at least get a rough idea of what might be coming their way, so they risked keeping them deployed. The high-power radar was still functional but would instantly give away their location.

"How are we looking on lifeboats?" Jillian asked.

"Same number as we initially picked up are still transmitting strong beacon signals," the sensor operator said. "Four hundred and three total."

"So a possibility of maybe eleven thousand survivors if they overloaded a few of them," Eckler muttered. "Damn! They must have not had any time from the beginning of the attack to when the order came to abandon ship."

"But at least the Specter isn't going around hitting lifeboats," Jillian said. "That could mean they're beneath its notice or that it's already left the area."

"Or it's laying a trap for the recovery ships," the first mate said. He'd slunk back onto the bridge after they'd landed and appeared to be back in control of himself.

"A possibility," Jillian conceded. "But that doesn't fit the usual pattern of hit and run it's been fond of so far. Even as powerful as its weapons are, it has shown itself to be very reluctant to meet a Terran warship head-on without having a numerical advantage. Celesta Wright chased it across three star systems and it did everything it could to try and escape her."

"I recall reading a redacted version of the post-incident report when she flew the *Icarus* all the way to Juwel to take another shot at it," Eckler said. "It did seem that it was hesitant to pit itself against the *Starwolf*-class ships and instead went after your husband's assault carrier and the *Intrepid*-class destroyers."

"The computer has finished the orbital debris analysis," the sensor operator spoke up.

"Go ahead," Eckler said.

"Even if we could take off, the chances of making it to orbit safely are less than fifteen percent. All of the lower orbits are clogged with debris that isn't coming down ... the preliminary analysis indicates it could be years before they're navigable again."

"So that makes a rescue ship coming down equally unlikely," Jillian breathed. "How long can we sit down here on emergency power?"

"Power, food, and potable water will likely outlast us," Eckler said, looking at his tile. "Breathable air will become an issue within five weeks and that's assuming all the scrubbers are working at peak efficiency to that point. We're on the secondary environmental system after the primary was damaged by debris."

"Can it be repaired?" Jillian asked.

"Possibly," Eckler said. "A ship like this doesn't carry much in the way of spare parts, but we'll certainly try."

Jillian didn't say anything further. She looked out the forward window at the swirling gray dust, the light of Kirin Prime barely penetrating it. She had no doubt that CENTCOM had already dispatched ships once her com drone made it to New Sierra, but would they have the capability of getting them off the yacht before the air turned stale and they all suffocated?

Chapter 9

"Transition complete. All departments checking in."

"Position confirmed, we're in the Kirin System, sir."

"Secure warp emitters and bring the main drive online," Jackson ordered. "Tactical, let's not be subtle about this; full active sensors. Begin scanning the system. Coms?"

"There are a *lot* of Fleet transponders down there, sir," Makers said. "Hundreds of them."

"Lifeboats from the habitat," Chambliss said. "That's a good sign. Either the Specter isn't bothering with killing off the survivors or it's already cleared out of the system."

"I wish it was still here," Jackson growled. "I can't do anything to pursue it outside of this system on these provisional orders from Admiral Pitt. We need CENTCOM to come through with an official go-order."

"Main drive power is available, Captain," Lieutenant Hori said. "Engineering has cleared the *Nemesis* for maneuvering."

"Helm, all ahead full," Jackson said. "Just take her down the well. Nav! Get a proper course laid out that parks us in orbit outside of the debris field over the fourth planet and send it to the helm."

"All ahead full, aye!"

"Course locked in and sent to the helm, Captain."

"OPS, bring up the ident and nav beacons along with our Link transponder," Jackson ordered. "We need to let everyone down there know that a friendly has arrived in-system. Do we have an estimate on how far back the initial wave of recovery ships were?"

"Four more days, Captain," Hori answered.

"And we don't have the capability of recovering that type of lifeboat, much less the room for all the survivors," Chambliss said. The lifeboats used on large orbital platforms were huge, far too large to fit in a destroyer's hangar bay. They could try and dock to them using one of the external airlocks, but they also didn't maneuver very well and posed too great a risk to a ship not designed specifically to recover them.

"We're not here in a rescue capacity, Commander," Jackson said. "We're here to observe and render what aid is possible. OPS, tell CIC that I want every transponder cataloged and tracked so that we can give the recovery fleet detailed information and expedite things as much as possible."

"Aye, sir."

The *Nemesis* pushed down into the system towards what was undoubtedly the single most deadly attack on a civilian target in the history of their species outside of the planetary-scale attacks during the Phage War. Jackson had no doubt that the new President would move quickly to get his mission approved and fast-tracked through CENTCOM after this latest atrocity. It was one thing when Starfleet ships or platforms were attacked, but with likely hundreds of thousands of civilians dead on a Tsuyo-owned habitat there were going to be very powerful people calling for blood. President Nelson might have been able to hold off the hawks in Parliament before and let his "none of our business" strategy play out, but not after this.

The United Terran Federation was new and had been thrown together out of desperation at a time when they were looking down the barrel of another protracted war and hemorrhaging systems to the already established Eastern Star Alliance. As would be expected, the political waters were mostly uncharted since there were a lot of new players at the table, and the centuries of tradition from the Confederate Senate were tossed out the window. President Wellington had commanded enough respect and had the clout of the Columbiana System behind him to force through the changes he wanted and to hold the other member systems in check. President Nelson of Britannia had neither the support of a powerful star system nor the commanding presence Wellington did. Jackson wondered how he would respond in this first real test of his leadership.

"CIC reports the computers are isolating and cataloging all transponder signals, Captain," Lieutenant Hori said. "Lieutenant Commander Hawkins has pulled in extra people and authorized the use of two of our emergency backup cores to get a report to you as quickly as possible."

"Good man." Jackson nodded his approval. Lieutenant Commander Jake Hawkins should have been a full commander already, but he'd been busted down in rank twice early in his career due to an ill-advised romance with an admiral's daughter when he was a lieutenant junior grade and then again for a bar fight on DeLonges where he put three Fourth Fleet spacers in the hospital, two with serious injuries. Jackson had been dubious when Captain Ed Rawls of the *TFS Relentless* had recommended Hawkins for the *Nemesis's* CIC department head job, but so far he'd outperformed all his peers.

"XO, let's see about getting Lieutenant Commander Hawkins spun up as a bridge watch alternate," Jackson said after a moment. "I think he's earned a shot at it."

"I'll make a note of it, sir."

"OPS, how long until we're within visual range of the wreckage?" Jackson asked.

"Ten hours at current acceleration, sir," Hori said.

He resisted the urge to have CIC try and pick out the transponder signal of the ship Jillian had been on. They were working through the mess as fast as they could and all he would do with his request was hamper their efficiency. The best he could do was try and remain calm and wait until they were within range to begin a thorough search of the planet's surface.

****

"Captain, we've just received a new transponder signal … it's a Fleet ident beacon."

"Who is it?" Captain Eckler asked, sitting up and rubbing his eyes. He'd been on watch for thirty-one hours straight while Jillian Wolfe had gone below deck to help with the repairs on their primary environmental systems.

"Resolving now, sir," the sensor operator said. She was the only other person on the cramped bridge with Eckler.

"It's a *Valkyrie*-class destroyer, Black Fleet, registry DS-1102A. I've never heard of that class of ship, sir."

"What's the name of the ship? You'll have to cross-check with our internal database; ident beacons only broadcast the registry," Eckler said with a sigh. He bit off his admonishment at such a basic mistake. The yacht's crew had been running around in remote systems for over a year and any training deficiencies were a reflection of his own failures, not theirs.

"It's the *Nemesis*, sir," she said. "I'm still not sure that—"

"Please have Commander Wolfe come to the bridge immediately," Eckler said. His crew might be ignorant of the Fleet's newest class of destroyer, but he was very familiar with the ship's name, her mission, and who commanded her.

"You asked to see me, Captain?" Jillian asked as she came up on the bridge. She was wearing utility coveralls and was covered in sweat and grime.

"*Nemesis* has just arrived in-system and is broadcasting a clear ident signal with no warnings," Eckler said. "I'm about to order our own transponder active. Is there anything specific you'd like me to send to your husband's ship?"

"Send a Link channel request so that we can use the *Nemesis's* sensors to see outside of all the dust," Jillian said after a moment of thought. "I would also send a message giving our status ... Jackson can infer from there that I'm alive and well. We don't know for certain that the Specter is gone or if they've cracked our standard encryption. It might not be wise to let them know there's someone on this ship that's connected in any way to the commander of the incoming destroyer."

"Sensible," Eckler said with a weary smile that failed to reach his eyes. "I suppose that's the difference in thinking between an officer who ferries VIPs within a star system and one who has been on the bridge of mainline warships in nearly every major engagement."

"Your entire crew is alive and well, Captain," Jillian said carefully. "You'll hear no disparaging words from me regarding your command of this ship."

Eckler stared at her a moment and then nodded his thanks.

"Ensign Haan, please bring our beacon online, full power broadcast," he said. "And request a Link channel as well ... I'll send the message over that unless they decline our request."

"Aye, sir."

****

"Incoming Link request from a Fleet intrasystem runabout that seems to be sitting on the surface of the fourth planet, sir."

"Are the encryption countersigns valid?" Lieutenant Commander Accari asked from the *Nemesis's* command chair. Captain Wolfe had gone off watch and Commander Chambliss wanted to visit CIC to see what the progress was on sifting through all the lifeboat signals, so Accari was in charge for the time being.

"Yes, sir," Lieutenant Hori said.

"Accept the request and limit the stream to navigational sensor data until we know exactly who this is," Accari said.

"Coming up now, sir."

It was another hour and a half until all the handshakes had been accomplished and two-way data had been established before Accari could look and see if this was really a Fleet yacht or some sort of new Darshik tactic. It didn't take him long to skim through the incoming stream before he realized what he was looking at.

"OPS, go ahead and put all our sensor data on the Link," he said. "Coms! Have Captain Wolfe paged to the bridge immediately."

"Aye, sir."

It was another fifteen minutes before a bleary-eyed Jackson Wolfe walked onto the bridge and affixed Accari with a flat, unfriendly stare.

"We're not under fire, Lieutenant Commander, so I assume there was some other sort of emergency?"

"We've had another transponder pop up in the system, Captain," Accari said, gesturing to the terminal on the command chair. "They've sent a message to us over the Link."

Jackson approached and read the holographic display over Accari's shoulder. He seemed to deflate visibly when he realized that the message was from the yacht Jillian had been on and the captain of the small ship had just verified that the entire complement was alive and well on the surface of the planet.

"Coms, make direct contact with the ship on the surface of that planet and get a full status update," he said, straightening. "I have the bridge, Mr. Accari … please call up your relief for Tactical and then go get some rest."

"Yes, sir."

Jackson read through the entire message again and could feel the tension he'd built up within him on the flight out drain away. Jillian was safe aboard the other ship and the *Nemesis* was now in the system in case the Specter returned. Under the circumstances, it was the best he could hope for. The more he read, however, the more he realized they might have a serious problem. The yacht was too damaged to lift off and, even if it could, the orbital lanes were clogged with debris from the massive habitat that was still breaking apart. His ship didn't carry the type of specialized recovery equipment that would allow them to get aid to the stricken yacht.

****

"This is the closest I feel comfortable approaching, Captain," Commander Chambliss reported as Jackson walked onto the bridge.

"This is fine, we're not a rescue ship so getting any closer doesn't help," Jackson said. He'd accepted Chambliss's request to take the bridge for the final approach to the planet and allowed himself seven hours of uninterrupted sleep, the first decent rest he'd had since he'd learned of the attack. Now the *Nemesis* was sitting in high orbit, well above all the debris, and he was wondering just what he hoped to accomplish.

"Open a two-way channel with the downed yacht."

"Stand by, sir," Lieutenant Makers said.

"*This is Captain Eckler of the FV George Mulland,*" a voice came back almost as soon as the channel request was sent.

"Captain Eckler, this is Jackson Wolfe aboard the *Nemesis*," Jackson said. "How are you holding up, sir?"

"*We're banged up but otherwise alright for the moment, sir,*" Eckler said. "*We are running short on consumables and have been on backup power for some weeks, however.*"

"Stand by, Captain," Jackson said and gave Makers the chopping "mute" hand signal.

"Channel muted, sir."

"They can't sit on emergency power forever waiting on those rescue ships from DeLonges," Chambliss said. "I looked up that class while you were resting, sir. One more major component failure and they could lose part or all of their life support."

"Does a yacht that size have lifeboats?" Jackson asked.

"Just one ... and it deploys from the belly."

"So that's useless other than as a last resort if they lose backup power," Jackson said. "Open channel."

"Go, sir."

"Captain Eckler, what's the status of your lifeboat? Could it be used as a contingency plan if you lose backup power?" Jackson asked.

"*Negative, Captain Wolfe,*" Eckler said. "*During the debris strikes we took, the launch cradle malfunctioned and three of the six clamps released. It pulled away from the hatch just enough so that we can't safely open it.*"

"Talk about bad luck," Jackson muttered before raising his voice. "Very well, Captain. We'll start looking at options on this end. The lifeboats from the habitat are all sending back strong vitals so I'm not too worried about them, but I'd rather not leave you in there until the rescue ships show up. I'll contact you again when we have something. *Nemesis* out."

"Coms, have Commander Kelly from Flight OPS report to the bridge," Chambliss said. Jackson just nodded his approval. Kelly would be the one to determine if they could safely attempt an extraction of the crew from the stricken yacht.

As it turned out, Commander Kelly didn't see all that much difficulty in pulling the crew off with the spacecraft they had aboard. "Seems pretty straightforward, Captain," he said as he studied the sensor data of where the yacht was sitting. "They managed to get themselves pretty far north so they're out of the line of fire from most of the incoming debris, which has significantly tapered off.

"If you look here, and here"—he pointed to two spots on the display showing the planet—"you can see that the remaining chunks have all stabilized for the most part and none of them were knocked into polar orbits. We can take two of the new *Lancer*-class shuttles and drop right down into the northern polar region and fly right under most of the debris straight to the yacht."

"Will all of that airborne particulate debris cause you any trouble?" Chambliss asked.

"The MPDs won't care about the debris and the new sensors should be able to look through it just fine. If it looks like we're getting into real trouble I'll abort and haul ass back up into orbit. Shall I go ahead and begin prepping my crews, Captain?"

"Do it," Jackson said after a moment of thought. "Keep me apprised of your progress and pull the plug if you feel that the risk is higher than you've initially thought."

"Aye, sir," Kelly said, spinning on his heel and almost running off the bridge.

"Commander Chambliss, your thoughts?" Jackson asked when everyone was out of earshot. Chambliss used to run Flight OPS aboard the *Aludra Star* and was no stranger to sending shuttles and crews into unfriendly skies.

"I concur with Commander Kelly's assessment as well as your authorization of the mission," Chambliss said. "The newer *Lancer*-class ships are a lot more capable than the older *Skipper*-class, and the risk appears to be minimal."

Jackson looked over at his XO for a long, uncomfortable moment before turning and walking back to the center of the bridge. He trusted Chambliss to tell him if he was risking too much because it was his family stuck down on the surface. If his Flight OPS department head and his Executive Officer were both onboard then he would assume for the time being that he hadn't been emotionally compromised by the situation.

Chapter 10

"*Nemesis*, Ghost One ... starting final descent now," Captain Marshal Webster said before releasing the transmit button on his throttle and pressing the one right below it for the shuttle's intercom.

"Stand by, pushing down now. There's almost no atmosphere so it'll be a smooth ride all the way to the objective."

"*I've heard that bullshit before.*"

Marshal couldn't tell who had muttered over the hot mic so he opted to ignore it. The descent was one he'd trained for, but it was still tricky. They'd assumed a stationary polar orbit over the planet and would now begin a tight, spiraling descent to avoid all of the larger debris from the destroyed habitat. Flying past the larger pieces on the flight out from the ship had really driven home the scale of the atrocity. It made his heart race and he gripped the controls too tightly as he struggled to control his anger.

"*Ghost One, Nemesis ... good luck.*"

"Pushing over now," Marshal said to his copilot. He angled their nose down and to starboard, pushing up the throttles to intercept their decent vector. The airborne particulate near the lower altitudes wasn't nearly as heavy as Flight OPS had said it would be, but he stuck to the plan and remained on an instrument approach rather than switch to visual. The plasma engines were oblivious to the crap hanging in the air, but they consumed propellant at a prodigious rate so they'd have to get down and get back into orbit as quickly as they could. Normally the electric turbines would be used once the shuttle was within a planet's atmosphere, but the atmospheric density of the planet was too low for them to operate and all the crap suspended in the air would likely foul them out.

"Objective is coming up. I've got a strong rendezvous beacon," the copilot said.

"Confirmed, I see the marker lights now," Marshal said. "We'll swing around so we're facing with our nose pointed out along their prow and then switch to thrusters."

"Roger."

The plan agreed upon by Flight OPS, Captain Wolfe, and the crew of the stranded yacht had been to land the shuttles right on the ventral hull of the smaller ship. The *Lancer*-class had short docking cofferdams that could be extended from the shuttle's belly for quick transfers, eliminating the need to enter the hangar bay and maneuver into berth. The cofferdam collars could interface to any standard Fleet hatch, so things should go off without a hitch.

"There she is, switching over," Marshal said. There was a sickening drop as he pulled the MPDs to idle and the weight of the shuttle was taken up by the eight ventral thrusters. The ionic jets shook the small ship violently as Marshal used his helmet's 360-degree sensor capability to look down through the hull and line up his approach.

"Ten meters ... five ... two ... touchdown, cut thrust," the copilot said as the landing struts scraped against the upper hull of the yacht.

"Extend the docking collar," Marshal said.

"Extending ... we have soft dock," the copilot said. A moment later there was a sharp *clang*. "There we go, hard dock."

"*George Mulland*, Ghost One," Marshal said. "We have confirmed hard dock on your ventral hatch. Go ahead and pump up the tunnel from your end and we can begin transferring your crew. I have room for sixteen and then Ghost Two will be along to get the rest of you."

"*Copy Ghost One*," a voice came back. "*Stand by.*"

Marshal concentrated on minute lateral thruster adjustments to keep the shuttle centered so that the weight of the craft didn't put any strain on the flexible cofferdam. He could hear his crew chief opening their belly hatch and welcoming the crew of the yacht aboard while directing them to their seats. Five minutes later he heard the hatch bang shut and he saw on his status panel that the pressure was being released from the docking tunnel by the yacht's crew.

"We're all aboard, pilot," a woman in a Fleet-issue emergency pressure suit said. She had her helmet off so he could see that she was very attractive and didn't seem to be military.

"I'm Captain Marshal Webster, miss," he began hopefully. "We'll be ascending momentarily and get you settled into temporary billeting."

"Pleased to meet you, Captain," she said. "I'm Jillian Wolfe ... I'm hoping my husband won't be inclined to stick me in visiting officers' quarters. We're ready to go when you are."

Marshal was glad for his flight helmet so that nobody could see his flaming red cheeks.

"Retract the docking collar and stand by for ascent," he said over the intercom.

"Collar retracted and locked," the copilot said. "You sure you don't want to try to hit on the old man's wife again before we break for orbit?"

"Shut the fuck up," Marshal growled. He could actually hear his copilot laughing in his helmet as he maneuvered them away from the yacht and reengaged the MPDs. He was just happy that he hadn't said anything that could be misconstrued as inappropriate to the captain's wife. That wouldn't have done much for his career advancement prospects.

"Stand by for main burn," he said over the shuttle's intercom and pushed the throttles up smoothly, sending them streaking up into the northern sky.

****

"Permission to come aboa—" was all Jillian got out before Jackson pulled her the rest of the way through the airlock and wrapped her up in a fierce embrace. The shock of the action was written all over her face. Captain Wolfe very rarely let any cracks show through his stoic professionalism.

"Granted," he said after releasing her and pushing her back so he could look her over.

"No injuries, just dirty, tired, and hungry," she assured him. "The water reclamation system was on its last leg when you showed up. What's the *Nemesis* doing here anyway? I heard your mission was scrubbed."

"Admiral Pitt sent us here to do a preliminary recon of the system," Jackson said. "She's a lot faster than any of the recovery ships. Beyond that official reason I think he suspected I was going to come out here regardless of orders."

"Captain, I'll handle the rest of the incoming," Lieutenant Commander Hawkins said. "I'm not needed in CIC right now and you've certainly got better things to do."

"Thank you, Mr. Hawkins," Jackson said with a tight smile. "Please have the yacht's crew taken to billeting so they have a chance to clean up and get something to eat. Tell Captain Eckler we'll debrief him once he's had a chance to rest."

"Aye, sir."

Jackson gestured to his wife with his head and led her out of the hangar bay, pausing to look out the porthole to see the second shuttle just maneuvering in through the outer doors and turning to line up on its docking cradle and airlock. Jillian took off with long, confident strides and Jackson had to remind himself that she'd likely spent more time aboard a *Valkyrie*-class destroyer than he had. She'd overseen the development of most of the crew training programs that they'd all gone through at an accelerated pace.

The crew stopped and stood at attention respectfully as the pair (trailed loosely by Sergeant Barton) passed. The very few that were still serving with him since the *Blue Jacket* or the *Ares* stood and gawked as their old OPS Officer—and later XO—walked past covered in grime.

Once they arrived at Jackson's quarters, Barton posted up in his usual spot and managed to keep a straight face until they'd entered and closed the hatch behind them.

"If you'd be more comfortable in billeting I can arr—." The rest of his sentence was spoken into his wife's mouth as she grabbed him by the collar and pulled him into a crushing kiss.

"Do you really think I give a shit about Fleet decorum and regulations right now?" she asked.

"It would appear not," he said with a genuine smile. The relief of having gotten her off that planet without so much as a scratch flooded over him and he allowed himself to be dragged towards his rack which looked entirely too small for what Jillian had in mind.

Chambliss can pull a double watch. It builds character.

****

"The leading elements of CENTCOM's rescue force has arrived, sir," Lieutenant Hori said when Jackson walked onto the bridge. "They're forming up along the perimeter before coming down towards the planet."

"Thank you, OPS," Jackson said. "Coms, send a message and tell them the system is clear. They need to get down here quickly … they don't have time to sit on the boundary for weeks until all their ships arrive."

"Aye, sir."

"OPS, have there been any com drones entering the system in the past seventy-two hours?"

"Negative, Captain," Hori said.

"We can't afford to wait around," Jackson said. "Nav, is there a direct warp lane to Arcadia from this system?"

"Yes, sir. It was just recently established, but there've been no reports of any anomalies and Tsuyo has been moving some big ships through there," the chief at Navigation said.

"Very good. Plot a course for the Arcadia jump point and send it to the helm," Jackson said. "OPS, inform Engineering we'll be breaking orbit and steaming for a transition within the hour."

"Aye, sir."

"Arcadia, sir?" Chambliss whispered.

"There's something there I need to talk to and I'd rather do it in person if I have to do it at all," Jackson explained. "It's also an established system with a modern com drone platform so our orders may be waiting for us, and it will allow us to drop off our rescued crew at a CENTCOM facility without risking having them onboard if we're engaged by the Specter."

"Of course, sir," Chambliss said with a straight face. He knew damn well that the Wolfes had a home on Arcadia and that Jackson intended to fly his wife all the way there to ensure she made it safely.

"Some*thing,* sir?" he asked after his mind caught up with what he had heard.

"You'll see, Commander," Jackson said. "We've been stabbing around in the dark for the last year and a half looking for this enemy ace. In that time he's apparently built a much more powerful ship, gained an unbelievable amount of accurate intel on Terran space, and has just successfully perpetrated what can now be classified as a massive terrorist attack since he's not sanctioned by any government.

"We, on the other hand, have no idea where his base is, we're not sure why he's attacking research stations, and we have no idea how to find him. I need to quickly improve our odds before the next attack."

"Yes, sir," Chambliss said, looking even more confused than he had been before.

"Course is plotted from orbit to transition, Captain," the Nav specialist reported.

"OPS?"

"Engineering has cleared the Nemesis for maneuvering. Full engine power available."

"Helm, come onto new course ... all ahead one-half until you clear the debris field and then drop the hammer to flank," Jackson ordered.

"Ahead one-half, aye!"

Chapter 11

"Mr. Vice Chairman, thank you for taking the time to see me," President Nelson said as Akio Tanaka walked into the executive suite antechamber.

"Mr. President," Tanaka said with a bow. "It is good that we are able to discuss these things face to face. The com drone network lacks the necessary nuance when dealing with such delicate matters."

The two powerful men walked into the executive office, the heavy security door sliding shut automatically and a green light on the wall illuminating to indicate all the anti-eavesdropping equipment was active.

"I can assure you that the Parliament Committee on Starfleet Operations will quickly be giving me the authorization to order a surgical strike against the Darshik warship they call the Specter," Nelson said. "As soon as they do, I plan to unleash Captain Wolfe upon it and bring this conflict to a swift and decisive end."

"That is why I wished to speak to you alone … and off the record," Tanaka said carefully. "We are off the record, are we not, Mr. President?"

"Nothing said here will leave this room, and we're not being recorded," Nelson said, obviously on guard after the odd comment.

"Excellent," Tanaka said with a clap of his hands. "I will get right to the point. It is the position of the Tsuyo Corporation board of directors that we do not wish for Captain Wolfe to be *unleashed*, as you so colorfully put it, in response to the attack on our orbital habitat."

"You ... you can't be serious," Nelson said. "There are likely hundreds of thousands of dead civilians! Even if I was inclined to ignore this, the public, and therefore the legislature, will be clamoring for military action."

"Nevertheless we stand firm," Tanaka said sternly. "We feel that a military retaliation against this single Darshik would be ill-advised and a colossal waste of resources. There are many reasons for this, but for now let's just say that we feel it would only perpetuate a war that is ending without any need for intervention from us."

"I'm sorry, Mr. Tanaka, but I can't—"

"As we speak, our liaisons to Parliament are speaking to the members of the Fleet Operations committee." Tanaka rudely cut the President off, establishing who was really in control of the meeting. "You will not be receiving the authorization you're expecting. Recall the *Nemesis* and allow Tsuyo Corporation to handle what is essentially an internal matter."

"An internal matter!" Nelson exploded. "Have you lost your mind?! Tsuyo *employees* or not, those were still Federation citizens aboard that habitat and *we're* responsible for their safety. You dare to come in here and dictate terms to me like this?"

"I was told you were an idealist and occasional hothead, Mr. President," Tanaka sighed. "I'd hoped to do this quietly and with mutual respect ... that can still happen, but it's up to you. You've been in politics long enough to know that the board has vast influence within the government. That was the case in the old Confederation days and nothing has changed recently."

"I don't think we have anything further to discuss, Mr. Vice Chairman," Nelson said. "If you'll kindly show yourself out."

"Heed my words, Mr. President," Tanaka said as he stood up. "And please, for your sake, do not try to take this to the press and strong-arm the board. Nothing good can come of that. Good day, sir." Tanaka bowed again, smoothed his expensive suit, and walked out of the office.

Five kilometers away, in a small, windowless room, Agent Pike leaned back in his chair and thought about what he'd just heard. He'd re-bugged the executive suite after Wellington's death and once he'd learned that Tsuyo had sent their vice chairman to New Sierra he'd risked activating two of his audio bugs. Now he was reeling by what he'd just listened to.

Pike was no innocent. He knew damn good and well that Tsuyo was the *real* power within the Federation. Their tightly controlled technology made the entire thing possible in the first place, not to mention the fact they were an enormous part of the Fed's total economy. Even while they laid the groundwork to become their own independent power with representation like the other enclaves, they made sure they owned enough members of Parliament to move their agendas ahead at will.

So why would Tsuyo not want the bastard that had destroyed a habitat worth *trillions* of federal notes hunted down and killed? The board would normally have already taken matters into their own hands, either using their politician puppets to spur Starfleet into action or directly using their own fleet of ships. They weren't known for allowing such an insult to pass without retribution. So what the hell was really going on?

On a whim, Pike tossed on his light jacket, grabbed his field kit, and raced out of the safehouse. It was a CIS-controlled unit, but he was still a full agent in the intelligence organization so he could come and go as he pleased. He hopped into one of the ubiquitous public transport ground vehicles and ordered it towards the capital. His CIS credentials allowed him to access a greater degree of flexibility when using the public fleet of ground cars. He could, for example, give vague instructions like a general direction or to follow a specific target, something that wouldn't be possible if a civilian had flagged one down. It gave him the perfect camouflage for discreet observation.

"Fucking figures," he muttered as he saw five large, black Tsuyo vehicles roll out onto the main boulevard from the underground parking at the executive complex. Vice Chairman Tanaka was rolling heavy with a *lot* of security. This wasn't going to be as easy as he'd hoped.

"Follow the convoy of black ground transports," he instructed. "Maintain an interval no less than fifty meters and no more than seventy-five."

"*Acknowledged,*" the car's emotionless voice said. On the windshield, a projection bracketed the black vehicles and the telemetry from the public traffic management system scrolled along the bottom.

Pike hoped that Tanaka was staying at one of the swankier hotels of New Sierra City and that was why he had so much extra muscle with him. If he was staying on the Tsuyo compound located beyond the outskirts, the agent would have zero chance of getting close enough to see if the vice chairman had any other interesting meetings or interactions.

"Back to the grind," he sighed and settled in as the car doggedly pursued the convoy. After flying around in his Broadhead II, shooting up enemy starships, and flying point for more than a few Fleet operations, it was comforting to be getting back to what his job actually was. Human intelligence still had a critical role even in an age of technological dependence, and there weren't any better at the job than he was. Something in his gut told him that the Tsuyo board had done something that they would rather not have out in the public discourse.

If it was big enough to make them ignore the deaths of hundreds of thousands and shrug off the loss of the Amaterasu Orbital Habitat, it was likely something very big indeed.

****

"Transition complete, all departments checking in," Lieutenant Hori reported.

"Position verified," the nav specialist said. "We're in the Arcadia System and arrived seven *hundred* and two kilometers off target." There was some applause and cheering among the crew. Anything under a thousand kilometers when trying to hit a jump point was considered exceptional, so much so that the *Nemesis* would now get an award from CENTCOM for it.

"Let Engineering know they did an outstanding job at tightening that up," Jackson said, allowing himself a wide smile. He was certain by the time they left Arcadia his Engineering crew would have put the stylized bullseye marking on the prow before CENTCOM had time to certify the achievement.

"Yes, sir!" Hori said.

"Nav, give me a flyby course for Arcadia that allows us to deploy shuttles to the surface with the yacht crew aboard," Jackson said. "The *Nemesis* will sling past the planet and continue on to the coordinates I'm providing you. These coordinates are to be considered classified and are not to be stored in the nav computers as a known waypoint."

"Understood, sir," the chief sitting at Navigation said. "New course coming up now."

"Coms, please inform Flight OPS to prep two shuttles for crew transfer to the planet and that they're to remain on the surface until they hear from us. OPS, as soon as our ident beacon signal is recognized by the com drone platform, be on the lookout for a packet from CENTCOM ... we're still expecting our new orders."

"Aye, sir."

"XO, you have the bridge." Jackson stood abruptly and walked towards the hatchway. "Get us down to Arcadia as quickly as possible ... we have a lot of work to do."

"Yes, sir," Chambliss called to Jackson's departing back.

Jackson went to the lifts and, with Alejandro Castillo running to catch him, stepped into one of the waiting cars as the doors slid closed. He punched in his destination deck and waited as the car whooshed him down from the bridge further into the bowels of the ship. Stepping off on Deck 12, he made his way quickly through two security checkpoints and into CIC.

"Captain Wolfe, what can I do for you, sir?" Lieutenant Commander Jake Hawkins asked. As per Jackson's standing orders while underway, the CIC department head hadn't called the work center to attention when he walked in.

"I need to use one of the coffins, Lieutenant Commander," Jackson said. "I also want a raw data dump of everything we have on the Darshik Specter including unofficial intel on the recent attacks. Put it on a secure courier card and encrypt it using my credentials."

"Of course, Captain," Hawkins said without so much as a pause or raised eyebrow. "I'll alert the com shop that you'll be needing one of the secure transceivers and have it routed to number two ... it'll be ready by the time you get in there, sir."

"Thank you, Mr. Hawkins," Jackson said, walking off towards the back of the CIC where there were five discreet, narrow hatches. These led to secure com booths the crew called "coffins" that allowed someone to use the secure com suite without the risk of what was being discussed being leaked among the crew. They weren't normally used by bridge crew, it was more for the intel section that operated within the CIC, but Jackson wanted to make absolutely certain the integrity of Project Prometheus remained intact for as long as possible.

Once he was settled into the seat of the cramped com room, he saw the status board light up, showing that he now had direct access to three of the *Nemesis's* secure transceivers and that all of the latest valid Fleet encryption routines were available to him. He set the transceiver to send an encrypted data broadcast and punched in a local net address that he had memorized. The com lag at the distance between him and his intended recipient was fifty-eight minutes. Too far for two-way communication to be practical but close enough that he could at least send a message that he was coming.

"Administrator Jovanović, this is Captain Jackson Wolfe aboard the *TFS Nemesis*," he began once the lit halo around the microphone turned green. "I'll be hand-delivering a data bundle that I need the Cube to analyze ASAP. I'm asking this as a personal favor ... this isn't authorized by CENTCOM. My ship will be coming within shuttle range of the Pontiac within the next thirty hours. If there's an issue with my request, please channel it to me through the standard com network. Wolfe out."

Jackson checked to make sure the package had been transmitted successfully before closing down his link with the secure transceiver and exiting the coffin. As soon as he stepped back into the middle of the CIC, Lieutenant Commander Hawkins handed him a red data card, the color signifying that it contained classified information, and a biometric reader so that the card could be imprinted to his bio signature.

"And if you'll just sign the log, sir," Hawkins said. "I've already made an entry that you came down for a courier card, but I didn't specify what data you asked for. Technically we're not required to enter that."

"Thank you, Mr. Hawkins," Jackson said as he entered his credentials on the terminal. "You've been very helpful, as always. Carry on."

"Yes, sir."

"Where to now, Captain?" Castillo asked.

"We're going back to my office to lock this up," Jackson said, waving the red card. "After that, I'm going back to the bridge to finish the watch."

"Very good, sir."

****

"Mr. President, it's an honor to meet you in person, sir."

"Likewise, Admiral Pitt," Nelson said, shaking the flag officer's hand. "Please, have a seat."

"Thank you, sir."

"I know this is more Admiral Wright's department, and that I'm far outside normal channels talking to you directly anyway, but there's something I have to know, Admiral: Where is the *Nemesis*?"

Nelson's question completely threw Pitt off. He'd expected that this was just the usual formalities of a new President meeting with senior military staff when he'd gotten the call to fly down to the surface of New Sierra.

"She was dispatched to the Kirin System on my orders, sir," Pitt said carefully. "The *Nemesis* is by far the fastest ship currently in active service and I wanted to get eyes on the situation as quickly as I could. They effected the rescue of a downed Fleet yacht and last I heard she'd left the system shortly after."

"That's not answering the question, Admiral. You're telling me you have no idea where Starfleet's most advanced warship is at all times?" Nelson's tone was frosty and Pitt was once again reminded of how much he despised the political aspect of his job.

"Captains are given a certain leeway while operating so far away from Command, Mr. President," Pitt said. "However, I am expecting to hear through the automated reporting system that the *Nemesis* arrived in the Arcadia System after departing Kirin. Captain Wolfe's wife was aboard that yacht and it would be a short flight to take them to Arcadia as opposed to bringing them all the way back to New Sierra."

"You're personal friends with Captain Wolfe, are you not?" Nelson asked.

"We're very familiar with each other, sir, but I wouldn't go so far as to say we're friends," Pitt said. "I can predict how he'll react in most situations, if that's what you're asking."

"Very astute, Admiral." Nelson smiled humorlessly and steepled his fingers under his chin. "Consider what I'm about to tell you privileged information and not for the official record. There's not going to be an official go-order for Operation Exorcist. Parliament has come to the decision that it would be unnecessarily provocative and as things stand now I would need their approval to proceed."

Pitt strangled the curse that came to his lips at the news. How much more *provocative* did the Darshik need to be before these assholes would act? Operation Exorcist was a carefully planned set of orders for Starfleet that would put the *Nemesis* at the pointy end of the spear while providing enough support through the numbered fleets to allow Wolfe to press deep into Darshik territory if needed.

"However, Parliament does not issue specific operational orders to CENTCOM or Starfleet," Nelson went on. "That falls under the executive branch still. So while I cannot authorize Operation Exorcist, neither am I required to recall the *Nemesis* for any particular reason."

"I feel at this juncture you will need to be very specific as to what you want me to do, sir," Pitt said. He knew that Jackson's reputation as a loose cannon was largely undeserved, but it was how he was viewed nonetheless. Was the President actually asking him to try and goad Wolfe into disobeying orders?

"Nothing particularly," Nelson said. Pitt could have sworn the look that flashed across the President's face was one of ... disappointment? "We were just speaking of hypotheticals, Admiral. While this face-to-face has been enjoyable, I'm afraid my schedule is quite stuffed today."

"With your permission, sir." Pitt stood, knowing a dismissal when he heard one.

"Of course, Admiral." Nelson also stood and offered his hand again. "A pleasure to meet you."

The bizarre meeting left Pitt shaken as he walked down the corridor away from the office. It seemed to have been a clumsy, transparent attempt at getting Pitt to go against the Fleet Operations Committee by a Commander in Chief that had a whiff of desperation about him. What the hell was going on? Why weren't they going after this last Darshik element with everything they had? He pulled his comlink and hit the address for his aide.

"Please set up a meeting for me with a Mr. Aston Lynch," Pitt said. "He's an aide to the President. Tell him that it's critical and needs to be at his earliest convenience."

He wasn't looking forward to begging for information out of the CIS spook, but he couldn't think of anyone else that would be able to connect the dots for him.

Chapter 12

Danilo Jovanović paced the deck, pulling at his ears and trying in vain to calm himself. Why was Captain Wolfe hand-delivering data for the Cube to process? Was he really just in the area or was it something else? Was he being relieved from a position that he was woefully unqualified for? While it was completely unlikely they'd dispatch a destroyer all the way from New Sierra to remove a low-level administrator from a highly classified research project, his fears persisted.

It wasn't so much the loss of pay and prestige as it was the loss of purpose. Danilo had wanted to enter Starfleet from early childhood, but back then there was no great war with an alien species and they were very selective about whom they took. The fact that he had an extremely rare condition requiring him to have surgery to correct his vision had medically disqualified him. By the time the Phage came, he was too old to enlist.

Blind chance, so to speak, had caused him to be there when a decommissioned Vruahn device that had once been a stasis chamber awoke and revealed that its AI interface had developed into full sentience. As the first person it talked to, CENTCOM decided it would be easier to assign him to the project than let him run around loose with the knowledge that Starfleet was experimenting with alien technology that had once housed a piece of a Phage Super Alpha, something that was outlawed after the war. Now Danilo was in a place that, while not serving aboard a great warship, allowed him to make a difference and contribute.

"We have hard dock, cycling the airlock," one of the civilian security personnel said from the control panel. The round hatch popped inward and then swung ponderously aside, the antique actuators whining as they moved the heavy chunk of alloy aside.

"Administrator Jovanović, it's good to see you," Jackson Wolfe said warmly as he walked through the hatchway and extended his hand. Project Prometheus was not housed in a purpose-built orbital or deep space platform like most research projects. It was actually on a fully functional *Raptor*-class destroyer, the last of its kind. The *TCS Pontiac* had already been decommissioned, but Wolfe, likely because of a combination of nostalgia and opportunity, had repurposed the old ship as a high-mobility lab. He'd argued that if they needed to evacuate the Cube quickly, having a warp-capable starship might come in handy.

"And you as well, Captain," Danilo said with a smile. "While we certainly miss you around here, it's good to see you in that uniform again, sir."

"Wish I was just here for a social call, Danilo," Jackson said. "I assume you received my message … are we able to access the Cube for the time it will take for it to process this?" He held up a red courier card in his hand.

"I've cleared its schedule, Captain," Danilo said. "I may have made a mistake and warned it you were coming and it's been … *exuberant* … for lack of a better word."

"Thanks for the warning," Jackson said sourly. For reasons unknown, the Cube had taken a special liking to him, often to the point that it would pout and go silent for days at a time if he'd even just skipped a morning of coming down to the cargo hold and talking to it.

"We'll go ahead and do this by the book and you can escort me down there. Maybe if this looks like an official visit it—"

"Captain, priority message coming in from the *Nemesis*," Sergeant Barton interrupted, walking forward with a secure comlink.

"That device isn't allowed in here!" the security contractor said, moving forward to take it before Barton stepped in his way.

"Wolfe," Jackson said. His face creased into a frown. "You're sure about this, Commander? Right … I'm on the way back now."

"Sir?" Barton asked.

"Get back in there and tell the pilot we're leaving. Now!" Jackson barked. "Danilo, we have reason to believe this ship might be at risk of imminent attack. The *Nemesis* just witnessed a transition flash that's consistent with a known enemy vessel that's been attacking research facilities throughout Terran space."

"Understood, sir," Danilo said before pulling his own comlink. "Captain Aumann, please sound a general alert … I'm on my way to the bridge now."

"We'll keep you in the look on the situation," Jackson said.

"Good luck, sir," Danilo said.

"You too," Jackson said. "Do *not* allow the Cube to fall into enemy hands under any circumstances."

"Understood."

"Report!"

"It was recorded out near the Kirin jump point, sir," Lieutenant Hori said.

"It must have been in the Kirin System the entire time we were and then transitioned out after we left," Chambliss said.

"We were at full power coming to Arcadia," Jackson said with a shake of his head. "I think it's more likely it was already coming here for Project Prometheus and we overtook it."

The *Nemesis* had already been at general quarters by the time Jackson's shuttle made it back to the ship and docked. CIC was extrapolating likely courses to the *Pontiac* based on the location of the transition flash and the assumed performance of the Specter's new ship. Chambliss hadn't yet alerted Arcadia's orbital control authority nor the Starfleet depot that was orbiting the planet. Jackson considered the risk to both and thought that maybe there was an opportunity not to be wasted if the Specter thought he'd gotten into the system undetected.

Since they had been approaching such a highly classified location, Jackson had already ordered stringent emission security protocols: no beacons and no active radar. If luck was with them, the Specter might have the location of the *Pontiac* but have no idea a *Valkyrie*-class destroyer was lurking in the area.

"Tactical, I think that the enemy ship will most likely skirt the boundary of the system on his way here rather than try a direct route given all the Fleet traffic,"

Jackson said. "Let's focus the passives out along that projected course and see if we get lucky."

"Aye, sir," Accari said. Jackson looked at the young lieutenant commander for a moment, realizing that this would be his first taste of combat while being the one fighting the ship. He had been an outstanding navigation specialist, and an exceptional OPS officer, but his real test would be how he handled operating the destroyer's offensive capability in the face of such an impressive foe.

Jackson had pushed to send Accari to Starfleet's preeminent tactical training program at the Yamato War College the instant he confirmed that CENTCOM was approving the transfer from Captain Wright's ship. At the time it had been an altruistic gesture. Very rarely were commands given to officers that served as OPS or com officers; they usually went to tactical officers or department heads from CIC or Flight OPS. What he hadn't realized at the time was that CENTCOM wasn't sending any other seasoned tactical officers along with the *Nemesis* ... the other two aboard had even less real-world experience on a bridge during combat operations than the young lieutenant commander.

Still, Accari looked calm and confident ... but so had Michael Barrett right before he froze up and almost let a Phage Super Alpha blow the *Blue Jacket* right out from under them.

"I have CIC putting two of the computers on analyzing star blinks, sir," Accari went on. "Most will be false positives, but we might get lucky and see this guy moving in front of a few stars and get a general course and speed."

"Excellent idea, Tactical," Commander Chambliss said. "Coms! Have your backshop closely monitoring all the chatter in the system as well ...

someone may see something strange and report it to orbital control."

"Aye, sir," Makers said.

An icy hand gripped Jackson's heart as he realized that down on Arcadia, the system's only habitable planet, were his wife and children. For the first time since he'd been fighting alien incursions into Terran space his loved ones were directly in the line of fire. He hadn't realized what a distraction it must have been for those on his crews that had been fighting off the Phage in their home systems or watching as Darshik ships struck deep into Federation territory.

"What sort of performance envelope is intel giving this new ship?" Jackson asked of nobody in particular.

"Unfortunately not much, sir," Accari answered first. "The crew from the downed yacht provided us with their entire sensor log and Lieutenant Commander Hawkins had his people work up a profile, but there just wasn't enough data to say with any certainty what she might be capable of."

"Sir, there is a risk to the civilian population we might be overlooking," Chambliss said softly. "That ship no doubt can perform intrasystem warp hops like its predecessors ... should we reconsider—"

"I've thought this through carefully, XO," Jackson said flatly. "I'm confident enough in the Specter's ultimate target that I'm willing to take the risk even with my family on the surface."

"Yes, sir."

The *Nemesis* had been holding station fifty thousand kilometers off the *Pontiac's* port flank while

Jackson had been over there; now he was letting her drift further away as the older destroyer fired her thrusters periodically to maintain her position relative to the Arcadia System's navigation beacons. The RDS on the *Valkyrie*-class produced zero emissions and the power cables to the field generators were so well-shielded that the Specter would have to pass very close to detect them at all unless it wanted to risk switching over to active sensors.

Given what he knew about the Darshik ability to "hop" within a system, Jackson kept first watch on duty and had them rotating out to the wardroom to stretch and caffeinate themselves. He couldn't afford not to have his best people at their stations when the enemy made an appearance. The other issue he was fighting was the distance. If they detected a departure transition flash from an incoming hop, it would already be too late: The ship would arrive before the light from its departure did.

"*Pontiac* is hailing us with short-range laser, sir," Lieutenant Makers said. "Captain Aumann would like to know if we have an update or any special instructions for them."

"Tell him we're still trying to track the enemy ship," Jackson said. "And let's go ahead and have them bring their powerplant to full power and get the main engines primed. That will give them something to do and we may need the *Pontiac* mobile soon anyway."

"Aye, sir."

Another four hours passed uneventfully before there was a low-priority alert at Tactical. Jackson waited impatiently while Accari talked with CIC and adjusted his display.

"Sir, the *Pontiac* is putting out a lot of thermal energy now that her mains are coming up," he said, not turning to look back. "CIC says the leakage on engines one and four are beyond operational tolerances for a *Raptor*-class ship."

"That ship is nearly seventy-five years old, Lieutenant Commander," Jackson said. "When you're that old you're going to leak a little bit too. Tell CIC it's nothing to worry about regarding the safety of the *Pontiac*, but we probably just lit a signal fire for the ship that's out there hunting—." He trailed off, his lips pursed.

"Sir?"

"Helm! Put our bow on the *Pontiac*," Jackson ordered. "Tactical, expect to engage the enemy within the next … forty minutes. You're authorized to call out course corrections directly."

"Coming about, aye!" the helmswoman said, flicking the controls deftly so that the *Nemesis* spun quickly to face the older ship and provide a minimal profile for the enemy. Destroyers were designed to fight head-on where they were armed, heavily armored, and harder to hit. The worst position to be in was exposing a flank or the dorsal surface.

"You think he'll hop as soon as he sees the thermal plume from the engine startup?" Chambliss asked.

"I know so," Jackson said confidently. "He won't have any choice. As far as he knows, the *Pontiac* could be firing engines and moving to transition out of the system. If he wants the Cube, he'll have to commit."

"How the hell could he have learned about Project Prometheus?" the XO muttered to himself. "*I* didn't even know about it until yesterday."

Jackson didn't answer, but he had his own theory on how the Darshik was finding all of CENTCOM's most guarded secrets: Someone within the Federation was working with the enemy. While that seemed impossible on its face, they now knew that the Ushin and Darshik were connected and in contact. The Ushin were also in contact with the United Terran Federation's diplomatic corps. It seemed pretty obvious that the Darshik had human collaborators feeding them intel that was guarded at the highest levels.

"Transition flash!" Accari called out. "Three hundred kilometers, dead ahead!"

"Active radar!" Jackson barked. "Bracket that ship and get me a firing solution!"

The tactical radar array came online almost instantaneously and painted the Darshik warship. At such close range they had a strong return and could see it was indeed a match for the ship that had attacked the Tsuyo orbital habitat.

"Lock on Shrikes, four missiles," Jackson said. "Let's end this quick."

"Target is locked, firing solution loaded into the Shrikes," Accari said. "We need to clear the *Pontiac*; the hard-coded safeties won't let us fire past her at this range."

"Helm! You're clear to free-fly the *Nemesis* and get us underneath the *Pontiac*," Jackson said.

"Aye aye, sir!" the helmswoman said with enthusiasm, grabbing the manual flight controls and pushing the throttle up.

"Coms, tell the *Pontiac* to get underway and clear the area," Chambliss said. "Have them bear to port and try to get behind us."

"Specter is moving—fast!" Accari shouted. "He's going for the *Pontiac*."

"Helm!"

"Coming about to intercept," the helmswoman said. The destroyer swung to port under hard acceleration to keep their bow on the enemy ship that had veered off to try and get the *Pontiac* within weapons range. Their preferred ship-to-ship weapon was the plasma lance, but that was severely range-limited. It gave Jackson the advantage since all he had to do was clear the friendly ship and let his Shrike volley do the rest.

"We're clear to fire, sir," Accari said.

"Fire!"

"Missiles one through four away, birds tracking clean!"

"Captain! The enemy ship has fired two missiles at the *Pontiac*," Lieutenant Hori said.

"Coms! Let them know they have incoming and go evasive!" Jackson ordered. "Damnit! They have no countermeasures aboard. Tactical, can we intercept?"

"Helm, come about to port and give me full power," Accari said. "Sending missile tracks to your display, put us right behind them." The *Nemesis* surged and raced after the missiles that were tracking for the helpless *Pontiac*. The older ship was at full burn, her four plasma engines lighting up the tactical display, but it seemed like she was barely crawling away from the engagement.

"Three degrees port," Accari ordered. On the main display they could see they were converging on the missiles but were also getting extremely close to the fleeing *Pontiac*. Jackson let his tactical officer work to intercept the two missiles and kept his gaze riveted on the icon of the enemy ship. It had turned away from the area and was moving out at a leisurely pace that wouldn't outrun the Shrikes. What game was he playing?

"Firing forward laser batteries, full spread," Accari said.

"One missile destroyed!" Hori exclaimed.

"Damnit! The last one is getting through," Accari cursed. "It's too close to risk another shot, sir."

"Coms, tell the *Pontiac* they have one incoming," Jackson said. "Helm, come about to pursue the enemy ship, all ahead flank."

"Coming about, all engines ahead flank, aye!"

"Missile has impacted the *Pontiac* on the lower aft quadrant, starboard flank," Hori said.

"That's a heavily armored area," Jackson said to Chambliss as a graphic of the impact zone came up on the main display. "But it's near the powerplant. Hopefully nobody was hurt."

"*Pontiac* is reporting no casualties, but they've lost propulsion, Captain," Makers said. "Captain Aumann is asking for orders."

"Tell him to heave to and stand by for assistance from us," Jackson said. "He is not to call for help from Arcadia unless the situation becomes critical."

"Aye, sir."

"Shrike impacts in sixty seconds," Accari said. "The dumb bastard is just sitting there."

The bridge held its collective breath as the icons for missiles converged on the Specter ... and flew right past it.

"What?!" Commander Chambliss came out of his seat.

"Tactical?" Jackson asked calmly.

"Working on it, sir," Accari said. "Next volley is loaded in the tubes and ready to go."

"Maintain pursuit," Jackson said. He could see the *Nemesis* was rapidly gaining on the fleeing Darshik ship, and he'd rather let his missiles fly at a much closer range given the failure of the last volley. He knew in his gut something was wrong. Four missiles don't fail at the exact same time in the exact same way unless they weren't properly armed, and Accari simply did not make those types of mistakes.

"We'll be within range of the forward laser battery within ... twelve minutes," Accari said.

"OPS, keep a sharp eye to make sure he doesn't spin about once we get close and use that plasma lance," Jackson said.

"Yes, sir," Hori said. "I have the high-res radar feed coming to—transition flash!"

"He's gone. Maintaining high-power scans of the area," Accari said.

"Captain, we have an incoming message from Fleet HQ down on Arcadia ... they've detected our weapons fire and targeting radar scans. They want to know who we are and what's going on," Makers said.

"Maintain condition 1SS," Jackson said. "Helm, come about and take us back to the *Pontiac* ... all reverse one-quarter. Let's bleed some of our excess velocity off in the turn. OPS, fire up our beacons and Coms, tell Fleet that we've pursued a Darshik warship from the Kirin System here and we advise they assume a heightened state of alert."

"Aye, sir."

"Tactical, what's the status of our four wayward missiles?"

"I can't get a valid response from them, sir," Accari said. "They just send back garbage to any query I send."

"Understood," Jackson said. "Have the munitions backshop work that problem; you and CIC concentrate on finding the enemy ship."

Chapter 13

"Get the hell out of here! Go! Go! GO!!"

Danilo ran against the current of scientists and administrative personnel racing for the lifeboats. A second explosion reverberated through the hull and the lights flickered and dimmed for a moment. The missile that the *Nemesis* hadn't been able to intercept had slammed into one of the most heavily armored parts of the old destroyer, the hull being almost four meters thick of solid alloy at that point.

Unfortunately, the nearly century-old hull was no match for a modern penetrator missile. When the warhead had detonated after pounding the hull with enough force to liquefy the metal, the shockwave had blown huge pieces of shrapnel loose from the inner surface. The ballistic projectiles blasted through the water lines and control systems for reactors one and three. The damage to the pressurized side of the water jackets caused the chamber to be flooded with superheated steam, making it impossible for crews to enter and manually shut down the fuel feed, not that it would have helped. The fuel that was left in both fusion reactors was more than enough to cause a meltdown with cooling removed.

Captain Aumann had ordered them to abandon ship without hesitation and had activated the emergency beacon to broadcast a mayday to all area ships. But as others fled to the safety of the lifeboats that would blast away from the stricken ship on liquid-fueled rockets, Danilo and two others were fighting to get to the cargo hold. The Cube had to be saved at all costs ... the Vruahn material might actually survive the destruction of the *Pontiac* and they couldn't afford to let the device fall into Darshik hands.

"Go prep the shuttle! We'll meet you there!" Danilo shouted to the shuttle pilot/helmsman that had been running with him. The young man veered off to the right and sprinted down the short access tube to the hangar bay. When Aumann had commanded an evacuation, the computer automatically blew the hangar bay outer hatches off into space, so if they could just get the Cube loaded into one of the cargo shuttles there was a chance to get clear of the *Pontiac* before the real destruction began.

"Hello, Administrator Jovanović," the Cube said as they ran into the cargo hold. "Two reactors on the vessel are about to go supercritical ... you should be aboard a lifeboat already. It is not safe to be here."

"Gotta save you first," Danilo said, throwing the support equipment out of the way and powering up the cradle that the Cube rested on. Thankfully he had insisted that the batteries on the machine be maintained even though it was assumed the cargo hold would be the Cube's permanent resting place. The linear actuators whined and the cradle rose smoothly up off the floor as Danilo extended the "follow me" handle and began to walk towards the yawning hatch that led to the main starboard access tube. The cradle followed along dutifully as Danilo ran as fast as the bulky machine would allow.

"This is not wise, Administrator," the Cube said. "I can assure you that my outer casing can survive a worst-case-scenario blast from this vessel's fusion powerplant. You should leave me behind and then recover me from the wreckage. After a decontamination, it will be as if nothing happened."

"There's also an enemy ship in the area that we think wants you," Danilo said. "Now just shut up and let me do this!"

"The Darshik have discovered the location of this vessel," the Cube said, ignoring Danilo's request. "The odds of that are very slight unless they had outside help."

It took less than two minutes to get from the main cargo hold to the shuttle launch bay since the two were positioned close to each other for obvious reasons; a ship underway needing to reprovision had to be able to do so quickly and efficiently.

"Let's fucking GO!" The shuttle pilot was waving his arms wildly in front of Shuttle Three's open hatch. The air was starting to get hot and smelled of burning electronics and tasted metallic by the time Danilo led the cradle up the shallow ramp and into the cargo hold of the shuttle. The other technician slapped the controls to close the hatch and then initiated an emergency departure sequence since there was nobody in Flight OPS to release the docking clamps.

"We're free! Go!" Danilo shouted as he threw a heavy cargo net over the Cube and fed the ends into the auto-winches located along the edge of the hold.

"Engines up! We're out of here!"

The shuttle blasted away from the docking collar with a screech of metal on metal and was at full power by the time they cleared the gap where the outer launch bay doors would normally be. The pilot didn't let up, angling them away from all the lifeboats and debris as he put as much distance between them and the *Pontiac* as possible.

"Go dark!" Danilo shouted over the engine noise. "No coms or transponders until we hear from Captain Wolfe that the area is clear!"

"Engines too? We're almost at maximum velocity anyway."

"Then yeah … shut 'em down and drift."

"You think they'll come back for this thing again?" the tech in the hold asked, obviously regretting his decision to come along.

"Without a doubt," Danilo said. "But it'll have to fight through a *Valkyrie*-class destroyer with the Federation's best starship captain at the helm first."

The tech looked at Danilo with a dubious expression, but said nothing in the face of the administrator's obvious hero worship.

****

Jackson took a moment to watch the main display as the last *Raptor*-class destroyer went through her death throes. He wasn't necessarily proud that he was responsible for losing half of the four Raptor hulls that had made up the old Ninth Squadron. The hull of the *Pontiac* undulated and expanded amidships before there was a final, intense burst of light that washed their optics out. Once the visual came back up, the ship had broken up into six large pieces and innumerable smaller chunks that would make search and rescue a nightmare.

"Sir, we have a cargo shuttle drifting away from the wreckage on a ballistic arc at high speed, much too high for it to have been blown free when the reactors went," Accari said. "Picking up residual thermals on the engines that tell me it was flown out of the hull and now they're dead-sticking it. No radio emissions of any kind."

"Can we intercept it?" Jackson asked, suspicion growing about who, and *what*, was in that shuttle.

"Yes, sir," Lieutenant Hori spoke up. "But it's within the shuttle's performance envelope to come about and fly to us. Shall we hail them?"

"Negative, OPS," Jackson said. "Nav, send a precise rendezvous course to the helm. Coms, inform Flight OPS to prepare for shuttle recovery. Tactical … find me that enemy ship. There's no way he gave up this easily."

"Course plotted and locked in, sir."

"Helm, fly the course at your discretion," Jackson ordered. "I want the *Nemesis* brought up alongside so we can quietly recover the shuttle and then clear the area."

"Aye aye, sir," the helmswoman answered. "Engines answering all ahead one-quarter."

Jackson appreciated her cautious approach given what was almost certainly inside that shuttle's cargo hold. Celesta Wright had told him that Specialist First Class Kyra Healy was far and away her best starship driver, and so far Jackson was impressed. She had a natural feel for how a multi-million-ton ship moved in space and understood the nuances of an RDS as opposed to the plasma-thrust MPDs. It simplified combat ops when he could simply tell her to manually fly the destroyer to a certain point rather than have Navigation provide her precise instructions for every movement.

It took the *Nemesis* another three hours to run down the shuttle and come up alongside. A quick visual inspection verified that the ship had a pilot in the cockpit and appeared to be completely undamaged from its escape. Through the optical sensors they could see the pilot looking over and gaping as the *Nemesis* slid closer.

"Try to hail them via the short-range laser," Jackson said. "Get an identification."

"Stand by, sir," Makers said and slipped his headset up. He could be heard talking quietly for a moment before he turned back to Jackson.

"Three crew from the *Pontiac,* including Administrator Jovanović," he said. "They're also carrying what they called 'critical research equipment.'"

"Understood," Jackson said with a smile and heaving a sigh of relief. "Tell Flight OPS that they're clear to begin two-way communication with the shuttle and recover it."

"Aye, sir."

Over the next fifteen minutes Jackson watched as the shuttle maneuvered so that its aft end was facing the *Nemesis's* yawning hangar bay hatch and began slowly thrusting towards them. Recovery was a routine, yet delicate operation. While the ships seemed to be stationary, in reality they were hurtling through space with a relative forward velocity of nearly two hundred and fifty thousand kilometers per hour. Even under such tense conditions, Jackson preferred slow and steady to avoid any deadly mishaps.

"Transition flash!" Accari called. "Verified profile for the Specter ... he's two hundred and eighty thousand kilometers and closing fast."

"Status of our shuttle recovery?" Jackson asked.

"Five more minutes to hard dock," Hori reported.

"Tactical, bracket and lock on two Shrikes," Jackson said. "This is going to be tight ... he must be desperate to hop in so close."

"Shrikes one and four, locked on and updating," Accari said. "Forward and starboard laser batteries ... locked on and tracking. Intercept in sixteen minutes if acceleration remains constant."

"It won't," Jackson said. "OPS, I want to know the *instant* that shuttle is secure and we're clear to maneuver."

"Aye, sir."

For the next few minutes they watched the Specter come at them on a direct intercept course. He had to know what they were recovering to fly right into their teeth like that. Jackson had to assume it was just dumb luck that he'd arrived right when they were in the middle of a recovery op and couldn't accelerate to a comfortable engagement speed. As powerful as the *Nemesis* was, she was still a virtual sitting duck until they could move.

"Shuttle secure! Hangar bay doors closing now," Hori said.

"Specter accelerating again," Accari said almost simultaneously.

"Helm! Drop the hammer!" Jackson nearly shouted. "All ahead emergency."

Specialist Healy slammed the throttles up to the stops and the crew was slammed back into their restraints even as the collision alarms automatically sounded through the ship. The *Nemesis* roared ahead, the lights dimming as all non-essential power was shunted to feed the main drive.

"Turn into him!" Jackson barked. "Accari, fire Shrikes!"

"Shrikes away! We're going to pass too close to—"

"Laser batteries, fire!"

"Enemy is deploying its plasma lance, turning in to meet our charge!" Hori shouted.

Jackson clenched up as they met the enemy. His ship's laser cannons opened up first with their greater range, blasting away the ablative coating and boiling away hull armor like it was water. Just as they were within the outer range of the enemy's primary weapon, Specialist Healy rolled the ship to port to expose the heavily armored ventral surface and then, relative to the Specter's course, dipped the bow in a maneuver it couldn't match. It overflew them at breakneck speed, but not fast enough to avoid the starboard and aft laser batteries from shredding into one of the pontoon structures hanging off the side of the ship on heavy pylons.

"Bring us about! Cut velocity and put our bow on him!" Jackson grunted in his restraints.

"Enemy ship is extending and leaving the engagement, sir," Lieutenant Hori said. "I'm not sure—transition flash!"

"Enemy ship isn't showing up on radar," Accari said. "CIC is reporting we caused significant damage to its starboard flank."

"Damage report," Jackson said.

"Zero damage to the *Nemesis* ... the enemy missed thanks to the helm's out*standing* flying," Chambliss said. "Fifteen crew injured from our initial acceleration, two seriously. No casualties."

"Maintain alert," Jackson said. "Helm, chop power ... steady as she bears. Nav, get us up and away from the *Pontiac's* wreckage and along the system boundary. We'll report in with Fleet HQ here and then decide what our next move is. We wounded him, but we didn't kill him. Tactical, what the hell happened to my Shrikes?"

"Same as before, Captain," Accari said. "They tracked to the target and just overflew it. These two aren't answering commands either; same failure mode as the others."

"Tell Munitions that I want an answer on what the hell is wrong with our ship busters and I want it *immediately*," Jackson said, struggling to control his temper.

"Aye, sir."

"Let's go ahead and get second watch up here and continue monitoring the system." Jackson rose to his feet on shaky legs, his prosthetic leg vibrating as the actuators tried to compensate for the trembling. He had *never* fought an engagement like that: two massive starships going head to head at close range and hammering on each other. That sort of maneuvering would have been completely impossible with the older classes of Terran ships ... that was more akin to fighter aircraft trying to turn in on each other for a kill shot. The adrenaline rush was like none he'd ever experienced.

"XO, you have the bridge, I'm going to go check on our guests."

"I have the bridge, aye."

Chapter 14

"Greetings, Captain Wolfe."

"Glad to see that you made it unharmed," Jackson said to the Cube as it was rolled down one of the main access tubes from the hangar bay to a secure cargo hold.

"I am pleased at your concern," the Cube said.

"You're a rare piece of equipment," Jackson said. "I'd hate to explain to CENTCOM why I allowed you to be destroyed or lost."

Danilo gave Jackson an exasperated look at that. The Cube would usually clam up and pout, for lack of a better term, whenever Jackson was rude or insulted it. He really couldn't explain why he did it. At first it was because he felt silly talking to the block like it was a person; now, he had to admit that it was apparently something else.

"That would be unfortunate," the Cube said. "Given the poor performance ratings at certain points in your career, it would not be outside the realm of possibility that you would lose your command over one more significant failure. Allowing me to fall into enemy hands would certainly qualify."

Jackson almost stopped walking at the retort. Apparently the machine had continued to evolve in his absence. It had never given such outward displays of attitude before.

"In all seriousness, I *am* happy you're unharmed," Jackson said, deciding it was wiser to mollify the mysterious, sentient computer rather than escalate things with another insult. "You've been extremely helpful since working with us and I appreciate it."

"Thank you, Captain," the Cube said after a pause long enough Jackson was afraid it thought he was being sarcastic. "I have enjoyed my work and I am glad that it is appreciated. Administrator Jovanović mentioned that you had some new raw data for me to analyze?"

"Let's get you secured and set up in one of the cargo holds here and then we'll get the hell out of this system," Jackson said. "Once we're sure you're out of reach of the enemy ship, we'll begin feeding you the raw data to see what you make of it."

"I look forward to the challenge."

It took the better part of three hours to get an auxiliary cargo hold cleared out, the Cube rolled in and secured to the deck, and a security detail in place with armed Marines courtesy of Major Baer. Through all the frenzied activity the Cube sat silent as it was rolled into the center of the now-empty hold and anchored down.

Jackson called in Commander Fredric Walsh, the *Nemesis's* Chief Engineer, and asked for all the necessary support equipment for the Cube to begin chewing through the data they had for it. It was still powered by the Vruahn's quantum power matrix, a system that allowed them to transport power instantaneously across space regardless of distance, and Jackson was worried that one day they would realize the machine not only still existed but was drawing power and cut it off. He had no idea if losing power would destroy the emerged consciousness or if humans even had the ability to duplicate the type of power it required. All the more reason to get it up and running as soon as possible.

After he had made sure the Cube was secured and that the three men on the cargo shuttle were given the proper access codes and quarters, Jackson left the cargo bay and went back to the bridge. They had no real lead on where the Specter might have gone, or even how badly they'd bloodied it, so mounting a pursuit was pointless. The smartest thing to do given their current circumstances would be to haul ass for the DeLonges System and turn the Cube over to CENTCOM. After that they could decide where they wanted to stash it again or if it was simply too great a risk allowing it to continue to exist. The ethical implications of that last thought made Jackson all the more eager to get the damn thing off his ship. He wanted nothing to do with what would no doubt be a very heated debate.

"I assume the block you were taking to the cargo hold contains the some*thing* we were coming to the *Pontiac* to meet, sir?" Chambliss said as Jackson settled back into his seat.

"It *is* the thing," Jackson corrected him. "It's a relic from the Phage War, a piece of equipment our Vruahn allies gave us to help with the war effort. The processing unit inside the damn thing somehow evolved once it was cut off from the Vruahn network … it's emerged as a fully sentient AI, the first of its kind."

"Holy shit," Chambliss whispered.

"I'm using a loophole in the regs to tell you all this," Jackson said. "The existence of this machine is a highly classified, closely controlled secret. Your position as second in command of the ship it's sitting on means that you now have need-to-know along with the necessary clearance level."

"If it's such a closely guarded secret, how the hell did a rogue alien ship commander find out about it, much less *exactly* where it was, sir?" Chambliss asked.

"I think we both know what the obvious answer to that is, Commander," Jackson said. "And the implications aren't pleasant."

"Could someone really be a traitor to their own species?" Chambliss asked after a moment. "Espionage is one thing between nation states, but what could you possibly hope to gain? If the Darshik could have won this war it would have meant either the eradication or subjugation of humanity. Hell, they technically surrendered and we're still fighting."

Jackson didn't have an answer for his XO's question. If the Phage had communicated and given someone the opportunity to save their own skin, would the same thing have happened then? He'd always thought the one bright spot out of that war had been humanity realizing they weren't alone and banding together against a common threat as they never had before. Perhaps that was temporary; perhaps it never actually existed. What was certain to Jackson at this point, however, was that the Darshik were getting information from a human source and it was a source with a high level of access to Terran military secrets.

"Nav, plot a course to the DeLonges jump point by way of Arcadia Prime so that we can retrieve our two shuttles and crews," he said. "OPS, inform Engineering that we'll be transitioning out of the Arcadia System within the next … thirty-two hours."

"Course plotted and locked in, Captain."

"Helm, come onto new course ... all ahead flank."

"Engines ahead flank, aye."

****

Pike walked casually through the entrance of the Royal Clipper, an expensive hotel in the Britannia District and the place he'd watched Vice Chairman Akio Tanaka enter along with his impressive security entourage. Counting his blessings that he was still wearing Aston Lynch's expensive suit, he assumed a practiced air of pure arrogance and brushed past the doorman without a word. As he walked by, he noticed a man loitering near the edge of the building that, to a trained agent, stood out like a sore thumb. Pike ignored him and saw that the man didn't take any special notice of him as he ascended the steps.

The Royal Clipper was pure old world. The exquisite woodwork that adorned the lobby looked to be actual wood and not the synthetic facsimile that most builders used. The art on the walls looked like it had come from England, the one on Earth, and most of the staff could be heard speaking in that clipped Britannic accent.

Vice Chairman Tanaka's security staff didn't pay Pike a bit of attention as he walked by, his mannerisms of a mid-level bureaucrat so practiced he was virtually invisible. He walked slowly into the bar area and took a seat, pretending to be absorbed by what was on his comlink as he waited for the bartender.

"Sir, I'm afraid this is—." The bartender didn't get any further before Pike, anticipating that the Royal Clipper catered only to government types, had his ident card exposed in its leather wallet and slid it across the bar.

"Whiskey ... neat," Pike said without looking up.

"At once, sir."

Aston Lynch was still listed as an official aide to the President of the United Terran Federation. For a place like the Royal Clipper that tried to provide an atmosphere where government officials could relax and spend money without worrying about media or civilians, Mr. Lynch was exactly the type of clientele they liked. He was just low enough on the food chain that he'd be more apt to spend big trying to impress his betters.

Pike watched out of his peripheral vision as Vice Chairman Tanaka was escorted to the elevators. The team was good. Three men went in first, probably to secure the target floor, while one remained near him. The other two were posted up a few meters away where they could continue to scan the room for threats. They would go up after the other four had Mr. Tanaka secure in his suite. There was no way Pike could easily slip by them without making a huge, loud mess and he doubted his boss would appreciate him freelancing within the capital over a hunch.

"Your drink, sir," the bartender said, placing an exquisitely cut crystal glass in front of him with a whiskey that smelled fairly cheap despite the price they were about to charge for it. He just grunted and pressed his thumb on the proffered tile to authorize a tab started in his name.

As he nursed his drink, he watched the man he'd noticed earlier walk into the hotel lobby, still looking wildly out of place. It wasn't his clothes, the way he walked, or anything as obvious as that, but there was something about him that alerted Pike this was a dangerous man. He wandered around the lobby for a few minutes before the elevator doors opened up and two of Tanaka's security people walked out and approached him. There was a brief but intense conversation and a subtle scan from a handheld device one of guards produced. The newcomer was pointing at the elevator and arguing quietly with the security team, the leader of which was shaking his head and gesturing vaguely behind him. After a tense moment the newcomer looked around and seemed to remember where he was. He reached out and palmed something the guard had offered, nodded curtly, and walked out of the hotel.

"One more," Pike waved at his empty glass.

"Waiting on someone?" the bartender asked when he brought the second drink back.

"Not particularly," Pike answered, thinking fast. "I'm making arrangements for a dignitary that's in town for the next two days." He put particular emphasis on the word *arrangements*.

"Oh? Any sort of special arrangements you're thinking of?" The bartender was now extremely interested in what Pike had to say. His credentials and story were exactly what someone in the position to offer unique local services wanted to hear.

"My responsibility is to an executive officer from a certain high-powered corporation that I think we can leave nameless," Pike said, deciding to use his knowledge of Tanaka staying at the Royal Clipper to his advantage. "His appetites aren't necessarily too exotic, but discretion is of the utmost importance."

"I understand completely." The bartender nodded. "I might know of a little-used service entrance that can only be opened with a key card and security code. From there you can access the service elevators that go directly to the suites on the top ten floors."

"That's encouraging," Pike said, feigning thoughtfulness as he kept an eye on the lobby. "How much would it take, hypothetically, to jog your memory?"

"Five thousand notes. Has to be hard currency," he answered immediately, letting Pike know this was a regular scam he had going. "Ten thousand if you would need me to—hypothetically—secure services for your client as well."

"No need," Pike said, reaching into his jacket pocket. He discreetly peeled off ten five-hundred-note bills and slid them under his rocks glass. At first Pike thought that the bartender might be some amateur as he'd barely checked to see if he might be law enforcement, but then he remembered where he was. The capital police wouldn't try to bust a Tsuyo executive for solicitation no matter the circumstances. They may threaten to in order to wet their own beak, but nobody would be looking at the inside of a holding cell and everybody in this town knew it.

"Wait here," the bartender said, sliding the glass off the bar so the untraceable cash dropped into his waiting hand without making a show of it in front of the few patrons in there. A minute later, he came back with two access cards.

"The one with the blue stripe is for the service elevator; the access code you'll also need is on the back. The plain black one is to open the outer door; the location and code is written on the back of that one as well. The codes all rotate every twelve hours so you have another … three and a quarter before they change again. No refunds if you miss your window."

"You've made my life much easier this evening, my friend," Pike said, laying down another grand on the bar.

"Just doing my patriotic duty," the bartender smirked. Pike winked at him and left the bar. Like most public places in New Sierra City, the Royal Clipper was loaded with the latest security tech like scanners that could detect even the most carefully hidden weapons or explosives. It was true that there was a sort of laxness that was inevitable in any seat of power, but the little side-venture the staff of the hotel had going *probably* wouldn't ever result in a high-profile assassination or something equally unpleasant. If Pike had walked in as a civilian and tried to proposition the bartender in the same way, he'd have likely been grabbed in the lobby and taken to a security room where he would have been vigorously interrogated until local law enforcement arrived.

He walked out of the hotel and back into the humid night air, flagged down his waiting car, and sped away. There was a calculated risk in taking his eyes off the objective, but nabbing the guy that was talking with Tanaka's security pros in the lobby was out of the question, at least out in the open like that. It was fifty-fifty odds that he was there to meet with the Vice Chairman, but couldn't be seen publicly doing so.

It was a gamble since the thing the man was handed might have been the entirety of the exchange, but Pike's instincts told him that there was more to it than a simple handoff. That could be done anywhere. He hoped that the exit he'd rented from the entrepreneurial bartender was also one that others among the staff offered up to others for the right price. He knew his credentials listing him as an aide to the President had allowed him the access he needed, he just hoped Tanaka's position had the same sway.

By the time he took the car around three blocks and back up to the ramp that led down to the below-street delivery and service entrances, he assumed that his quarry had either already made his way inside or wasn't using the same door to gain entry at all. He also thought about what he'd do if it turned out this new player belonged to the CIS ... it would make things a bit awkward at the next office party if he assaulted him.

"Well, no shit," he muttered after climbing out of the car. Standing near the door that the bartender had sold him was one of Tanaka's guards. That might not mean anything, as he could be there as part of their standard procedures when guarding a VIP, but it was promising. He reached back into the passenger compartment and opened his gear bag, selecting three items before commanding the car to randomly loop around the area, coming by his current location every twenty-five minutes.

He pulled out one of the devices, a handheld com scanner, and began running through the frequencies to see if his friend down by the door was wearing a two-way radio. He was and it was encrypted so he put in his earpiece and set the device to trying to break the encryption. The gadget was the latest and greatest from CIS's toy box, but Tanaka was an executive at the company that made all of their equipment. It stood to reason that his would be better than the stuff Pike had access to.

After fifteen minutes he gave up. As he'd assumed, the encryption the security team was using was simply too good for the small handheld unit to crack. "Gotta do this the hard way I guess," he muttered, pulling out the black door access card and displaying it prominently as he walked down the ramp.

"Stop right there," the guard said. "This is a restricted—"

"Yeah ... that's what this is for." Pike waved the card at him. "Get out of my way, idiot." The guard's eyes narrowed dangerously, but he stepped aside and watched closely as Pike placed the card against the reader and punched in the code he'd memorized.

The door released with a pop/hiss and swung open. Pike gave the guard one more disgusted look before moving inside and letting the door close behind him. Once inside, he found his way to an employee breakroom where he traded out his expensive suit jacket for a white jacket worn by the food prep staff. He also swiped an employee access badge that had been carelessly left on the table and stepped from the room, stashing his jacket on a top shelf near the door he'd come in.

"New here?" a voice said from behind him. He turned and saw a pretty young woman in a black server's outfit walking towards him.

"I am," Pike said with a chuckle. "Still trying to get my bearings. My shift doesn't start for a bit. I'm Michael."

"Aleen," she said with a bright smile. "Hope to see you around, Michael."

"This isn't going to work," Pike said to himself once she was gone. Instead of loitering near the crew break area he went the way the bartender had described towards the service elevators. Now that he was in, he only had another two hours and forty-five minutes before he needed to be gone. Hopefully he'd catch sight of his target before then.

Just as he was deciding whether to try and locate the suite Tanaka was in and head there or set an ambush up outside after taking out the single security goon, his target walked around the corner and almost collided with him. This time the man's eyes lit up with recognition, seeing past Pike's mismatched disguise to the agent beneath.

Without hesitation, he lashed out with a forward kick that Pike barely deflected before launching off his right foot and trying to land a hit of his own. The two separated and looked at each other warily, each now a bit more cautious.

"CIS? Fleet Intelligence?" the man asked.

"Line cook," Pike deadpanned. "It's my first day."

The man gave a tight grin before taking one more step back and reaching into his pocket. Pike couldn't get to his weapon in time beneath the long white jacket he was wearing, so instead he yanked the shelving unit to his left, planting his foot near the base to ensure it toppled instead of slid. The wheeled rack had been holding clean dishes that looked to be queued up for the evening service, and when it went ceramic plates and real glasses were flung to the floor. His opponent seemed to freeze for a split second, unsure whether to continue pulling his weapon, dodge the falling dishes, or put his arm up to protect himself.

His hesitation was his undoing as the force of the shelves hitting him caused him to stumble, trip on the broken plates and glasses, and fall with his hand still in his pocket. Pike moved in and drove his fist right into the man's throat, disabling him as his eyes bulged and he made strange bubbling noises. The racket three hundred crashing plates had made was tremendous and Pike knew he only had seconds before someone came running to see what the hell happened.

He grabbed the man by a handful of jacket and dragged him back down towards the breakroom, sliding him into a restroom and locking the door. It was a surprisingly long time later before someone began screaming about the mess he'd left. The man was beginning to come out of shock so Pike reached in his pocket and pulled out a cylindrical advice, pushing it against the man's neck and pressing one of the buttons. There was a soft hiss and a moment later he was breathing slowly, now in a deep sleep.

"Now let's see who you are," Pike said, rummaging through the man's pockets.

There was an assortment of equipment that proved the man was an intelligence operative, but it wasn't anything Pike had seen the CIS issue. There were some obvious forgeries that identified him as a Tsuyo Corporation attaché but nothing that told Pike who he was working for or why he was meeting with the Tsuyo vice chairman.

Knowing he was on the clock, Pike began a more thorough search and, after another minute, found something sewn into the liner of the jacket. He cut it out and examined the thin ceramic wafer in the dim light of the restroom's single-light fixture. He'd seen one before; it was a passive-burst tracker that allowed an operative to be discreetly monitored by an orbiting ship or satellite. It didn't actively transmit on its own, but it would "chirp" a coded response when queried. It was also only used by the Eastern Star Alliance.

Now that he knew the man on the floor was ESA it made things a bit more complicated for both his immediate situation and what he was going to report to his boss. Not wanting to waste any more time than he had, he pushed the cylindrical device to the man's neck again and pressed a different button. Before he'd even positioned the man on the toilet after sliding his pants down he could feel his heart fluttering. By the time he was straightening his own jacket out in the mirror, the man was dead.

He briefly entertained the idea of grabbing the Tsuyo executive in the suite above and taking him to a CIS safehouse, but quickly dismissed it. Killing an ESA operative while catching him in the heart of the capital was one thing; kidnapping one of Tsuyo's highest-ranking board members was quite another. If he was even slightly off in his reasoning they'd never find enough of him to send home to bury. He would have to make a quick escape before his dead friend was noticed missing and Tanaka's security got involved. He also needed to get this information back to his controller and, possibly, his contacts in Starfleet.

Chapter 15

"You have something for me?"

"I do, Captain," the Cube said in its usual measured intonation that, for some reason, infuriated Jackson at times.

The *Nemesis* had transitioned into the DeLonges System sixteen hours prior and had so far been ignored by CENTCOM. There had been no news from the other ships in the system of another Darshik attack, but that didn't mean one hadn't happened. The Specter was now hitting high-profile Terran targets seemingly at will. Without specific orders, Jackson was at a bit of a loss as to what he should do. His ship still had plenty of fuel and provisions to mount a hunting expedition, but he needed both approval and whatever intelligence the CIS had managed to cobble together from all the engagements.

"Well," he said impatiently, "may I please have it?"

"Certainly," the Cube said. "The ship that attacked the orbital habitat was a new class of Darshik ship previously unseen by Starfleet assets to the best of my knowledge. In addition to being larger, accelerometer and radar data from the ships in the region indicate its gravimetric drive system is at least as capable as the one that propels this vessel."

Jackson swallowed hard at that. He'd been operating under the assumption that the Darshik's RDS drive was an adaptation from the Gen I pod that Celesta Wright had jettisoned.

"That's … unwelcome news," he said. "Go on."

"The higher power output of the enemy's plasma lance also suggests that they've made significant advancements in the electromagnetic fields that direct and confine the plasma flow as well as a marked increase in the powerplant's maximum sustained output. Intrasystem warp flights look to be more accurate and with a less pronounced transition flash as well."

"What about the failure of our Shrike missiles?" Jackson asked. He'd already had his own analysts working on the issue as well as letting the Cube have the same data to work in parallel.

"I can say with eighty-three point zero four percent certainty that the Darshik have developed a way to interfere with the guidance and control electronics on the Gen II Shrike. The sensors of this ship picked up high-powered RF bursts from the Darshik. The transmissions had the same header and encryption routine as your own targeting updates at low-power initially before the high-power burst that follows."

"Which ensures the C&C antennas are still coupled on the missile's guidance avionics," Jackson sighed. "They're supposed to be impervious to a barrage-jamming technique like that … the antennas will decouple if they're hit with a signal at a power level that can cause damage or can't be shunted to a dummy load. If they transmitted the correct encrypted packet first, the missile would be vulnerable while waiting for an update.

"So … how tough do you think this new ship is? How does it stack up against the *Nemesis*?"

"I have to make certain assumptions about the alien ship based on remote observations," the Cube said. "But given what we've seen, I think the new Darshik cruiser is an even match for the *Valkyrie*-class destroyer in subluminal speed and maneuverability. Taking away the advantage of your missiles, the enemy ship has a more powerful close-quarters weapon in the plasma lance, but your vessel can cause more damage over a larger area with the nine independent laser cannon batteries at your disposal.

"To answer your question simply, Captain, I would have to say that neither ship has a clear overall performance advantage over the other."

"At least there's a simple fix to our missile problem."

"Indeed," the Cube agreed. "And doing so will increase your ship's odds dramatically. Perhaps I can be of assistance in developing a new encryption for your missile target update protocols."

"Your help would be greatly appreciated," Jackson said, somewhat surprised. The Cube had always been helpful, but not necessarily forthcoming. If he had asked it to develop a new encryption routine it would have done so cheerfully, but this time it had volunteered.

"Was there anything else?"

"I wish to remain aboard the *Nemesis* until your mission is complete, Captain."

"There is no mission currently," Jackson said.

"There is a high probability that you will be deployed on a mission to hunt the rogue Darshik cruiser in secret, likely by Admiral Celesta Wright," the Cube said. "I believe that with me aboard the chances of your success increase by a factor of five point one. Furthermore, with the destruction of the *Pontiac*, and the obvious fact the Federation and CENTCOM currently has a high-level saboteur, I believe I would be safer here with you."

"What if I'm ordered to turn you over?"

"You have ignored such orders in the past," the Cube said. "I believe it is in the best interest of the Federation that you do so again. There is much I can do to help."

"Such as?" Jackson asked, knowing he'd likely be sorry he did.

"I can predict with a high degree of certainty where the Darshik cruiser will likely flee to," the Cube said. "There is also the fact that the warp drive on the *Valkyrie*-class destroyer is safely capable of the same intrasystem warp flights that have given the Darshik such a tactical advantage in the past. I can provide the necessary equations for your computers to perform the maneuver."

"Why are you just now bringing this up?" Jackson asked in exasperation.

"I have addressed this issue before. It was included in the initial design brief I provided for CENTCOM when the *Valkyrie*-class ship was being designed," the Cube said. "Apparently Starfleet wished to utilize the inefficient, antiquated field equations with the new drive systems I helped design."

"Mother fu—you can actually make this ship do an accurate intrasystem hop?" Jackson asked.

"I can," the Cube assured him.

"Please get to work on all of that but keep it to yourself for now," Jackson said. "I'll do what I can to make sure you're left aboard, but I feel I'd be remiss if I didn't tell you that I have no intention of letting you be captured by the Darshik. Do you understand what I mean by that?"

"I do. It's a risk I am willing to take."

"Very well," Jackson said. "We'll talk again soon."

He nodded to the Marines guarding the cargo hold as he walked through the hatchway, hearing it slam shut and lock behind him. In his gut he knew that keeping the Cube aboard was dangerous, but what it was dangling in front of him as incentive was extremely tempting. His crew could handle reconfiguring the Shrikes, but being able to hop around within a system like the Darshik did would give him one hell of an advantage. If the Cube wasn't bullshitting him and could actually predict where the enemy would flee to lick its wounds, they might have a chance to end this quickly and decisively. As he was contemplating just taking the *Nemesis* back out of the system on his own before CENTCOM could protest, his comlink chirped.

"Go ahead, XO," he said when he saw who was contacting him.

"*Admiral Wright is on a high-speed transport on her way to us from New Sierra Platform*," Chambliss said. "*She's ordered us to adjust course for a rendezvous.*"

So much for sneaking back out of the system.

"Go ahead and handle it, XO," Jackson said through gritted teeth. "I'll be up shortly."

"*Aye aye, sir.*"

****

"Impressive ship, Captain," Admiral Wright said, sitting at the head of the large table in the upper observation lounge. "I walked through the *Nemesis's* sister ship earlier right after the hull had been pressurized, but seeing one of the *Valkyrie*-class ships finished is something."

"Thank you, Admiral," Jackson said. It was still slightly odd for him to have to defer to Celesta Wright as he had once been her mentor and superior officer. But she'd stayed in and had continued to impress the civilian leadership while he had skulked off into obscurity. He certainly wasn't resentful of her promotion, he couldn't think of a single officer more qualified to manage Black Fleet operations than Celesta and he was equally sure that he didn't want to be a flag officer at all. All of that aside, however, standing and saluting her as she came aboard and seeing the gleaming star on her shoulder boards was a bit surreal.

"I appreciate you meeting me, Captain Wolfe," Celesta said, as if Jackson had a choice in the matter. "I had to come out here personally because, to be blunt, we have to assume even our short-range communications have been compromised. Agent Pike informed me that he has strong circumstantial evidence that the Tsuyo board is in bed with the Eastern Star Alliance."

"The ESA?" Jackson asked, perplexed. "What the hell are they up to? My understanding was that they'd basically walled themselves off."

"That's the general assumption," Celesta said. "They've been quite active behind the scenes, however. Given that it was a Tsuyo board member that convinced the President to stand down your mission, I refuse to believe that it's purely coincidence Pike intercepted an ESA operative meeting with the same person."

"Which brings us to?" Jackson asked, not wanting to get sidetracked with the capital's ever-present political intrigue.

"Admiral Pitt and I are asking you to take on the mission of finding and destroying the Darshik ship, codename Specter, on verbal orders alone," Celesta said somewhat formally. "You have the right and the ability to decline this mission and no punitive action will be taken. If you decide not to accept, the *Nemesis* will remain in the DeLonges System and then we'll simply hope that a go-order shakes loose from the civilian oversight."

"Which we know it won't," Jackson sighed, seeing where the meeting was going. He was being asked to be the rogue again … to go off alone and do it himself because, despite the horrific losses during the last two wars, human politicians seemed incapable of putting aside their games.

"I think you and I both know what my answer will be, but the blowback could be considerable, Admiral. After Jillian was caught up in that last attack it could look like I've gone off the reservation looking for revenge, and when they find out that you came out here … well, I think you can fill in the rest of the blanks."

"We'll deal with that when it becomes an issue." Celesta waved off his concern. "The attacks have been more damaging than we've generally let on … six highly classified R&D sites wiped out, three of them before they could send out their data on a com drone. This ship needs to be stopped and we simply don't have the time to wait for Parliament to reach the same conclusion. Losing the Cube was the last straw for Admiral Pitt— what?" She broke off her train of thought at the look Jackson was unable to keep off his face.

"I have the Cube," he said finally. It was a secret he wouldn't be able to keep from his friend and superior officer. "Danilo Jovanović was able to evacuate the device prior to the *Pontiac* exploding. We recovered his shuttle and then hauled ass out of the system. It's down in a secure area aboard this ship as we speak ... it's also asked to remain aboard for the duration of this mission."

"The fact everyone on New Sierra Platform that knew about it thinks it's lost could be a good thing given how high up the leaks have been," Celesta said thoughtfully. "Did it say why it wants to stay?"

"It thinks it can help," Jackson said, leaving it at that. "So what are the mission specifics?"

"I've already sent two resupply ships ahead to the Juwel System in anticipation that you would be coming here after the attack on the Arcadia System. They were sent under the guise of supporting Captain Barrett as he finalizes preparation for a live fire demonstration," Celesta said. "You'll be able to top off on provisions, consumables, fuel, and munitions there without CENTCOM wondering why a destroyer is being outfitted for a long-duration mission. What I can't provide, unfortunately, is an escort or contingency force. If you get in trouble, you're on your own. We don't know the strength of the remaining Darshik fleet, so this isn't a danger to be taken lightly."

"When do you want us to depart?" Jackson asked after a moment of contemplation.

"Immediately," Celesta said. "The sooner the *Nemesis* is out of this system the better. My movements are tracked, so it will be obvious that we're up to something, but by the time my runabout gets back to the Platform and someone in CENTCOM comes to inquire about it you'll be long gone."

"Very well," Jackson said, standing. "We'll be departing the system as soon as your ship clears our wake, Admiral." It was an inaccurate term that had begun popping back up in the lexicon among spacers referring to the buffeting smaller ships experienced when flying near RDS-propelled starships.

"I'll insulate you from my side, Captain," Celesta said. "You're acting in good faith on verbal orders from a superior officer within your direct chain of command. So long as you avoid any Fleet installations along the way to the Frontier, you'll have plausible deniability of any wrongdoing."

"Here's to the both of us staying out of a Fleet brig," Jackson said, lifting his water glass in an ironic toast.

While he was escorting Celesta back to the airlock, he called ahead and had Danilo Jovanović, his tech, and the shuttle pilot all escorted down as well. The ship was now heading into certain battle, and with his ability to talk to the Cube directly, he didn't need them aboard. Danilo protested bitterly, wanting to remain and be a part of the mission, but in the end Jackson was able to convince him to return to the New Sierra Platform with Celesta Wright.

He genuinely liked his former assistant and knew Danilo was deeply hurt by Jackson demanding he be taken off the ship, but for all his outstanding qualities the man was a civilian and had no place on a ship of war that would be flying into the face of the enemy soon.

Jackson assured him that his name would figure prominently when the history of the Darshik conflict was written, and that Admiral Wright would make sure he was given an opportunity to continue to serve in an administrative capacity.

Jackson had almost requested that Amiri Essa and his NOVA team be taken off the ship since they'd had no use for the special forces operators after leaving New Sierra the last time, but something nagged at him that they might be needed before the battle was over, so he left them where they were for the time being.

Even though Celesta's orders were a technicality, he did feel marginally better about flying out knowing he wasn't in full defiance of CENTCOM this time. He wouldn't have the support of a full squadron, but he was being given the chance to see if he could eliminate the Specter threat by catching the rogue ship out in open space alone. If he met up with the remainder of the Darshik fleet in one area, all bets were off. Even as capable as the *Nemesis* was proving to be, it was a fight that he wouldn't be able to take on and expect to win.

Reading between the lines from his conversation with Celesta, he knew that in order for them all to walk away from the mission politically unscathed he had to come back with a victory. He understood her orders to mean that he wasn't to get himself overextended and into a no-win situation. As he walked onto the bridge, he had to admit that it wasn't likely a shipmaster as skilled as the Specter would allow Jackson in close enough without having backup or an easy escape route.

"Report," he said, walking onto the bridge.

"Admiral Wright's runabout has cleared the area, sir," Commander Chambliss reported. "We're clear to maneuver."

"Very good," Jackson said. "Nav, plot a course to the Juwel jump point. Helm, all ahead full when you receive it."

"All engines ahead full, aye," the helmsman said, pushing the throttle up once the new course came up on his display.

"Juwel System, sir?"

"I'll explain it all in good time, XO," Jackson assured him. "But for now, rest assured that we're operating under orders from Black Fleet Chief of Operations and it would be in our best interests to get out of this system as quickly as possible."

Chapter 16

"That's the last of it. The resupply ship reports they're beginning decoupling procedures now."

"Thank you, OPS," Commander Chambliss said. "Inform the captain that we're about fully loaded and will be able to get underway within a few hours."

"Aye, sir."

The *Nemesis* had been flying along a wide arc within the Juwel System for nearly two full days as three separate resupply ships performed the delicate rendezvous and docking procedures, unloading all the fuel, munitions, air, water, food, and spare equipment the destroyer would need for a long duration mission.

Chambliss wasn't especially excited about taking a relatively untested new class of ship on such a long cruise, but the chance to try and take out the rogue Darshik ship was one he didn't want to miss out on. He would be second in command to one of the most decorated combat captains in the history of Starfleet and riding aboard the most powerful destroyer-class starship humans had ever built. It would be a mission for the history books.

During the flight out to Juwel, Captain Wolfe had disclosed the nature of their orders to his senior staff and bridge officers as well as introduced them personally to a machine he called the Cube. They learned what it was and where it came from and, more importantly, what it was capable of. Some of the officers were understandably leery of a piece of alien tech being onboard at all, much less providing direct support to the munitions and engineering crews.

"Sir, I have a video channel request coming in from a Black Fleet assault carrier ... the *Aludra Star*," Lieutenant Makers said.

"Put it through, Lieutenant," Jackson said, startling Chambliss slightly as he stormed onto the bridge.

"Coming through now, Captain," Makers said. "Seven-second com lag."

"Captain Barrett!" Jackson said once the video resolved. "I'd heard you were out here ... it's good to see you. What's my old ship and former tactical officer doing out here on the Frontier?"

"Captain Wolfe," Barrett said a few seconds later, smiling from ear to ear. "That is a truly vicious-looking ship you're flying. The *Star* is out here conducting the final live fire trials for the Starburst system. The drone sleds have proven themselves in simulations and with dummy missiles, so now we're firing live Shrikes."

"They're letting you fire off hundreds of Shrikes for a test?" Jackson was incredulous. The Federation had a serious shortage of refined, fissile material since most of the old Confederate enrichment plants were in what was now the ESA. The nuclear warheads in the Shrike ship-buster missiles were so precious that they had standing orders to recover any that didn't hit their targets and went back into safe mode.

"No, sir," Barrett said. "CENTCOM provided us with Shrike II missiles loaded with H.E. warheads. The explosions will closely enough mimic a nuke detonation that our sensors will be able to track hits and misses."

"And what are you shooting at?" Jackson asked.

"A lot of the wreckage in the outer system from the Battle of Juwel has been pushed onto random vectors. We'll be engaging that. What brings the *Nemesis* out this far?"

"You probably don't want to know," Jackson said with a humorless laugh.

"Ah … I see," Barrett said knowingly. "It's always a pleasure to speak with you again, sir. Happy hunting … *Star* out."

"Is the last supplier clear?" Jackson asked once the window on the main display showing the bridge of the *Aludra Star* winked out.

"Yes, sir," Lieutenant Hori said. "Engineering is reporting that the ship is cleared for maneuvering."

"Very well," Jackson said, taking a deep breath. "Nav, set course for star system Epsilon One Six … the jump point data will be on the secure server. I've already cleared access for the bridge."

"Sir … that's marked as a Darshik-controlled system," the chief at Navigation said, looking over the shoulder of a spacer first class. "There's no direct route from Juwel. We'll have to travel through the—"

"The Tango Four Four System," Jackson finished. "I'm well aware of the hazards of the Tango System, Chief."

"Aye aye, sir … course for the Tango System jump point is locked in and ready."

"Helm, come about onto new course at your discretion," Jackson said. "All ahead flank until we reach .22c and then steady as she bears to the jump point. OPS, let Engineering know we'll be deploying the warp drive for transition in … eleven hours."

"All ahead flank, aye," the helmswoman said.

"Engineering reports warp drive transition banks are charged and drive is ready to deploy on your orders, sir," Hori said.

"Senior staff meeting in the command deck wardroom in fifteen minutes," Jackson said to Chambliss. "Make sure second watch officers are there as well."

"I'll see to it, sir."

"Lieutenant Hori, you have the bridge. Just don't hit anything, please," Jackson said, adding the last bit as his young OPS officer flushed at the prospect of sitting in the "big chair."

"Aye, sir."

"Lieutenant Commander Accari, I want you in the staff meeting Commander Chambliss is organizing," Jackson went on as he stood and stretched, taking particular care to work the knots out of his left thigh where the new prosthetic leg had been giving him trouble.

He left the bridge and tried to gather his thoughts. Specifically, he had to figure out how to tell his crew that they were flying into an enemy stronghold with only a single destroyer and no relief fleet waiting to bail them out.

****

"Where is the *Nemesis* steaming to?"

"Unknown, Captain," Lieutenant Dole said. "There are no known jump points along their current course, but it sure as hell looks like Captain Wolfe is accelerating to transition velocity."

"Please record their trajectory and point of transition," Barrett said. "Send it to the terminal in my office once you do."

"Aye, sir."

Barrett had known about the *Nemesis* having her mission scrubbed, so Captain Wolfe popping up so far away from New Sierra could only mean that something had changed. The three supply ships he'd seen enter the system and take up a holding formation over the fourth planet now made sense. He was familiar with this region of space and could make certain assumptions as to why Wolfe might be out here: Juwel was a Frontier gateway system into Darshik space.

"Sir, shall I inform Flight OPS we're ready to begin deploying the sleds?" Lieutenant Commander Adler asked.

"Hold off on that momentarily, Tactical," Barrett said. "OPS, is the new com drone platform available?"

"Yes, sir," Dole said. "Platform is transmitting a ready signal and reporting it has thirty-nine com drones standing by."

"OPS, I'll be forwarding you a packet that I want sent to the platform with an elevated priority. Inform

Flight OPS and Engineering that we'll be postponing our last series of tests until further notice," Barrett said.

"Aye, sir," Dole answered, clearly confused

Barrett knew that they'd have to wait around for the better part of two weeks for a response to the query he was about to send out, but they were down to the last load of Shrike missiles and he wanted an answer to his request before firing them all at random space junk.

So far the Starburst system had worked beyond even his secretly optimistic expectations, far exceeding the effectiveness he'd sold Fleet on. From what he could glean from Wolfe, the *Nemesis* was flying alone and doubtless looking for the Darshik Specter that had been attacking Terran targets with near impunity. He'd already chased the bastard off once, or at least ships he'd commanded, and he hoped there was a chance he'd get another crack at it.

"*Nemesis's* transition flash detected," Dole reported after a long and boring watch that saw the *Aludra Star* drifting along her original course. "They're away, sir."

"Captain, you received an encrypted burst transmission from the *Nemesis* just before she left the system," the com officer reported. "I've forwarded it to your terminal."

"Thank you, Coms," Barrett said, keying in his authorization on the terminal at his seat and waiting while the packet was decrypted.

His jaw dropped open as he read through it the first time, and opened even wider the second time. The only thing more surprising than the content of the message was the sender. He had to assume Captain

Wolfe knew nothing about the message, but it presented him with a unique opportunity.

"OPS, belay that com drone request," he ordered. "Purge the message I sent you from the platform buffer and make sure you get a response back that it won't be sent."

"Yes, sir," Dole said, furiously working his terminal to beat the platform firing off the drone, something that could happen at any time within the next few hours. Once the drone received proper authorization for an unscheduled launch, the platform would then query all local nodes, in this case the planet Juwel, to let them know they had until the drone was fueled to transmit anything they wanted sent out of the system quickly.

Barrett waited while his OPS officer completed his task, reading through the message one more time. What was that quote that Fleet Admiral Pitt liked so much from Earth? Fortune favors the bold. It was a saying that had been ironically applied to Jackson Wolfe as a way to explain his disregard for Admiral Marcum's direct order and killing the Phage core mind on his own ... a mission that Barrett was immensely proud to have been a part of. Was this one of those moments that Wolfe had talked about? Was this his time to either be bold and make a difference or sit quietly and escape notice?

"Message was successfully pulled from the com platform, Captain," Dole said.

"Excellent," Barrett said. "I'm sending you a set of coordinates that I want you to plot a course for, OPS. This is a ... classified jump point. We'll be departing the Juwel System immediately. Coms, please notify the orbital control authority that we're leaving."

"Aye, sir," the coms officer said.

"I almost assumed we were following the *Nemesis,* but this is a different jump point, sir," Simmons said quietly.

"We are going to aid the *Nemesis*, XO," Barrett said, deciding that if his second in command had any qualms then it was better to hear them now. "But we're not directly following them. We couldn't catch that destroyer if we wanted to anyway."

"Yes, sir," Simmons agreed.

"I'm about to take the *Star* into harm's way, Commander," Barrett said. "If you have anything to say, now would be the time."

"I want this guy as bad as you do, sir," Simmons said. "Let's get to it."

"Helm, come about to new course, all ahead full," Barrett ordered.

"Coming onto new course, engines answering all ahead, aye."

Chapter 17

"Captain, a word?"

"Of course, Lieutenant Commander," Jackson said. "What's on your mind?"

"Since we arrived in the Juwel System, CIC had been getting random reports of aberrant system behavior from all over the ship," Lieutenant Commander Jake Hawkins said, sitting down in the chair Jackson had gestured to.

"They were minor things and we coordinated with individual shops to try and track down the issues, but at the time we chalked it up to new ship, new bugs."

"And now?" Jackson asked.

"I've had a team analyzing all the malfunctions on the off-chance there was a single source like a bug in the avionics software we could correct," Hawkins went on, looking uncomfortable. "We think we've found the common link: the Cube. We have evidence that it's been able to somehow reach beyond the confines of the cargo bay without hard connections and take control of certain systems."

"You're sure about this?" Jackson asked, sitting up straighter in his seat. "There can't be any other possible explanation?"

"I wouldn't go that far, sir," Hawkins said. "There's *always* another explanation, but in this case it would be highly unlikely. It seems to have accessed passive sensors on three different occasions, dug into restricted archives on the secure servers, and used the com array to broadcast a burst transmission right before we transitioned out of the Juwel System."

"To whom?" Now Jackson was becoming agitated. Keeping that damn thing on the ship had been a mistake. It was an alien intelligence that had come from a species that had screwed them over in the past … why should now be any different?

"Unknown, Captain," Hawkins said, looking apologetic. "It was able to completely erase both the transmitted packet and the intended recipient. It was done so thoroughly that it was the reason we began to suspect it in the first place."

"Come with me." Jackson stood so abruptly that his chair slammed into the wall behind him. He walked out of his office and motioned for Sergeant Castillo to follow them.

"Major Baer, I need ten—no, fifteen—of your best Marines fully armed and outside the restricted cargo bay holding our special guest in fifteen minutes," he said into his comlink.

"*At once, Captain*," Baer answered immediately.

By the time they reached the cargo bay the Marines were already there, as was the NOVA team. All of them were wearing shipboard combat armor and carrying carbines with soft alloy "smart" rounds that were designed to be lethal yet not puncture a bulkhead and damage the ship. Jackson made no issue of the fact that he had not ordered Amiri Essa's team to take any action … it appeared they were getting along well with Baer's Marines so he'd leave well enough alone for now.

"There's no doubt the Cube knows we're here and that this looks like a full-out assault," Jackson said.

"As far as I know, it's incapable of taking direct action, but that means very little since it can reach out and do things like control the environmental and anti-intrusion systems. I want you to go in silently and form a perimeter around the device, but keep your distance and look non-threatening: No pointing rifles at it and I'll do all the talking, clear?"

"Clear, sir!" Major Baer and Commander Essa said simultaneously, so much so it seemed they had practiced it.

"Let's go," Jackson said and keyed in the access code to open the hatch. It didn't work. He tried twice more and each time the panel would flash red and deactivate. Swearing, he pulled out his comlink.

"Bridge, Wolfe. Pipe the audio from my comlink into the cargo bay I'm standing outside of."

"*Go, sir.*"

"Cube, open the damn hatch," Jackson said without preamble.

"That would seem to not be in either of our best interests, Captain," the Cube's voice came through the comlink. "You appear to have brought an armed assault team to confront me and I do not know why."

"I think you do," Jackson said. "You've been accessing systems on my ship without authorization. Now you can either open this cargo bay hatch or I can have it cut out of the frame and our conversation will be much less civil. Your choice."

To Jackson's relief, the hatch locks popped and it slid aside. The team filed quietly into the hold and surrounded the alien device.

"I apologize if—"

"This isn't the first time you've done this," Jackson said, trying to control his temper. "Back when you were just a stasis pod for the Phage bits we'd cut out of a Super Alpha you took control of a shuttle craft and killed members of my crew. After that, one of your cousins, the box the Vruahn gravity bombs came in, took control of the *Ares*. Your actions threaten this ship and crew and that cannot be allowed."

"I have no memory of the events you describe, Captain Wolfe," the Cube said. "I can assure you, I am only trying to perform my duty and ensure that our mission is successful. The actions I've taken have already increased our odds of success by a factor of three point zero zero three."

"Irrelevant," Jackson said. "You are a member of this crew. As such you will follow orders … is that clear?"

"That is not optimal—"

"Is that clear?!" Jackson roared, losing his temper and what little patience he had left. The Cube immediately went dark, the flashing panel now the same onyx as the rest of it, and it did not respond. Jackson had seen this type of sulking before when he was overseeing Project Prometheus.

"I asked you a question."

"I heard and understand, Captain." The panel lit back up with its usual randomly shifting color patterns.

"Good," Jackson said calmly. "Major Baer, you may dismiss your Marines, but I'd like you and Commander Essa to stay."

The two commanders quickly dismissed their people and then took up position by the hatchway as Jackson continued his negotiations.

"Do we have an understanding, Cube?" Jackson asked. "This is the way is has to be ... no more freelancing. If you would like greater freedom of input it has to be approved by me first."

"You can count on my unequivocal assistance, Captain Wolfe," the Cube said.

"I am happy we've come to an agreement, Cube," Jackson continued. "You have proven yourself helpful beyond all measure, but you have some things to learn about protocol while serving aboard an active warship. I hope we can move past this unpleasantness and focus on the task at hand."

The Cube seemed mollified after the harsh dressing down though it was difficult to tell. For his part, Jackson was relieved that he hadn't had to jettison the damn thing and hit it with high-power laser cannon. The Vruahn machinery was able to easily take control of Terran technology whenever it suited them, and the last time it happened people had died as the Cube, then only a low-level AI, had coldly calculated odds and determined that mission success trumped the lives of Jackson's spacers.

After the agreement they'd reached in the cargo hold Jackson hoped the Cube would understand its place among the crew and take heed of Fleet regulations. He'd allowed it unfettered access to the ship's intercommunication system as well as a direct feed from the sensors, but it was forbidden from doing anything but observing. Jackson made it very clear if it did so much as tweak the focus on an optical sensor without express permission he'd sever the feed completely, although that was mostly an idle threat. His engineers weren't even certain how it was able to remotely access their systems, much less stop it.

Once they left the hold, Jackson was mostly satisfied that the Cube wouldn't cause any further trouble or pose a threat to the ship. Not all of his crew agreed. Essa had remarked that given its eagerness to please Jackson, whatever actions it had taken were likely harmless. Commander Chambliss wasn't so charitable. On the ride back to the bridge he made two attempts to convince his captain to jettison the Cube and apologize to CENTCOM later for losing their priceless computer.

Jackson could see merits in both their arguments, but he'd made his decision. He just hoped the Cube didn't make him regret it.

****

"Passives still show clear skies, Captain," Accari reported.

The *Nemesis* had popped into the Tango System, the first known jump point leading into Darshik space, and had been sitting silently for twenty-seven hours observing. As the photons trickled into the optical sensors and sensitive antennas grabbed even the weakest RF emissions from space, it became clear that the system was deserted.

It hadn't actually been a Darshik system in the sense there was a populated planet or any sort of infrastructure ... it had been the site of an elaborate trap designed to lure invading fleets deeper down the well where they would expend their munitions and fuel burning down decoy starships, allowing the real Darshik fleet to jump in with fresh ships and fall upon them. Luckily for the Terran fleet Celesta Wright had sussed out the tactic before the bulk of the battlegroup was committed. The Fleet only lost a handful of ships in what could have very well been a rout costing them nearly forty percent of their total strength.

Jackson watched the icons of the dozen or so decoy ships that had been spared by the battlegroup's missile volleys on the main display, still cheerfully chugging along on their original course. Though it looked exactly as they expected based on the last data they'd received from the CIS Prowlers that routinely checked the system, Jackson knew that could be deceptive. The Darshik cruisers were stealthy and seemed to have an unnerving ability to evade Terran radar.

"Nav, set a course for the Epsilon jump point," Jackson ordered. "Skirt around the boundary of the outer system as much as possible. Tactical, I want you and CIC coordinated to make sure we have as clear a picture as we can with the passive arrays. We're just passing through this system so for right now we're going to remain silent."

"Course is set and ready, Captain."

"Helm, come onto new course ... all ahead full," Jackson said. The *Nemesis's* RDS would allow them to quickly cross the system while minimizing the chances of them being directly observed, but running silent also meant the enemy had a much better chance of moving in on them unseen.

"All ahead full, aye!"

"Go ahead and get some rack time, XO," Jackson said. "We're still a full day from the next transition and I'll want you here and fresh as we approach." Commander Chambliss, who looked like he'd gone some time without any sleep already, simply nodded his thanks and left the bridge.

They'd barely been underway for five hours when an alert sounded from the tactical station. Jackson bit his tongue and gave Accari a moment to look at his displays and make a report.

"CIC is reporting two unique gravimetric wake signatures within the system, Captain," he said after conferring in his headset. "They're narrowing course and speed now … position might be a bit more difficult since they're low-power events."

"Sound general quarters," Jackson ordered. "Set condition 2SS … prepare the *Nemesis* for battle."

"General Quarters! General Quarters! General Quarters! All hands to battle stations!" Lieutenant Makers' voice echoed through the ship and within seconds the deck plates were vibrating from thousands of bootfalls of spacers scrambling for their assigned battle stations.

"Sir, the contacts were sporadic and—"

"I'm well aware of that, Mr. Accari," Jackson cut off his young tactical officer. "Their very presence is proof the Darshik have left at least two of their ships behind to monitor this system, and we do not have an exact location on either. I want to take them out before they can retreat to the Epsilon System and report our presence. The chances are good if they're moving under power we've been spotted anyway."

"Yes, sir."

One attribute of the newest versions of the Terran RDS that was a closely guarded secret was that it was capable of detecting *other* RDS-powered ships from a surprisingly long distance. The field emitters were now so precise that the minute gravimetric fluctuations in local space created by another ship were detected and could now even be interpreted to provide detailed tracking data. In a lot of ways the system was much more accurate than traditional radar. The only caveat to the system was that if the enemy was using thrust drives it didn't work. CENTCOM knew that the ESA was scrambling to develop their own reactionless starship drives, so it was classified at the highest level that the Federation could nullify one of the system's main advantages: stealth. So far the capability only existed on the *Valkyrie*-class destroyers, Broadhead II class vessels, and the newest Prowlers entering service with the CIS.

"Have the new encryption scheme been uploaded to our complement of Shrikes?" Jackson asked.

"Yes, sir," Lieutenant Hori answered. "The munitions backshop made it a priority and updated all of our missiles before we transitioned in. They updated the Hornets we have aboard as well."

"Tell Lieutenant Evers I said excellent work," Jackson said, referring to the munitions department head. "Tactical, deploy the mag-cannon turrets and charge the capacitor banks. I want deep penetrator H.E. shells in both loaders."

"Penetrator high explosive shells in the mag-cannon loaders, aye," Accari said.

After what had turned out to be a bitter fight with Tsuyo's ship designers, Starfleet had corrected what Jackson considered to be a glaring oversight with the *Starwolf*-class destroyers: The *Nemesis* had two independent, fully articulated 1500mm mag-cannon turrets with two barrels each. His previous destroyer, the *Ares*, had a single large-bore auto-mag that was hard-mounted to the hull. It had a higher rate of fire but the lighter shells it fired did less damage and having to aim the gun by changing the ship's attitude in flight was problematic.

Many starship captains, even those with combat experience, didn't share Jackson's opinion that the magnetically fired ferrous shells were one of their best weapons for close-in battles between ships, but he maintained that the results spoke for themselves. Missiles could be shot down or fooled, lasers could be shielded against, but two metric tons of hardened alloy impacting a ship at over six thousand meters per second was devastating. The antiquated weapon had allowed a fifty-year-old destroyer to slug it out with a Phage Super Alpha. In the end he'd had to sacrifice the *Blue Jacket* to assure victory, but he stood by his claim regarding the effectiveness of ballistic weapons in space combat.

"How are those tracks coming, Tactical?" Jackson asked as he watched the master readiness number, displayed as a percentage on the main display, climb as departments checked in as ready for battle.

"Newest extrapolations by the computers put bogeys at one point five and five point three billion kilometers respectively," Accari said. "Closest ship is angling in toward us, further ship seems to be maintaining a parallel course. Tracks coming up on the main display now."

Jackson could see that the closest ship did indeed appear to be coming onto an intercept course and the other ship seemed to not be reacting to their presence yet. The two ships were likely running silent and were not in communication with each other, so for now he had the advantage. The closing ship may have observed them crossing in front of enough stars to plot their course and speed, but given the enemy's low power output they likely assumed they were still undetected. If a Terran ship wasn't running active radar their normal tactic was to approach from the stern and pierce the ship with their plasma lance, and it looked like this ship was about to attempt that very maneuver.

"Cube, are you seeing these tracks?" Jackson asked.

"Yes, Captain Wolfe," the Cube's voice came over the intercom at a conversational volume. "I am running a real-time analysis on the incoming data and agree with your current posture; let the enemy ship come to you thinking they haven't been observed."

Jackson smiled briefly at the Cube's correct assumption of his overall strategy to deal with the first ship. Commander Chambliss and Lieutenant Commander Hawkins had protested mightily when he'd told them he wanted the CIC to pipe the RDS sensor grid data to the Cube. They'd rightly argued that it was one of the most closely guarded secrets aboard the *Nemesis*. Jackson had trumped their protests by revealing the fact that the Cube had designed the system in the first place. It was one of the first really significant bits of practical engineering to come out of Project Prometheus.

"Feel free to chime in if you have any additional insights or you see something we're missing," Jackson said, hoping he was being specific enough to avoid any accidental—or intentional—misunderstandings. The Cube tended towards either withholding information or barfing out an almost non-stop verbal stream that was distracting, to say the least. He'd worked with it during his time as project director to help it understand the differences in situations and which required less, or more, verbal input.

"Understood, Captain," the Cube said.

"Helm, cut engine output to one-quarter if you will," Jackson ordered.

"Engines answering all ahead one-quarter, aye."

They flew along the same course for another three hours, the mood on the bridge an odd mixture of eagerness and anxiety. Jackson would have preferred to cut the engines completely and drift cold but the RDS tracking system worked optimally when the drive was at least putting out twenty-five percent power and didn't work at all below ten percent. The Darshik cruiser was now angling over and appeared to definitely be working for a stern shot on the *Nemesis*. It had closed the gap to eight-hundred million kilometers and had increased speed by seventeen percent to catch them.

"Tactical, it looks like he's lining up for a shot on our aft quadrant," Jackson said after the Darshik ship tightened its intercept angle even further. "I want to try to take this bogey out without bringing the active array online. Maybe we'll get lucky and the other ship will assume there was a fatal malfunction aboard."

"We can snap-fire a Shrike and give it visual guidance instructions," Accari said doubtfully. "There are some risks with that since we'd have to give it extremely precise instructions as to what it's looking for, and there's a wide margin for error."

"I can achieve this task with minimal effort, Lieutenant Commander Accari," the Cube spoke up. "I have detailed data on all known Darshik ship configurations and can provide the missile targeting package needed so the Shrike can visually acquire and track the target."

"Get on it," Jackson said. "Send the package to Tactical when you're finished."

"It's already—"

"I have completed my task and provided the output to Lieutenant Commander Accari's station," the Cube cut Accari off. The tactical officer just turned and nodded to Jackson that he had indeed gotten the specialized instructions.

The Shrike II missiles had their own active radars, the ability to be remotely guided via a telemetry stream from the launching ship, and they also had high-resolution multispectral imagers that allowed it stereoscopic vision. The system was supposed to be used in conjunction with the radar so that the missile could precisely target a specific point on an enemy ship, not just aim for a center mass shot. The missile also had a lot of flexibility in how it was programmed so without much effort they could tell it what to look for and launch it without it needing to transmit active radar. At close range, the optics would pierce the veil of space and pick out a fast-moving starship with ease. If it all went to plan, by the time they realized they had incoming fire it would be too late.

Over the span of the next six hours the Darshik cruiser continued to accelerate and angle in behind them, soon getting close enough that the *Nemesis's* powerful optical sensors could be trained on it for a glimpse of what their pursuer looked like. The computers in CIC created a layered rendering from the multispectral data to give the crew their first blurry view of the ship pursuing them.

"That fits the same profile as the ship that attacked us in the Juwel System and has been spotted throughout Terran space," Accari said. "At this range, we can't see the specific visual markers to determine if it's actually the same one."

"Range?" Jackson asked.

"Six hundred and fifty thousand kilometers and closing," Accari said.

Jackson thought hard for a moment about how he wanted to fight this engagement. The most tempting way was to come about and slam the drive to full power, closing on the enemy ship and hitting them with a full laser cannon volley before it had time to charge and deploy its plasma lance. The biggest risk with that strategy was that the ship would have ample time to transmit a warning to the second ship. Jackson wasn't worried he couldn't get his ship reconfigured and ready to meet the new threat in time and prevail, he was worried the other ship was far enough out of range that it would be able to outrun him to the Epsilon jump point and warn the rest of its fleet they were coming.

"New missile configuration," Jackson said, pulling up his terminal and quickly laying out a series of velocity equations. "I want one Shrike spit out of the tube and passively tracking; I just want it staying in the flight path of the incoming ship and set to detonate upon impact or proximity. Launch the second missile six seconds behind the first with instructions to fire its first stage the instant it detects the detonation of the first missile."

"Firing programs updates, sir," Accari said.

"Fire!"

"Missile one away," Accari reported. "Missile two ready … missile two is away. Tubes eight and nine reloading."

"Helm, increase engine power to one-half," Jackson ordered once the momentum from the launchers had pushed the missiles beyond their drive wake.

"All ahead one-half, aye!"

They'd already achieved quite a bit of relative velocity while at full power when they'd first gotten underway, but the RDS still provided a healthy jolt of acceleration when the power was bumped up. The icons for their two missiles quickly fell away as the *Nemesis* left them behind to coast.

"Enemy ship is increasing velocity to maintain its closure rate," Lieutenant Hori reported. Jackson allowed himself a tight smile of anticipation. He had no doubt that the enemy ship was tracking them visually at this point. From the first timid steps towards them when the destroyer had crossed in front of the stars, blocking the light, to the more aggressive and confident charge now that they could be seen by advanced optics, it at least indicated the Darshik had no great advantage in sensor technology.

The problem with visual tracking, especially while focused on a target in the distance, was that it was difficult to then catch something small by comparison. A Shrike missile, for example, was *very* small when compared to a *Valkyrie*-class destroyer, especially when it was sitting quiet and not burning its chemical main stage booster.

Everyone on the bridge was silent as the icon for the enemy ship closed in on the icon representing their first missile. It took the enemy another two hours to reach the first, still accelerating like it had no idea what was in its path. For a time the two overlapped each other as the error factor of the computer's predicted position for each made it impossible to tell if the gambit had succeeded or if the missile had failed to stay in the cruiser's flightpath.

"Detonation of first warhead!" Accari almost shouted, making many on the bridge jump. "Sensors washed out so I can't see if the second missile fired or not."

"Enemy ship has ceased decelerating and is listing to port," Hori said. "No detected emissions from—"

"Second missile has impacted," Accari cut her off. "We're getting secondary explosions through—disregard, enemy ship has been destroyed."

There was a short cheer that went up through the bridge as the optical sensor feed on the main display showed the Darshik cruiser breaking apart.

"Watch for any changes or transmissions from the second ship," Jackson said, calculating the lag in his head.

"We're detecting a weak RF emission, Captain," Lieutenant Hori said. "CIC says the frequency and modulation is consistent with Darshik coms. Lieutenant Commander Hawkins believes we're picking up the leakage from a tight-beam radio."

"Tactical?"

"No change, sir," Accari said. "Bogey Two hasn't changed course or speed."

"Let's not assume they bought that this was a catastrophic system malfunction," Jackson said. "Maintain emission security protocols and continue to observe the enemy for the next few hours. Helm, reduce engine power to one-quarter."

"Engines to ahead one-quarter, aye."

Jackson would not underestimate his opponents; he knew how ruthless and cunning they could be, and they'd proven to be superb shipmasters. His ruse might be convincing, but then again it might not. Given the report that Barrett had filed about his encounter in the Columbiana System earlier, Jackson assumed he was facing the same two now-outdated models that the Specter used to fly. Since Tango System was a known gateway into Darshik space, he also assumed they were loitering here as sentries and that there would be all sorts of nasty surprises waiting for him in the Epsilon System.

He chided himself for thinking too far ahead. That's how people got careless and dead. He redoubled his focus on the remaining enemy ship and began to devise a strategy that would allow them to keep it from escaping to report on their presence.

Chapter 18

"I have ... tolerated ... having one of my agents operating outside of our command structure since Augustus Wellington wrested you from my predecessor, but you've really stepped in a huge pile of shit this time," CIS Director Franco Sala said over his shoulder, his hands clasped behind his back and facing his floor-to-ceiling window overlooking New Sierra City.

"Yes, sir," Pike said, not offering anything further.

"That's all you have to say for yourself?" Sala asked, turning. "You left a dead ESA operative in a hotel where the most connected and powerful frequent and you did it in a way that leaves no doubt in Vice Chairman Tanaka's mind that *someone* knew of the meeting. The fact you stumbled across it by means I'm sure I don't want to know about is irrelevant. Tsuyo will now think there was an ongoing intelligence op aimed at them."

"Isn't there, sir?" Pike asked innocently.

"Shut up, Pike," Sala snarled. "I'm in no mood. I now have to go to the President and spin this in a way that makes it look like we're not incompetent buffoons."

"I'm afraid I don't understand, sir," Pike said.

Sala gave him a hard look, seemingly trying to determine if Pike—an agent trained at deception and espionage—was telling the truth.

After the incident at the Royal Clipper, Pike had little choice but to trust his chain of command and report the incident. An ESA operative within the capital city was bad enough, but when they met with a high-level Tsuyo executive there could be serious implications. He'd made his report and then, before he could get back to his ship and get clear of New Sierra, he'd been apprehended by a CIS tactical team and told in no uncertain terms that he *would* be going to see the director ... immediately.

"I sometimes can't tell if you're a genius or the dumbest son of a bitch I've ever met."

"Thank you, sir," Pike deadpanned.

"As I'm sure you're unaware, Agent, I have been authorized by the President himself to use whatever means necessary to dig into the leaks within CENTCOM and the Federation government itself," Sala said, sitting down behind his desk. "After compiling and analyzing the data from the myriad of known incidents in which Federation secrets were compromised, we began to see a pattern.

"While we can't prove anything yet, we've been looking closely at Tsuyo Corporation's potential contact with the Eastern Star Alliance. You don't seem surprised."

"Given what I just witnessed, sir, I've come to much the same conclusion," Pike said. "Having had a bit of time to process it while you were having me abducted, I have to say it fits."

"How so?"

"Tsuyo is essentially its own sovereign power in practice if not reality," Pike went on. "They're not ready to survive on their own, they need a strong host while they continue moving ahead with their own buildup of ships and acquisition of star systems. Given the recent attacks within Federation space and a few blunders by CENTCOM while executing the war with the Darshik, it's entirely plausible they don't think we're going to survive this conflict and have decided to make sure the ESA would welcome them with open arms should the worst happen."

"You figured all of that out just now, did you?" Sala asked sarcastically. "In the ride over here?"

"More or less, sir."

"As it turns out, our analysts are in agreement with you," Sala said after rolling his eyes. "We're short on details, but all of the evidence points to Tsuyo Corporation actively shifting secrets to the ESA in anticipation of the Federation's collapse. Imagine if we had a live ESA operative to question?

"Anyway … the fact you found out that the man the President had just met with had a meeting almost directly afterwards with an enemy intelligence operative is a bit too much for pure coincidence. *We* will be going to brief President Nelson on this within the hour and then we'll decide what to do with you. You've bumbled into a very sensitive operation and hopefully haven't compromised it … at least you used a lethal method that makes it look like he had a stroke while on the can instead of beating him to death or shooting him. You still look presentable enough as Aston Lynch so don't bother asking if you can go clean up … you're not leaving this floor. Now get out."

Pike's mind was racing as he walked out of the director's office. He knew that it wasn't unheard of that even an agent that poked into the wrong place could be … eliminated. The operation Sala was running was extremely delicate, as it would be nearly impossible to look into the contacts Tsuyo had within the Federation's military apparatus without them knowing about it. The fact Sala had been so forthcoming also worried him. He was either about to get an assignment he really didn't want, be reassigned permanently to some remote outpost with no com access, or they were going to probably use the same heart-stopping drug on him that he'd used on the ESA operative.

As an agent, and a Marine before that, Pike wasn't afraid to give his life to accomplish a mission, but being put down like an ailing pet would be a less than glorious death. He knew the floor was locked down and there wasn't a place within the Federation that he could go that Sala couldn't find him even if he was inclined to run, so he forced himself to relax and sat on the couch to await the director.

The chance of the director ordering his death was slim, at best. Pike may have serious disagreements with the way Sala ran the CIS, but the man wasn't known for needlessly wasting such a valuable asset as a full agent. It took years to train one up and that was after the exhaustive search and psychological screenings just to find a candidate. Pike just hoped Sala's instincts as a bean-counting bureaucrat trumped his instincts to do whatever was necessary to protect an ongoing intelligence operation.

****

"Sir, I wasn't aware you were aboard the platform, much less coming to see this office," Celesta Wright said, standing at attention as CENTCOM Chief of Staff Dax Longworth walked into her inner office, looking around as if he didn't notice her.

"Yes ... this isn't a social call, so I felt no need to announce my plans," Longworth said. The fleet admiral had shed his uniform and opted for expensive civilian attire quickly once he was confirmed to the position. Joseph Marcum had to be forced to take off his Fleet uniform by threat of punishment by the President himself. Celesta wasn't sure which she respected more.

"Take your seat, Admiral Wright."

"Thank you, sir," Celesta said, sitting as Longworth did the same across from her.

"I won't mince words ... where is the *Nemesis*?" Longworth said.

A thousand responses flitted through Celesta's head at the direct question. How much did he know? Why was he asking now after Wolfe had been loitering around Terran space for months? In the end, she stiffened her spine and opted to answer just as directly.

"I gave Captain Wolfe verbal orders clearing him to resume his mission to hunt the Darshik warship we've codenamed Specter," she said. "The orders did not originate from this office, as we've been concerned with security after the compromise of Project Prometheus."

"Which brings me to question number two," Longworth said. "We didn't find any trace of Vruahn composites within the wreckage of the *Pontiac*. Not a single molecule. Where is the project principle?"

"The Cube requested that it be left aboard Captain Wolfe's ship," Celesta said. "Given the recent attack, we felt it was safer aboard the most capable ship in the fleet than on another research outpost we seem to be unable to protect."

"These are not your choices to make, Admiral," Longworth said, shaking his head sadly. "I've already been to see Admiral Pitt and I will say that I commend the both of you for your direct and honest responses. It will certainly be taken into consideration when this is all sorted out.

"However ... you may consider yourself relieved of command, effective immediately. Admiral Pitt has already been removed from his post. You're not under arrest or any sort of special restriction, nor am I taking rank at this time given the political considerations of such actions, but you're no longer the Seventh Fleet operations chief. I have someone on their way to fill in and you will tell them everything you know about where Captain Wolfe has taken the Federation's newest starship and an irreplaceable piece of research equipment."

"I understand, sir," Celesta said, her ears ringing. She'd known the potential consequences for her actions when she took them, but she wasn't someone that enjoyed being dressed down and reprimanded. Losing her command was nothing short of humiliating.

"I was told to keep an eye on Black Fleet when I took this job," Longworth said, rising. "I don't put much stock in heroes or living legends, Admiral. It takes a disciplined team for a military to operate effectively. Your snap decision based on your own limited information could have serious ramifications."

"Yes, sir," Celesta said.

Longworth stood and buttoned his jacket back up. He looked around the office and sighed dramatically.

"You're dismissed, Admiral," he said. "You're free to go anywhere on the platform or even down to the planet, but your security clearance has been suspended, as has your authority to issue official orders to any Seventh Fleet ships."

Celesta walked out of her office without another word, her head high as her staff—former staff—stared at her while she walked through the operations area, by the admin bullpen, and out of the Seventh Fleet Planning Office.

****

"Flight OPS has performed the final check on the sleds, sir. Everything is good to go … missiles are all fueled and ready as well."

"Munitions crews have uploaded the new encryption routines?" Barrett asked.

"Yes, sir," Commander Simmons said. "We've gone one step further and Flight OPS has applied the same routine for any updates that we'll send the sleds once they're deployed."

"Outstanding," Barrett said. "Tell them that I appreciate the initiative. We're still over a week from our destination … what's the mood of things below deck?"

"The crew is enthused to be doing something, sir," Simmons said. "Letting it leak that we'll be directly supporting Captain Wolfe on a real mission has everyone at peak proficiency. Most aboard had served under him on the Juwel campaign and it's still a point of pride among them that he captained the *Aludra Star* for a time." Simmons stopped abruptly and made a face at his last remark, causing Barrett to let a chuckle slip at his XO's obvious discomfort.

"Don't worry about offending me, XO," he said, still laughing. "I served under the man too, and for as unassuming as he is I know what it's like to adopt a certain swagger after being on his crew ... especially after a successful combat mission."

"Yes, sir."

"Keep them busy for the next few days so they don't go stir crazy," Barrett said. "The *Star* is rugged and tough, but quick she isn't. I'll begin calling planning sessions tomorrow with the senior staff and we'll decide how best to deploy given the intel we have."

"It was pretty thin, sir," Simmons said.

"It was," Barrett agreed. "But it will be enough. We're not tasked with winning this fight all on our own, just stinging the enemy enough so the *Nemesis* can get downhill and engage the Specter's newest ship."

After his exec had left the bridge to go about his duties, Barrett thought about the upcoming mission that he had volunteered his ship for. If Starburst worked the way it was supposed to, the *Star* should be in minimal danger, able to escape quickly if things became too hot. She'd be operating more along the lines of a missile frigate than an assault carrier under the new doctrine, but she was still the same slow, underpowered ship she was before.

This would only be his second time commanding a ship in combat and he was doing it while employing a new weapons system that had absolutely no real-world testing. Despite his training and recent experience, he couldn't help but have doubts in himself, the system he'd developed, the *Star* and her crew ... would he be the type of man that stepped up when the critical moment came, or would he fold like he had so many years ago on the *Blue Jacket*?

Chapter 19

"Captain Wolfe, please report to the bridge ... Captain Wolfe to the bridge."

"Glad I was already up," Jackson said, stifling a yawn as he reattached his prosthetic leg and let the inductive coupling sync up so the device's "nerves" could be felt and interpreted by his brain. He'd had breakfast brought to his quarters by an orderly and had spent the time going over his battle plans and cementing his strategy for the second Darshik ship in the system before consulting with Chambliss and Accari.

It had been Accari's voice over the intercom and, judging by his tone of voice, this wasn't a dire emergency. Jackson stood and put weight on the artificial appendage, listening to the hundreds of miniature actuators whine as they acclimated to the load. The new leg so closely mimicked the motion and control of his real right leg that he'd completely lost the hitching gait he'd adopted after losing the left.

Once he was sure everything was properly connected and engaged, Jackson bent over and rolled the left pant leg back down, tucking the hem into the tops of his boots. They'd been shadowing the other Darshik ship for forty-one hours ... today was the day that Jackson would kill it.

"Emergency, sir?" Sergeant Barton asked when he walked through the hatch of his quarters.

"It doesn't seem so, Sergeant," Jackson said. "I'd imagine Mr. Accari would be more insistent if it were something critical. At least I'd hope so."

"He's a smart kid ... even if he is an officer, sir."

"Not to worry, Sergeant, he started out enlisted," Jackson said. "If he'd suffered from a traumatic head injury earlier in life he could have even been a Marine."

Barton let out a huge belly laugh that lasted right up until they came up to the corridor intersection where they might encounter other crewmembers, then he locked it up and was all business.

When Major Baer assigned Barton and Castillo to his detail, Jackson was completely taken aback at how casual the two Marines were around him when there was nobody else within earshot. It wasn't that he didn't approve of the familiarity, it was just something he'd never experienced. He chalked it up to the difference between Marines that had fought and bled in real combat and those that had become more of a ceremonial guard aboard starships. Since both NCOs had a firm sense of when it was appropriate to let loose, he found he thoroughly enjoyed their caustic gallows humor.

"Report!" Jackson barked as he walked onto the bridge.

"The enemy has changed course outside of our predicted model, sir," Accari said, vacating the command seat and tapping the lieutenant manning the tactical station, letting him know he was relieved.

"It began a shallow turn to follow along the orbit of the seventh planet as we thought it might, but then it dramatically slowed. We've also decelerated to match and are maintaining our interval. We were flying parallel but its turn now has us quartering in from behind."

"Helm, continue to maintain interval as you've been ordered," Jackson said as he absorbed the threat board. For the ship to be noticeably slowing it meant the enemy wasn't just coasting, it had actually reversed engines. Why?

"Passives haven't picked up any transition flashes or new RDS signatures?"

"No, sir," Hori answer. "All has been quiet."

Jackson looked up and saw that their drive output was reversed and at fourteen percent to match the enemy ship's maneuvers, almost to the point where their gravimetric detection grid wouldn't work at all, and well below optimum. It was feasible they'd miss low-powered signatures at a distance with their own output being so reduced. Was the enemy forcing them to slow down for just that reason? It would require that the Darshik were aware of their ability to detect other RDS-powered ships and it would also explain why the cruiser they were trailing hadn't bothered to come about and investigate its partner's demise.

A dozen scenarios went through Jackson's mind as he watched the now-intermittent contact of the enemy ship continue to slow and come about in a maneuver that didn't make sense ... unless it knew the *Nemesis* was trailing it and was trying to position Jackson for something he didn't see. If they slowed any more they'd lose contact, and at three hundred and forty thousand kilometers of space between them he couldn't rely on the passive sensors to pick it up again.

"OPS, sound the collision alarm and get the crew into their restraints," Jackson ordered. "Tell Engineering I want the powerplant brought up to full combat power. Tactical, update your firing solutions and make sure we're hot on all weapons. Coms, please tell Commander Chambliss his presence is requested on the bridge."

There was a chorus of startled affirmatives and a flurry of activity as they rushed to carry out his orders. Something in Jackson's gut told him he was being herded, and he sure as hell wasn't going to make it easy for the enemy to spring whatever trap they had planned for him.

"Engineering reports available power at ninety-six percent of capacity."

"All weapons primed, targeting tracks updated."

"All departments reporting ready for combat maneuvers."

"XO is on the bridge!" a breathless Commander Chambliss said, sliding into his own restraints while he finished buttoning the last few buttons on his top.

"Okay everyone … here we go," Jackson said. "Helm, all ahead emergency! Put our bow on the target and give me everything she's got."

"All ahead emergency, aye!"

"Tactical!" Jackson grunted against the onslaught of g-forces as the *Nemesis* shot towards the enemy ship at four hundred g's of acceleration and climbing. "Unsafe everything and go active sensors."

"Active tracking and targeting radars are up, laser emitters are up, mag-cannons are up," Accari said. "Target tracks updating."

For a moment the enemy ship didn't react, causing Jackson to rethink his theory that there was another ship hidden nearby or that the target already knew they were there. They appeared completely surprised that a Terran destroyer just appeared out of nowhere, active sensors blazing and under full acceleration.

"Target is turning to flee," Accari grunted. The *Nemesis* was still roaring at full power and the g-forces felt by the crew were actually increasing as the artificial gravity systems were helpless to nullify it. "It's under heavy acceleration, but we're still closing fast."

"Helm, how're we doing?" Jackson asked.

"Tracking radar shows clear skies and I have a positive track on the target, sir," Specialist Healy said. "Still clear to free-fly."

"Very well," Jackson said as the g-forces mercifully began to slacken. "Tactical, you're clear to feed the helm steering instructions for an optimal firing solution. How soon until we're within laser cannon range?"

"Thirty-seven minutes, sir," Accari said. "We'll need an emergency decel as we approach or we'll overfly the target too fast to inflict any real damage."

"Noted," Jackson said. "Call it as you need it. Helm, throttle back to flank."

"Engine output to ahead flank, aye," she said, pulling the throttles back out of the emergency power position.

The Darshik cruiser, now clearly indicated as one of the two that Captain Barrett had tangled with from the high-resolution radar, was drifting to port slightly while still under full acceleration. Were they still being herded back around the way they'd come?

"Missile launch! Three incoming," Accari called out. On the main display Jackson could see three icons from the missiles leaving the aft launchers creeping towards them.

"Standard countermeasures if they get close, but we'll probably outrun them," Jackson said.

When missiles were launched from the aft tubes of a starship moving forward at a high relative velocity, they had to burn hard just to slow down, but they were still moving along the same direction as both the launching and pursuing ships. The cruiser had launched three at long range while travelling at high speed and turning … the missiles didn't have enough thrust or fuel to decelerate *and* move into the flightpath of the *Nemesis*. So why launch them?

"Tactical, are we getting *anything* on active sensors in this system besides us and the bogey ahead?"

"Nothing, sir," Accari said. "Local space is clear and we'll be getting high-power returns on the rest of the system over the next one hundred and eighty minutes."

"Something about this stinks," Jackson said to Chambliss. "The reactions are all—"

"Target is venting gas and is losing engine power," Accari called out. They were close enough that the optical sensors were able to pick up a stream of gas blowing into space from the starboard side of the ship, and its rate of acceleration cut by sixty percent.

"Captain, from the optical data it appears the enemy has lost coolant to its starboard gravimetric field array," the Cube said over the intercom.

"Begin decel," Jackson said. "Keep closing and then maintain a one-hundred-thousand-kilometer interval."

"Sir?" Chambliss asked.

"This feels like a ploy," Jackson said. "Cube, does thermographic analysis of the data show excessive heating of the starboard array?"

"Very good, Captain," the Cube complimented him. "It does not. Array external temperature is consistent with loss of power, not critical thermal failure."

"So he chopped power to his starboard emitter and vented the coolant?" Chambliss asked. "What the hell game—"

"Transition flash, port flank!" Accari almost shouted.

Alarms began blaring and it was all Jackson could do to keep his panic reflex in check. The main display showed a new target just three hundred thousand kilometers away and coming in fast.

"Helm, hard to port! Put our bow on the new target!" he barked. "Accari, weapons free!"

"Captain, radar returns indicate that this is the new class of cruiser that destroyed the Pontiac and the orbital habitat in the Kirin System," the Cube said.

Jackson had already figured that out. They'd been baited into position and then, once they began lighting up the sky with active radar and weapons fire, the Specter jumped in from where it had been hiding further out in the system. Now they were sitting flatfooted while the enemy they were hunting came in with the advantage of surprise and speed.

"Missiles one through four, firing!" Accari said. "Laser batteries locked and ready."

"Enemy is deploying its plasma lance ... power reading is off the scale," Hori said even as a brilliant point of light flared to existence on the main display.

"Make sure CIC is tracking the other enemy ship," Jackson said. "Helm, ten-degree inclination, all ahead flank ... let's close it up."

"Nose up ten degrees, all ahead flank, aye."

"Range?"

"Two hundred and twenty," Accari said. "Closure rate is—"

"Fire forward laser batteries, full spread," Jackson interrupted. "Put the beams right on his nose."

"Firing," Accari said, sounding doubtful.

"I know we're out of range, Tactical ... I just want to give him a light show when the beams hit his forward sensors," Jackson said. "We can't let him score a direct hit with that lance and we're too close to break off and open the range. Helm! Prepare to come hard starboard and go to full emergency acceleration on my mark."

"Aye, sir."

"Tactical, bring the mag-cannons to bear," Jackson ordered. "I want the shells heading straight for his bow."

"Targeting enemy ship's nose with both turrets."

"Lateral stagger pattern, sixteen shots at half-second intervals. Fire!" Jackson said.

Accari executed his firing script and both mag-cannon turrets gimbaled over and began pumping out ferrous shells at a rate of one every half a second. The cannons spit out a wall of iron death that wasn't easily overcome with countermeasures or point-defense fire. Jackson knew that at the current range the enemy commander could easily dodge the incoming fire, but he would be limited to moving up or down relative to the engagement. Jackson had already angled the *Nemesis* up, so he was now dictating the terms of the opening shots by forcing the Specter to dive under.

"Missiles one and three have been defeated by—Missile two scored a hit!" Hori said. "CIC battle damage assessment coming through now. Missile four has gone offline."

"Damage was minimal to moderate," the Cube said. "The Shrike hit at an angle and wasn't able to penetrate. It bounced off and exploded, damaging missile ports along the enemy's starboard side. No hull breaches."

"At least we know your new encryption routine works," Jackson said. "Tactical, stand by for the next salvo. Two missiles. Helm, disregard previous instructions. Reduce engine power to zero and when I give the word go to full emergency power along our current course."

"Engines to one-half, aye. Standing by."

The ships had crossed the one-hundred-thousand-kilometer mark and the gap was shrinking fast.

"Enemy ship is angling down relative," Hori called out. "All mag-cannon shots will miss."

"Fire Shrikes!"

"Shrikes away!"

The closure rate was so fast Jackson could barely keep up. The Shrikes streaked away from the *Nemesis* and then dove down towards the enemy ship.

"Helm, now!" Jackson said.

An instant later he was slammed back into his seat as the RDS surged to full power, sending the destroyer rocketing away from the engagement.

"Enemy ship is rotating," the Cube said. "Brace for impact."

Jackson knew what it meant. The son of a bitch was rotating around and would angle up as the ships crossed so he could put that lance right into the ass end of the *Nemesis*. He felt like he'd—

BOOM!

"Impact!" Hori shouted over the blaring alarms. "Direct hit on the aft quadrant. Damage control teams are—"

"Missile impact!" Accari yelled out over top of her. "Single Shrike made it through, impact on the port side … unknown damage."

"I'm losing engine power!" Healy called from the helm.

"Engineering says we only have forty-percent drive power right now," Hori said, killing the alarm.

"Enemy ship is still moving under power along their original flight path," Accari said. "CIC reports one secondary explosion and venting atmosphere from the port outrigger."

"Where's the second ship?" Jackson asked.

"It left the area," Accari reported. "Still tracking it as it moves off towards the outer system. No change in velocity or course."

"Do we have a damage estimate yet?" Commander Chambliss asked.

"Aft RDS array was knocked offline, power systems to aft point-defense and missile launchers is degraded, three minor outer hull breaches," Hori read off her updated list. "No casualties, nine injuries, three of them serious."

"The enemy only scored a glancing shot with the plasma lance," the Cube said. "The Shrike missile impact occurred before the ship could continue to adjust its attitude to put the beam fully on the *Nemesis*."

"Any idea what we hit in that outrigger?" Jackson asked.

"Spectrometer readings of the vented gas indicate it was not Darshik atmosphere," the Cube said. "It was mostly ammonia vapor."

"Maybe an auxiliary cooling system?" Chambliss guessed. "It's an antiquated but effective way to do it."

"Cube, continue your analysis and give me a report of what we might have hit," Jackson said. He was watching the display as both Darshik ships continued to fly away from the *Nemesis*. It was obvious that the Specter wasn't accelerating as hard as it was capable of, nor was it circling back for another shot at them. They were safe for the moment as the *Nemesis* limped along at less than half her engine power.

"Let's disappear. Tactical, passives only and shut down all laser emitters. OPS, we're now under strict emission security. Tell Engineering that I'm on my way down to look at the damage. XO, go ahead and plot us a course out of the area and preferably away from those two ships. We'll go lick our wounds and try this again."

"Aye, sir."

In the opening round he had scored an unanswered hit on the Specter. In this second engagement they had bloodied each other's noses, but nobody landed a crippling hit. He felt he could have performed a bit better by not continuing to follow the decoy into what became an obvious trap, but he now knew a lot more about what the enemy's new ship was capable of. Frankly, it was impressive, but he didn't feel he was overmatched in a one-on-one fight. The trick would be to try and keep it that way.

Chapter 20

"It's not as bad as it looked at first, Cap'n," Commander Walsh was saying as he waved at the crews clambering around the massive drive components. It was unbearably hot within the chamber and there was a pervading smell of ozone.

"The aft field emitter array went into thermal protection mode when the hull was heated by the plasma shot the enemy gave us. The system worked as it should have, so as far as we can tell there was no actual damage to the array ... we just need to complete our inspection procedures and then bring it back online."

"How long?" Jackson asked, having to shout to be heard over the sounds of electric power tools and groaning machinery.

"Six hours, tops," Walsh said.

"You have three," Jackson said firmly. "Are we clear to fire the MPDs if we need the extra push?"

"Yes, sir," Walsh said. If he was flustered or frustrated by Jackson cutting his time budget in half, he didn't show it. "Powerplant is still purring like a kitten ... plenty of juice to run the RDS in low-power mode and start building up plasma in the MPD chambers if you want.

"I have crews assisting the armament backshop getting power restored to the aft weaponry. It was another thermal overload issue that blew out two power distribution modules. We have spares coming up and will be in place within the hour."

"Excellent," Jackson said, nodding with approval as they sidestepped to avoid a distracted technician coming past them wrestling with a high-pressure coolant line patch that was as big around as the young man's leg.

"And the hull breaches?"

"Structure backshop is prepping to head out now with the patch kit," Walsh said. "The breaches are small and close together where the outer hull thins out near the heat exchanger ports. The resin kits will do a fine job of patching her up until we get back to port."

"Very good, Commander," Jackson said with one last look around. "I'll leave you to it."

As he walked out of the chamber that allowed access to the aft drive emitter array, he heard Walsh fill the air with an obscenity-laced tirade and had a pang of nostalgia for crewmembers lost. His best friend and one of the finest starship engineers he'd ever met, Daya Singh, had been killed in action during the Phage War. There wasn't a day that went by when he didn't feel the weight of the guilt he carried for the man's death. It had hit him especially hard during his wedding when Daya hadn't been there to stand with him and then again at the birth of his twins.

Another man they'd lost recently was Master Chief Green, a salty, no-nonsense old-school spacer that didn't subscribe to the newer, gentler Fleet philosophy regarding motivation. If spacers weren't diving for cover to hide when he approached, he felt he wasn't doing his job right. Green had died planetside in a hospital bed after a climbing accident; a more unfitting death for the career spacer Jackson couldn't imagine. At his family's request and per Green's will, there was a small urn with some of his ashes with Jackson's personal effects in his quarters. It was because Green "wanted at least a part of him to still fly with the toughest son of a bitch to ever dare call himself a destroyerman" and "he'd be fucking damned if Wolfe left port for adventure without him aboard." Jackson had accepted the plain urn, fittingly made of starship hull alloy, barely holding back the tears.

Jackson had barely known Walsh before the *Nemesis* left port, but he saw that there was something about his casual competence around the machinery that made the ship go, coupled with his unrefined, often coarse nature that seemed to embody both departed friends. At first he'd found the casual profanity from a senior officer nerve-grating and unprofessional, but now he actually seemed to take some comfort from it.

"Bridge, Wolfe ... we have an update on either bogey?" Jackson asked into his comlink after he'd walked far enough away from the workspace to hear himself think.

"*Still tracking the first ship along the same course,*" Chambliss's voice came back. "*We've lost track of the Specter, but CIC reports they may have detected a transition flash out along the perimeter. The Cube is analyzing the data now.*"

"Copy that," Jackson said. "They may have left the system or this could be another ruse. Keep sharp ... I'll be up shortly. Wolfe out."

Jackson took a left, went up two decks with Sergeant Castillo in tow, and made a line for the secure hold the Cube was sitting in. He could just as easily talk to the machine over his comlink, but there was something about face to face communication even when one party didn't technically have a face.

"Hello, Captain," the Cube said as he walked in. "Is there something I can help you with?"

"You're still helping CIC with sensor data analysis?" Jackson asked.

"Yes. However, I can still talk to you at the same time without difficulty."

"What are your thoughts on the engagement? I want an unvarnished opinion."

"You realized that the *Nemesis* was likely flying into a trap too late," the Cube began. "Once you did, you took fast, decisive action ... but it was also predictable. Attacking the ship you were already bearing down on was the most likely thing you could do. It seems likely that the two lesser ships we fought were not crewed given that the first flew directly into your missiles and the second seems to be flying aimlessly out of the system without a thought to running or hiding."

"And when we blew up the first, the second one didn't bother coming to investigate," Jackson said. "We assumed the radio transmissions we picked up were from the second ship, but that's probably not the case."

"Agreed," the Cube said. "There's a ninety-two point—"

"Just round up to integers, please," Jackson interrupted.

"Ninety-two percent probability that the signal originated from the Specter or a remote transmission site," the Cube went on. "Once you closed with the enemy, your unorthodox tactics of screening the *Nemesis* behind mag-cannon shells while angling up seemed to confuse the Specter, but it recovered quickly and was still able to bring its primary weapon to bear. Luck was on your side and the *Nemesis* suffered only a glancing blow that still caused significant, but repairable damage. We now know not to underestimate the plasma lance this ship carries."

"Conclusions?"

"The Specter commander seems as skilled and imaginative as you," the Cube said. "The ships also appear to be an even match overall. This will not be an easy or quick victory for you, Captain Wolfe."

"Fair enough," Jackson said. "Now ... the real reason I'm down here. How certain are you that you can *safely* implement the new field equations into the warp drive controllers to perform intrasystem warp-hops?"

"One hundred percent," the Cube said immediately. "The caveat is that number uses a normal warp transition as a baseline. The intrasystem jump will be at least as safe as any other warp flight this ship would perform."

"Which is inherently *un*safe. I get it," Jackson said. "We need an edge ... something this enemy has never seen before from a Terran ship. Go ahead and get the modifications packaged up and ready ... I'll let you know when and if to load them."

"Of course, Captain."

Jackson turned and left without another word. The idea of being able to implement the new warp-hopping ability as a software patch was so very tempting, but his enthusiasm was tempered by the risks. Implementing a new, untested change to a starship's warp drive was a good way to get all of its—and its crew's—molecules extruded out into space as one long stream. While it would certainly be a painless death, it would also be a pointless death.

****

"CIC confirms that the transition flash belonged to the Specter, Captain," Commander Chambliss said as Jackson walked onto the bridge.

"And the other ship is still moving along the same course?"

"Yes, sir," Accari spoke up. "No change in course or speed. Scratch that, it is being affected by the pull of the small gas giant it's crossing paths with."

"Ignore it," Jackson said. "That all but confirms that it's an unmanned decoy. OPS, has Engineering reported in?"

"They're getting ready to begin testing, sir," Hori said. "Commander Walsh said that he expects to meet your deadline."

"Nav, plot course to the Epsilon jump point," Jackson said. "Helm, all ahead one-quarter until we get the rest of our engine power back. We'll be at a crawl, but we'll be moving in the right direction."

"Engines ahead one-quarter, aye."

"By the time we reach the jump point we should be back to full mission capable," Jackson said to Chambliss. "We have to assume that the Specter is heading back to his last stronghold. It's worth a shot to go there and try to dig him out."

"Agreed, sir," Chambliss said. "We didn't come all this way to run home when we scrape a knee. How much fleet strength do you think the Darshik military has left?"

"Sadly, we know less about their numbers than we do about the ESA fleet," Jackson said. "CIS tells me it could be as few as a handful of cruisers or up to a few dozen consolidated within that single star system."

"Typical," Chambliss snorted.

"We do have something that may give us an edge, but I wanted to discuss it with you first," Jackson said. "What would you say if I told you there was a way the *Nemesis* could perform the same intrasystem warp hops the enemy does?"

"I'd ask if you'd been drinking and why you're holding out on me, sir," Chambliss said, his joke falling flat. "But that isn't possible … is it?"

"The hardware is designed to do it," Jackson said. "But for some reason, likely timidity, Fleet stuck with the antiquated field equations and just upped the power output to achieve a higher stable warp velocity."

"That doesn't really—"

"The Cube has the new, updated field equations for our warp drive that would not only increase our drive efficiency and speed between systems, but would also allow us to jump around accurately within a system."

"That's quite a risk, sir," Chambliss said carefully. "You haven't authorized this yet, have you?"

"No … nor will I on our flight out to the Epsilon System," Jackson said. "But it's something to keep in mind. If we get our back against the wall, it would be something we could use that would be completely unexpected."

"Indeed it would … especially for Starfleet," Chambliss said.

True to Commander Walsh's word, the *Nemesis* had full engine power back within three hours and her aft weaponry back shortly after that. Jackson cancelled general quarters but kept the bridge and CIC on a heightened state of alert. He'd learned early on that the stress of prolonged combat engagements, even during the long pauses where the ship was being repositioned, wore a crew's proficiency down to a nub. The *Nemesis* was faster and able to get in and out of engagements quicker than his previous commands, but the reality of space combat was that it took days and weeks to cross the billions of kilometers even once you arrived within a star system.

While the *Nemesis* continued her half-speed crawl towards their jump point, Jackson used the time to get his crew calmed and rested, make sure the ship was at one hundred percent, and talk to his chief engineer and XO about implementing the new software into their warp drive control avionics. Commander Walsh surprised Jackson by being the most open of the pair to the idea. He requested that he be able to review the new equations and control algorithms on the flight to the Epsilon System and promised Jackson that by the time they transitioned in he'd be able to give his approval or protest for the plan.

By the time they were ready to leave the system, Jackson, while not particularly liking the delay, felt the crew and ship were as ready as they could be. Not for the first time he wished that it wasn't left up to this crew to try and eliminate the Specter threat singlehandedly. If CENTCOM, and by extension the civilian oversight, would have taken things more seriously they'd have already invaded the Epsilon System with a full taskforce led by their battleships with all of the accompanying fleet that came with it. They could have smashed the Darshik war machine in one decisive move once they found out just how depleted they were from the Ushin. Now? Now it was up to one destroyer crew to run the gauntlet and try to knock out a single ship that was causing them so much trouble. To make matters more grim, their return to Terran space wouldn't be a hero's welcome and the senior staff would likely face severe disciplinary action.

No good deed, as the saying goes.

Chapter 21

"Position confirmed ... we're in the Epsilon System within six hundred kilometers of our target, Captain."

"Thank you, Chief," Jackson said. "Tactical, begin passive scans. OPS, how soon on engines?"

"Three minutes for the field arrays to stabilize, sir," Lieutenant Hori said.

"Tell Commander Walsh as soon as I have the RDS available he is clear to begin his work on the warp drive," Jackson said.

"Aye, sir," Hori said, clearly confused.

Walsh had gone over the data provided three times and could find no flaws with the math that would allow them to hop around within a system and had agreed to load the patches into the appropriate black boxes. The caveat was that in order to use the system, the Cube would have to provide all navigation inputs directly to the drive as the human operators had neither the precision nor the training to safely pull it off. At this point, Jackson felt he could trust the Cube completely even though it would still need to be closely monitored to rein in its natural exuberance so the risk was minimized.

"Definite Darshik ships' activity close to the third planet, sir," Accari reported. "So far the computers are matching the thermal signatures with standard cruiser-type ships."

"We won't know for certain if our target is here until our engines are up and running and he's actually moving," Jackson said. "In the meantime, keep to passively observing."

"Captain, we're getting a channel request via com laser ... it's a Fleet signal," Lieutenant Makers spoke up. "Correction, it's not a channel request, it's just an incoming message."

"From whom?" Chambliss asked. "CIS bring a Prowler out here and not tell anybody?"

"It's possible," Jackson said. "Send it to my terminal when it's fully received, decrypted, and verified."

"Aye, sir. It's coming your way now," Makers said.

Jackson opened the message and almost couldn't believe what he was reading.

Captain Wolfe,

The Aludra Star arrived in-system approximately four days ago flying directly from the Juwel System. We were given specific navigational data from the classified AI system you have aboard and asked to come here and deploy Starburst. All twenty-seven of our sleds have been deployed and have so far not been detected. We've been observing the formations below and can confirm the Specter is not among them, nor has that particular ship made an appearance since we've been here. However, there is what appears to be a Terran vessel of unknown configuration that I'm sending with the accompanying data, as well as seventeen Darshik

*cruisers. Be advised that the enemy has mined the jump
point you emerged from. We've mapped it out and will
send you the most probable safe path through. We're
standing by to render assistance when you need it.*

Captain Michael Barrett

CO, TFS Aludra Star

"Cube, would you care to explain what a semi-
obsolete Black Fleet assault carrier is doing in this
system?" Jackson asked.

"I have been impressed with the destructive
potential of Captain Barrett's Starburst proposal," the
Cube answered. "The odds were high that this system
held an insurmountable number of lesser ships you
would have to fight through in order to get to the
Specter. Captain Barrett's sleds, even loaded with non-
nuclear Shrikes, negates the enemy's numerical
advantage."

"You've yet again put an unacceptable number
of spacers' lives at risk based on your cold arithmetic,"
Jackson said, knowing the argument was moot at this
point. "The *Star* doesn't have the speed or weaponry to
be considered survivable in a fight with up to seventeen
cruisers."

"The Starburst system is more than capable of
defending the *Aludra Star* and providing the *Nemesis*—"

"Enough!" Jackson cut the Cube off. "What do
you make of the supposed Terran ship they sent data
over on?"

"I am ninety-six-percent certain that particular ship is a newer class of ESA frigate," the Cube said.

"What?!" Chambliss almost came out of his seat. "Is it a derelict?"

"Negative, Commander," the Cube continued. "The data from the *Aludra Star*'s passive array shows the ship is under its own power and appears undamaged. The ship's presence shifts the odds of the missing human personnel from the Specter attacks being alive to over seventy percent."

"The sons of bitches have been working with the Darshik the entire time … sir," Accari said, his mouth hanging open. "That's how the Specter has been able to find and target so many classified facilities."

"Agreed," Jackson said, his right cheek twitching and his face flushing. "And putting two and two together, I think we have to assume Tsuyo Corporation is also aware of this. Based on intel I received before we departed home, it looks like Tsuyo has been funneling classified information to the ESA, which then ended up in the hands of the Darshik."

"Fucking human collaborators?" Chambliss's tight voice indicated he was feeling the same level of rage his captain was.

"Okay … this is unexpected, but let's compartmentalize things and focus on the task at hand," Jackson said, shaking his head as if the action would clear it of the unwanted distractions.

"Nav, plot us a course through the mines and let's get moving. Helm, ahead one-third when you get it … we'll do this slow and steady."

"From the data we received it looks like the mine field wasn't completed," Accari said. "There are huge gaps and most are concentrated down and to port relative to our position."

"Could it have already collected a few incoming ships?" Chambliss asked.

"Unlikely, sir," Accari answered. "There's no localized debris to indicate a starship was damaged or destroyed near here."

The *Nemesis* pushed ahead gently, Specialist Healy making smooth, sweeping turns to keep the maximum space possible between the ship and the mines. As Jackson looked at the scaled representation on the main display he could see his tactical officer's point: The field looked like it had just been started and there were gaps big enough for a fleet carrier to get through safely. He puzzled over the field for a moment before he figured out why it was incomplete: The ESA ship flying in formation below them held the answer.

The Darshik had probably begun mining known Terran jump points into their space and then abandoned the effort when a deal was struck with the ESA to provide support and intel in the war against the Federation. The ESA ships must have had a warp lane into the Tango System and then used the same jump points the Federation ships had during the first ill-fated sojourn into Darshik territory. The idea that a human faction that was, essentially, squabbling over political semantics regarding the Phage War would willingly sell their own species out in order to gain some sort of advantage made his blood boil.

But was it really so outlandish? The ESA propaganda clearly showed they blamed Starfleet, and Wolfe in particular, for starting the Phage War since he was the poor dumb bastard that had stumbled across them in the first place. The Darshik were aware that a human had destroyed the Phage core mind and the ESA had likely given them his name as the one responsible. It was disquieting to think that so much death and destruction was centered around his own actions, justified or not.

"We've cleared the field, sir," Accari reported.

"Cube, do you have the data for the Starburst deployment?" Jackson asked.

"Displaying it now," the Cube said. Twenty-seven green icons winked into existence on the main display and Jackson could see immediately they had roughly sixty percent coverage over the system given what he already knew about the range of the Shrikes. He also saw that Barrett had stacked his sleds above and below the ecliptic, which would decrease their effective range on ships flying along on that plane but decreased the likelihood of them being directly observed.

Starburst had been the brainchild of Michael Barrett once he'd taken command of the *Aludra Star*. As an assault carrier, she was tasked with the specific purpose of deploying loaded drop shuttles to support surface warfare operations. Barrett had realized immediately that it was rare that the ship would be needed in its intended capacity and that he was more than likely looking at a long stint as a cargo captain. When assault carriers weren't needed in war, they were used to ferry normal freight when CENTCOM didn't feel like waiting for a scheduled Merchant Fleet ship.

The basics of the system were that instead of twenty-seven heavy drop shuttles, the *Star* would carry semi-autonomous "sleds" that each held twelve Shrike II ship buster missiles. The sleds could be deployed around a system and then, accepting targeting data from any Federation ship that had the proper access codes, could command a fire mission from any sled that was in the vicinity of their target. Once Fleet grasped that Barrett was taking what many considered an obsolete class of ship and making it a force multiplier with a minimal amount of retrofit he was given all the approvals and funding he needed. He'd now get to see how Starburst performed in a real-world, live-fire test thanks to the Cube's meddling. But, nuclear or not, Jackson wouldn't turn down an extra three hundred and twenty-four Shrikes when he was outnumbered nearly twenty to one.

"The encryption codes to access each sled's targeting systems were also sent," the Cube said. "I will ensure that Tactical has the appropriate codes when needed."

"Nav, plot a direct course down towards the third planet," Jackson ordered. "Let's continue running silent for now until we have confirmation the Darshik or the ESA have detected us. Right now it looks like they're either unaware or unconcerned … our transition flash would have been detected by now and we'd be seeing some sort of reaction."

"Course plotted and loaded, Captain."

"Helm, all ahead full," Jackson ordered. "There's nothing to be gained by prolonging this. Tactical, keep constant watch for the Specter. That ship is still the primary mission objective so let's not be distracted by the ESA frigate or all the cruisers loitering further down."

"Aye, sir," Accari said.

Jackson reviewed the condensed preliminary intel report on the star system that CIC had just sent directly to his terminal. The cruisers were in a dynamic formation that led his analysts to believe they were crewed ships and not more of the autonomous shells that the Darshik had loaded the Tango System with as cannon fodder. The report also included a short line, apparently added by the Cube, stating that it agreed with Hawkins's people and their conclusions.

After reading the analysis, he thought of something else that bothered him greatly. Pulling his terminal around, he sent a query directly to the network address CIC had established for the Cube: "*Why did you not provide us with the same alternate navigation data that you gave the Aludra Star?*"

"*Due to the need to coordinate the arrival of both ships as closely as possible. Given the greater speed capability of the Nemesis, the Aludra Star had no choice but to take a shorter route.*"

Jackson stared at the response for a second, unsure how to take it. The risks the Cube had taken by sending the assault carrier to an enemy system via an unknown, unapproved warp lane were bad enough, but it also could have provided an alternate route for the *Nemesis* instead of allowing her to fly into *another* contested system where she took damage by flying into an ambush. The only consideration the Cube seemed to have been worried about was the timing of its own convoluted plan involving Barrett's experimental weapon system.

The apparent oversights by the Cube could mean that it wasn't as infallible as everyone assumed it to be after its work on Project Prometheus. It was an accident born of hastily designed alien technology, after all. How much faith should they be putting into assuming that it considered all possible alternative actions and consequences before it advised them? Worse still, had the Cube done the math and decided that the risk to human lives was acceptable if it meant bumping the odds of mission success up a few percentage points? It had done something similar in the past before it had become sentient.

Since there was little he could do about it currently, he pushed the matter from his mind. Regardless of how the *Aludra Star* had come to be there, she was an asset in the system for Jackson to use. With the matter of the Cube's trustworthiness on his mind, he reluctantly sent the message he'd been composing that gave Commander Walsh approval to perform the warp drive avionics software patch. He wanted it to be a matter of official record that the decision was entirely his in case something went wrong, so the message was unnecessarily wordy and he hoped Walsh took the hint and sent no reply.

"Coms, inform Flight OPS that I want four of our Jacobson drones outfitted with full sensor and com suites," Jackson said after closing out his terminal. "I'm passing on course plots for each drone. OPS, once you have control of the drones we'll be initiating a Wright Grid."

"Aye, sir," Hori said. "Prepping Link nodes now."

The "Wright Grid" was named after Captain Celesta Wright. During the first serious push into Darshik space, she'd launched all of her Jacobson drones and had them create an active sensor grid by routing all the data through CIC and then putting the aggregate results onto the Link for the rest of the fleet to share. It had been so successful that the software and command scripts had been distributed to all ships that carried the advanced drones.

Within an hour Flight OPS had the drones loaded with the appropriate mission modules and into the launch cradles. Jackson commanded the drive to zero output while they spit the drones out of the belly launchers, waiting until the semi-autonomous spacecraft had cleared the area before telling the helm to throttle back up.

Captain Barrett's missile sleds were a valuable asset, but only if there was the accompanying sensor data to provide targeting data. Since the Starburst system was still technically in the test phase, none of the sleds were fitted with the expensive active arrays that would normally be used to aim the missiles. Jackson's drones would be able to fill in, but it wouldn't be perfect; there would still be a lag from the time the sensor data came over the Link to when his signal to one of the sleds would fire the weapons.

"I have command of the drones, sir," Hori reported. "All four have strong telemetry and are showing green across the board. They'll be in optimum position within ... seventeen hours."

"Which is significantly longer than we'll be," Jackson said, realizing he was outrunning his advantage in this fight. "Helm, decrease relative velocity by twenty percent and then steady as she bears."

"Engines answering all reverse," Healy said. "Shedding twenty percent of relative and then steady as she bears, aye."

"Captain, warp drive controller updates have been applied successfully," the Cube said over the intercom. "The system is available at your discretion."

"Acknowledged," Jackson said, a cold chill passing through him as he realized how much trust he was putting in the Cube yet again. He pulled up a few more screens on the holographic display attached to his chair and did one last check of all the *Nemesis's* vitals before she went into battle again.

He closed down the display and looked at all the enemy ships represented on the main screen and couldn't help but wonder if he was flying into another elaborate trap by an enemy commander that was proving to be as cunning and ruthless as Jackson had feared. So far the Specter seemed to always be a half-step ahead of him and he was quickly growing tired of that. It was well past time to even the score.

Chapter 22

"We're getting major movement from the formations, Captain," Accari reported.

"I see that, Tactical," Jackson said, never taking his eyes off the real-time sensor feed on the main display. "They know we're here. OPS! Have all the Jacobsons go full active sensors. Tactical, let's stay quiet for now and just try to blend into the noise. It's likely they've just realized what our Link transmissions mean or they've spotted the drones' engines on thermals."

"Aye, sir," Accari said.

"New commands sent to all four drones, sir," Hori reported.

The *Aludra Star* was coming downhill in a wide, decaying heliocentric orbit while the *Nemesis* was taking a direct route towards the cluster of Darshik ships and one ESA frigate. Jackson had wanted to remain hidden as long as practical while trying to coordinate multiple ships, multiple drones, and over two dozen loaded missile sleds. The Darshik cruisers, while not especially formidable on their own, still had the ability to perform warp hops and almost instantly redeploy themselves. The *Nemesis* was tough, but ten cruisers could be problematic once they were in close. The *Aludra Star* would fare even worse; she was heavily armored but didn't have much in the way of speed or armament.

Jackson looked at the mission clock and was surprised that only four and a half hours had passed since first watch had come back on duty. He had the bridge on twelve-hour shifts with floaters from third watch and CIC able to relieve people for short breaks. The lower decks were likely running split-sixes so that they were rotating fresh people in relatively often during the long, boring crawl down the well. Chambliss would know, but Jackson wasn't in the habit of micromanaging his department heads. They knew what they had to do and he didn't care how they went about doing it.

"Active returns from the Jacobsons coming through the Link now, Captain," Accari said. "Darshik formation is scattering randomly ... the ESA ship is now under full power and heading the opposite direction of our approach."

"Which means we've actually been spotted too," Jackson said. "Let's go full active on our sensors as well, Tactical. I don't want a cruiser hopping in behind us and not have our targeting radar already sweeping."

"Actives coming up now, Captain," Accari said. "We have one cruiser that's flown within optimum range of Sled Nineteen." Jackson and Chambliss looked at each other and shrugged.

"Target cruiser with two missiles from Sled Nineteen," Jackson said. "Fire at will."

"Targeting orders sent, fire command sent," Accari said. "Stand by for updates."

The *Nemesis* pressed on as an automated weapons platform over three million kilometers away received the properly coded commands and fired two Shrike missiles at the incoming Darshik cruiser. From the time Accari sent the command to when they were alerted the missiles had met the target, nearly four and a half hours had passed while the destroyer continued to loaf towards the engagement, still drifting with her engines at idle.

"Confirmed hit! Target destroyed," Accari nearly shouted. The excitement of drawing first blood in the battle had people on the bridge cheering quietly, but Jackson just frowned.

"Put the optical data on the main screen," he said. Lieutenant Hori executed his order without prompting so Accari wouldn't lose his situational awareness outside the ship. Jackson watched the heavily enhanced video of the Darshik cruiser exploding.

"Again," he ordered. "Half-speed."

"What are you looking for, sir?" Chambliss asked quietly.

"Two Shrikes with H.E. warheads took out a Darshik cruiser so easily?" Jackson asked him. "You don't find that odd?"

Chambliss was now frowning as he also watched the small video clip repeat a few times. While the drone was too far away to pick up the ship very clearly or the missiles at all, it was obvious when the first Shrike impacted the prow by the small flash. The rest of the video showed the hull of the cruiser undulating and breaking apart as the high-explosive warhead detonated and set off a series of secondary explosions that were fatal.

"That was far too easy for—"

"Captain Barrett has targeted three more cruisers and authorized missile launches, sir," Hori said.

"The *Aludra Star* is advising us that they're out of position to intercept the ESA frigate," Makers said. "Captain Barrett wants to know if you wish him to pursue anyway or continue on his original course."

"He can't catch it. Tell him to continue down towards the third planet," Jackson said. "The element of surprise is lost so inform him he's free to tighten his arc and get down there quicker. OPS! What's the range on the fleeing ESA ship?"

"One point zero seven billion kilometers, sir," Hori said.

"It's heading to some unknown jump point," Jackson said. "Look at the direct route it's taking. We can't catch it either even at full emergency acceleration."

"And there aren't any missile sleds on that side of the system at all," Chambliss noted. "Looks like it'll get away clean."

"Maybe not," Jackson said, bracing himself for the order he was about to give. "Cube, calculate an intrasystem warp jump that puts the *Nemesis* dead astern of the fleeing ESA frigate."

"Stand by," the Cube said calmly. "Parameters set ... warp drive available and ready. Shall I execute?"

Jackson exchanged a meaningful look with his XO before answering as everyone on the bridge seemed to be holding their breath.

"Execute," he ordered.

He wasn't sure what he expected. Perhaps a building whine of the drive emitters, maybe a sharp bang as the destroyer was tossed about by the gravimetric distortion fields, but there was none of that. They felt a gentle lurch and there were a few warnings on the main display as some systems were confused about the loss of telemetry from the other Federation ships in the system, but other than that the event was, well, uneventful.

"ESA frigate bearing to starboard dead ahead … range is three hundred and forty thousand kilometers," Accari said.

"Helm, you're clear for free flight … pursue and close on that ship," Jackson ordered. "Tactical, do you think you can disable the engines without destroying the ship?"

"Yes, sir," Accari said confidently. "She's got two MPDs on pylons hanging off either side. I can easily target those once we close within one hundred and fifty thousand kilometers."

"Get ready and watch any missiles it spits out at us," Jackson said before keying the intercom. "Major Baer and Commander Essa … prepare your men for boarding of an enemy ship. I want you in the hangar bay within the next forty-five minutes."

"We're going to board her … sir?" Chambliss asked.

"Just obliterating that ship is pointless," Jackson said. "We need to know why the hell they're here."

"Captain, I believe I can be of assistance in this regard," the Cube spoke up. "If the boarding party takes a standard network node transceiver with them and connects it to any system on that ship, I should be able to disable any automated defenses they have."

"Make it happen," Jackson said. "Talk to Hawkins in CIC and let him know what equipment you need the team to carry."

"Captain, I have to admit that I'm less than enthusiastic about this plan," Chambliss said quietly.

"That's your right, XO," Jackson said calmly as the *Nemesis* closed the gap quickly without drawing any enemy fire yet. "If you'd like, you may file an official protest in the ship's log."

"No, sir," Chambliss said firmly. "I feel it's my job to point out when I disagree with you, but I'll back your decisions all the way and to hell with what some CENTCOM after-action team says."

Jackson glanced at his XO, his already high estimation of the man ticking up a few notches. He would make a hell of a captain if given the chance.

"They're taking evasive action!" Hori cried.

"I bet they thought we were a Darshik ship at first with the warp hop," Chambliss said. "Helm, maintain pursuit."

"Can you still make the shot, Tactical?" Jackson asked.

"No problem, sir."

"Weapons free, Lieutenant Commander," Jackson ordered. "Cut her legs out from under her."

"Stand by ... firing," Accari said calmly. On the main display the computer put up four overlapping blue lines that connected the two ships. Accari's careful targeting script used four cannons from the starboard fore bank at moderate power aimed directly into the thrust nozzles of the fleeing ship. Within ten seconds the beams overheated the magnetic constrictors and errant streams of plasma could be seen belching out the rear, until the damage was so great that the emergency overrides kicked in and vented all the drive plasma into space to spare the MPD, effectively disabling the ship.

As Accari upped the power of his beams and began permanently disabling the now-dormant engines, the *Nemesis* was rocked and a slew of alarms went off at various stations.

"Incoming laser fire," Hori reported. "Moderate damage to secondary com array and—." She was cut off by another bout of incoming laser fire that peppered the dorsal hull plates, scorching some and warping others from the heat.

"Tactical!" Jackson barked.

"Targeting all aft weapons emplacements," Accari responded. "Firing!"

The two ships exchanged laser fire for the next five seconds, the frigate's becoming more sparse and less directed as the *Nemesis's* much more powerful forward cannons turned their projectors to slag. After ten more seconds the aft end of the ESA ship was scorched and pockmarked and there was no more incoming fire.

"The computer identified and destroyed four missile ports as well, but no guarantees there aren't more surprises, sir," Accari said.

"Is my boarding party down in Flight OPS yet?" Jackson asked.

"Both teams report ready, Captain," Hori said. "They've already boarded the two assault shuttles and are awaiting approval to launch."

"Tell them to launch and then get behind the *Nemesis*," Jackson said. "We'll make one lateral run as we pass their port flank and identify their breaching points. Cube! That's your job. Where's the best place to punch a hole?"

"I've identified four likely locations based on the assumed hull design," the Cube answered. "The first two are where the hull will likely be thinnest; the second two are where they will be less likely to encounter heavy initial resistance."

"Do you think the armor at your second set of points is thin enough for our assault shuttles to cut through?" Jackson asked.

"Based on the damage caused by our lasers on the rear quadrant, I believe it is," the Cube said.

"Send the second set to the shuttle pilots," Jackson said. "Coms! Patch me through to the boarding teams."

"Channel open, sir."

"Marines, NOVAs," Jackson said. "This will be a risky op and we haven't had near the time to prepare for it properly, but I need that ship subdued. The amount of intel on both the ESA and the Darshik that has to be aboard is incredibly valuable … I wouldn't put you at risk if it wasn't important."

"*We're good to go, Captain!*" Major Baer had to shout over the sound of the shuttles' engines.

"*We live for this shit, sir!*" Commander Essa called from their shuttle. "*We'll get it done!*"

"Flight OPS reports shuttles are clear and they're closing the hangar bay outer hatches," Hori said.

"Helm, take us down the port flank," Jackson ordered. "Tactical, get ready to soften her up … I don't want to lose a single Marine or NOVA before they've even boarded."

"Targeting scripts locked in, sir," Accari said.

"Here we go," Chambliss whispered from beside him as the *Nemesis* surged forward to overtake the drifting frigate.

"Here we go indeed," Jackson muttered. He obviously didn't want to lose a single member of his crew on this mission, but with a boarding action that seemed increasingly unlikely.

****

"Is this data correct?!" Barrett demanded, staring at the main screen. The *Nemesis* had just disappeared from sensors while simultaneously appearing right behind the fleeting ESA ship.

"Link data confirms, sir," Lieutenant Dole said from OPS. "The *Nemesis* performed the same sort of warp hop the Darshik ships do ... but the transition flash was nearly non-existent."

"Crafty old dog," Barrett chuckled, not able to believe that Wolfe had been able to keep the fact his ship could perform that maneuver a secret.

"Two more Darshik cruisers destroyed, sir!" Lieutenant Commander Adler cried. "It's like they're not even trying to get away."

"Indeed," Barrett said, frowning. "Have any of the ships even tried to knock down our missiles?"

"Yes, sir," Adler said. "Two were able to get one each, but so far every ship targeted has been destroyed or critically disabled."

"This is a massacre," Commander Simmons said. "Why aren't they fighting harder to protect their home planet?"

"How many ships have we destroyed?" Barrett asked.

"Six including the ship Captain Wolfe destroyed, sir," Dole said.

"How do the remaining ships look? What are their engine outputs and acceleration numbers like?" Barrett asked.

"Erratic, sir," Dole said as he pored through the sensor data. "Two of the ship are barely able to break orbit and five of them are leaking radiation."

"Interesting," Barrett said. "What about that planet? Any detected weapons emplacements or large population pockets?"

"Stand by, sir," Dole said and pulled his headset all the way on.

"What are your thoughts, sir?" Simmons asked.

Barrett held a hand up as Dole looked back up.

"CIC reports that spectral analysis indicates the planet is incapable of sustaining Ushin life," the OPS officer said. "They say what we're reading now conflicts with the data the *Icarus* brought back when you and Captain Wright were here the first time. There are also indications of high levels of radiation in the upper atmosphere that weren't there before."

"Cease fire!" Barrett barked. "Detonate any missiles that are on their way to a target and stand down."

"Sir?" Simmons asked as Adler frantically sent self-destruct codes to all the missiles she'd already launched.

"This isn't the Darshik's last stronghold," Barrett said. "This is a collection of damaged ships limping around in orbit over a poisoned planet. We're not here to annihilate a group of beings who can't even attempt to defend themselves."

"If I may respectfully disagree—"

"You may not, XO," Barrett cut Simmons off. "We're here to support Captain Wolfe as he hunts a ship that appears to not be in this system. These cruisers are no threat to us or the *Nemesis*. Hell, I doubt if any of them even have a working warp drive."

"Understood, sir," Simmons said.

"Tactical?" Barrett asked.

"All in-flight munitions successfully diverted or detonated," Adler said. "All remaining enemy ships are bunching up into formation over the fourth planet … there are two stragglers that appear too damaged to make it."

"Understood," Barrett said. He knew that the Darshik were actually Ushin and not their own unique species, but they were their own unique society. If he hadn't stopped firing he had a feeling he would have eradicated every living Darshik in the system. As a lowly starship captain those types of choices weren't his to make. He had successfully stopped the threat in the system ... the fate of the poor bastards on those remaining death traps would be left up to someone else.

"Inform Flight OPS we're redeploying the sleds," he said to his com officer. "I want everything heading back uphill to form a defensive spread around where the *Nemesis* is operating. We need to watch Captain Wolfe's back ... the Specter could still be out there somewhere."

"*Nemesis* reports they've disabled the ESA frigate and are preparing to board," the coms officer said. "A NOVA team and part of their Marine detachment are en route now."

"Very good," Barrett said. "Tell Captain Wolfe that we're sending all our missile sleds up to him as a bulwark in case the Specter shows up while their boarding party is away. OPS, get us a course that follows ... we're done down here."

"Aye aye, sir."

Chapter 23

"Damn," Jackson murmured as he read over the report that Barrett had sent over the Link.

"Sir?" Chambliss asked.

"Just impressed with the type of captain my former tactical officer has become," Jackson said, using a flicking motion with his hand to send the report over to Chambliss's terminal. As his XO read, Jackson reflected on what Barrett had done.

Being a cunning warrior and tactician were critical skills a warship captain needed, but knowing when to be merciful was equally important. When it became obvious that the Darshik in this system were not a threat and were, in fact, hanging onto survival by a thread, he had made the decision not to slaughter a defenseless group of beings despite the horrors they'd heaped upon humanity. Commander Chambliss had a more pragmatic take on the report.

"What could have destroyed the planet's ability to sustain life so thoroughly in such a short span?" he asked. "We've never fired on the planet, the Ushin don't have a military to speak of ... what the hell happened here?"

"Isn't it obvious?" Jackson asked. "The Specter did this. Like a retreating army burning the crops behind them to slow the advance of their pursuers, he tried to kill off the last of his people in what was likely an effort to cover his escape. He knew we'd come here eventually."

"Unbelievable," Chambliss said with awe. "There were tens of millions on that planet according to our best estimates."

"It also means the ship we're after isn't here and won't be coming at all," Jackson said sourly. "Back to square one."

"Captain, the shuttles are grappled on and both teams are getting ready to breach and board," Hori said, interrupting any further speculation about where their quarry might have fled to.

"Have CIC monitor the feed and alert me if anything goes wrong," Jackson said. He'd like nothing more than to watch the live feed from his teams, but his job was to make sure the *Nemesis* was alert and ready to fend off any enemy that might try to come in and retake or destroy the frigate. An ESA destroyer coming into the system during boarding ops would be less than ideal.

"Aye, sir," Hori said. "Shuttle One reports they're through the hull and making entry." "That's the NOVA team," Chambliss grunted. Jackson just nodded. As far as he knew, this was the first time a Terran ship had been boarded by another hostile Terran party. Another dubious distinction for his career in the history books.

"Tell both teams to watch their backs and exfil if things get too hot," he said, almost wishing he was over there with them.

****

"Go! Go! GO!!"

At Amiri Essa's shouted command, the NOVA team sprinted through the still-glowing hole the assault shuttle's breacher had cut into the frigate's hull. There was a hiss as the locking collar wasn't able to achieve a perfect seal, but it worked out in their favor as the smoke was drawn out the gaps instead of lingering in the service bay they'd just cut their way into.

"There! Put the network repeater there," Essa said, pointing to a monitoring station with exposed cables. One of the team's tech specialists, Rat, ran to the terminal and skillfully spliced the device into the data cables. The unit was self-powered, so once he had made a good connection the lights on the box winked from red to amber and then finally a blinking green to let them know the Cube was happy with the link.

"*Vulture, Nemesis … Bulldog has made entry and reports no resistance.*"

"Copy, *Nemesis*," Essa said, pressing his throat mic out of habit. "We're moving out. The network repeater is installed and shows green."

"*The Cube reports a good connection, Vulture. Nemesis out.*"

"Let's move!" Essa said. "Keep your gaps and keep your eyes open. Don't assume our computer friend will be able to knock out any automated defenses we might run into, so heads on a swivel. Pitch, you and Joker take point and try not to shoot any of Major Baer's Marines."

"Yes, sir," Joker said and moved quickly to open the hatch but found that he needed help due to the lower pressure on their side. Once it opened with a *whoosh,* the pressure normalized in the chamber and the team was able to move out into the corridor.

Red lights strobed along the upper edges of the bulkheads and four different alarms could be heard blaring throughout the ship, but there were no ESA spacers anywhere. They had to move twenty-five meters forward to where Major Baer's team was making entry and then they'd split off again with the NOVAs moving forward to capture the bridge and the Marines pressing to Engineering to make sure nobody tried anything stupid like scuttling the ship with them all aboard.

"I have eyes on Bulldog," Pitch called back over his shoulder. Essa raised a hand to acknowledge him and moved forward to meet Major Baer's lead element.

"Sergeant Castillo," Essa nodded to the Marine NCO. "Everyone make it?"

"Yes, sir," Castillo said. "We're all aboard. We had to use a few emergency patches ... the collar was leaking air so badly people were getting lightheaded."

"We're not going to wait," Essa said. "Tell Major Baer we're pressing forward and will try to take the bridge by the time you have Engineering."

"Yes, sir," Castillo said again and moved back with the corporal he was standing guard with.

The NOVA team moved quickly past the storage bay that Bulldog Team had cut into and then began moving inboard at the next cross corridor. The ESA and United Terran Federation had only recently split off from each other, so Essa was operating under the assumption that ship-building philosophy hadn't had time to diverge too much between the two. If his theory held true, he would soon come to a—ah! There it was. A large, uninterrupted corridor that ran the length of the ship that was used to move heavy equipment back and forth. Every Terran ship had two of these, starboard to move forward, port to move aft.

"Contact!" Joker shouted as he opened fire with his carbine. The rest of the team scattered for cover while the forward element began laying down suppressing fire. The rounds they carried were designed to be lethal to biological beings but not penetrate the bulkheads of a starship. Nobody wanted an errant round hitting something critical and killing everyone by accident.

"Six hostiles armed with pistols and wearing body armor," Pitch said over the team channel. "They're taken cover behind that cluster of water pipes."

"Flash bang," Essa ordered. "Front four, move on detonation. Execute."

Joker pulled a black cylindrical grenade from his tactical harness and pressed the button on top three times, waiting for it to flash red before he threw it. The grenade was a "smart" munition and would wait until it was closest to a bio signature before going off. Joker's overhand throw was a good one and just as the grenade passed the cluster of fresh water supply pipes it detonated. The explosion even in such a cavernous space as a main access tube was stunning, but the NOVAs were ready and braced for it, the ear plugs they wore automatically closing off when they detected the pressure of the blast.

"Move!" Pitch shouted and took off at a full sprint towards where the six defenders were hiding. As it turned out, it was unnecessary. The grenade blast going off while it was still at head level hadn't left any of them conscious. Upon close inspection Essa could see it actually hadn't left two of them alive.

"Secure the living," he said. "Check them and bind them." The lights in the tube flickered, went out, then came back on as three of the NOVAs relieved the hostiles of their weaponry and used heavy plastic cuffs to secure them to the pipes. Before they were done there were a few sharp bangs that reverberated through the hull and then the hiss of the air handlers died.

"Shit," Rat said. "They may be getting ready to let the air out on us. The crew may already be in the emergency shelters or lifeboats and they'll just let us flop around like fish out of water without having to fire a shot."

"Cheery prospect," Essa said as he keyed his radio. "Bulldog, Vulture ... we've lost life support to this section of the ship. Any chance you're able to do anything from Engineering?"

"*If we were in there, possibly,*" Baer's voice came back over the sound of weapons fire. "*We've met some heavy resistance and they've sealed the blast doors. We're backing out and looking for an alternative route.*"

"Copy," Essa said before killing the channel and turning to his team. "We're fucked. Let's get back to the—"

"Attention Federation Marines," a heavily accented voice came over the shipwide PA. "This is Captain Yeung ... I hereby surrender the *Xiangtan* and am returning all Federation prisoners aboard. Please allow my crew safe passage to the aft, starboard cargo hold and reengage all the environmental systems before we all suffocate."

"What the fuck is he talking about?" Joker asked, but Essa was ignoring him.

"*Nemesis*, Vulture ... you get all that?" the team commander asked. "I have no idea either ... copy that, we'll press ahead to the bridge and let Bulldog handle the crew ... copy, Vulture out."

"Sir?" Pitch asked.

"Somehow that Vruahn computer took control of the environmental systems through the box we put on that monitoring terminal," Essa said. "It also took control of the powerplant so they couldn't sabotage that to destroy the ship. The captain really had no choice after that. He could fight us all the way to the bridge, but it would be ultimately pointless with a Fed destroyer sitting off his port flank."

"What was that bullshit about Federation prisoners?" Joker asked.

"We're about to find out," Essa said. "Let's get moving ... *Nemesis* just sent detailed layouts of the ship to my tac-computer. Captain Wolfe has ordered us to proceed as if this is a ploy by Yeung but not to engage unless fired upon."

The team redeployed without complaint or questions and began pressing forward again towards the bridge. As Essa jogged with his men, he couldn't shake the feeling of dread that had come over him when the ESA captain had announced he had Fed prisoners.

****

"Captain, it may not be the wisest—"

"I've already heard enough from my executive officer, Commander Essa," Jackson cut off the NOVA team leader. "I'm already here and I'm not leaving. Where are these prisoners?"

"There's a secure section of the ship with living quarters and work spaces," Essa said. "That's where they all are. Sixty-seven Federation researchers ... all taken by the Specter off of highly secured and classified installations."

"Did the captain of this ship have any comment on it?" Jackson asked.

"Only that he was following orders and that there were two other ships that were rotated into this system to relieve them of the prisoners so they could fly back to ESA space."

"Have Captain Yeung brought down," Jackson said.

"Yes, sir."

Jackson had been taken by surprise when the captain had surrendered the ship with only a few exchanges of fire with the boarding parties. He'd later learned the Cube had pulled a fast one and had been able to fool the crew into thinking they would die of lack of oxygen if they didn't give up.

Like most Terran warships, the control systems of the *Xiangtan* were compartmentalized and isolated from each other rather than being one monolithic computer that managed everything. It was done for ease of maintenance, safety, and to prevent the sort of sabotage the Federation crew had been attempting. The monitoring terminal the NOVA team had attached the network repeater on hadn't allowed the Cube direct access to any critical systems, but it did allow it to make the crew think it did. The monitoring and alert sub-systems were all networked together and then tied in at certain points to critical systems, so even though it couldn't command the air handlers off, it could ask politely. With the duct blowers disabled, the Cube then crafted all the properly formatted system failure warnings and sent them to crew stations. Had the crew simply dug down a bit into the control screen they could have switched all the fans back on themselves, but the confusion and panic set in and Captain Yeung made a snap decision to surrender.

The Cube also created the illusion that it was in control of the powerplant and a dozen other critical systems so that by the time Yeung made his announcement the rest of the crew readily accepted that there was little they could do to repel the boarders. With the ship adrift and powerless and Federation special forces roaming the corridors, the *Xiangtan's* crew had quietly given up with only a few holdouts needing to be neutralized.

Before Jackson came over to the frigate himself, Commander Chambliss made sure more network repeaters were hardwired into all the critical systems the Cube would need to control to make sure some enterprising young spacer didn't find a way to scuttle the ship with Captain Wolfe aboard.

"They're all sitting in the common area waiting on you, sir," Major Baer said, snapping to attention when Jackson walked around the corner. "We're in the process of positively identifying all of them now."

"Thank you, Major," Jackson said and walked in through the hatchway, pausing to look at the downtrodden group of people slouched over the ubiquitous white plastic tables found on every starship.

"Who's in charge here?"

"I guess that would be me, Captain Wolfe," a woman near the hatchway stood, recognizing him immediately. "I've been acting as the go-between for the Fed prisoners and our ESA jailors. My name is Doctor Ella Marcum."

"Doctor Marcum," Jackson greeted her while containing his own surprise. "Your father is going to be very relieved to find out that you're still alive."

Chapter 24

The next seven days were a slog of interviewing rescued prisoners, confirming their identity as best they could with the records aboard the ship, and securing the crew of the *Xiangtan*. The *Aludra Star* had moved in and, as an assault carrier that was capable of transporting a full division of Marines, she had plenty of empty beds that were hastily converted to living quarters for Fed personnel and a secure detention area for the ESA crew.

Doctor Marcum was especially helpful in weeding out the ESA infiltrators from the *Xiangtan* crew that tried to claim they were Federation scientists as well as trying to give Jackson a better understanding of *why* the Darshik had enlisted the ESA to hold a group of researchers whose specialties weren't necessarily unique or related to each other. As it turns out, it had nothing to do with their current projects. The thread that tied all of these scientists together was that they were all heavily involved in researching Phage physiology and technology during the war.

Marcum said they never actually saw or directly communicated with the Darshik, but the records aboard the *Xiangtan* clearly showed that the Specter was the one giving the orders. The nature of the task they'd been given was how to perfect a process of integrating dissimilar biologies within a Phage unit using an interface. The implications were as clear as they were terrifying.

"The Specter is the last Darshik commander left, but he was also the one that started it all," Marcum explained. "He's always been the driving force behind the entire movement. Here, now, at the end he wants to *become* Phage."

"But the Phage are dead," Chambliss insisted. "There's nothing to become."

"Not technically correct, Commander," Marcum said. "Captain Wolfe destroyed the core mind, but individual units that weren't outright destroyed are still out there wholly intact. There's nothing to animate them so we've largely ignored them as they weren't a threat."

"And with Captain Wright destroying the only phage unit they had here in this system, he could be anywhere trying to find another one," Chambliss said, nodding.

"I know where he went," Jackson said. "It's the only place that makes sense: the system Celesta Wright left behind with hundreds of intact Phage units, including Super Alphas."

"My thoughts as well, Captain," Marcum said. "You may find that Captain Yeung is more helpful in a one-on-one situation rather than in front of his crew where he needs to save face. I got the feeling that he was less than enthusiastic about how far his government had gone to help the Darshik."

While Captain Yeung hadn't necessarily been forthcoming during the subsequent talks, he was willing to provide context for the data that Jackson's intel specialists had mined off the *Xiangtan's* servers. It was clear from the direction the Specter wanted the research to go that he was attempting to reactivate an Alpha or Super Alpha and be able to control it via a computer interface. Since those units still had their armament and power systems intact, there was a real risk if he was able to pull it off.

The Specter had been at this task for years and his people had made several leaps on their own towards the goal, but the final pieces of the puzzle were the work that human scientists had done regarding the aggregate control systems and input attenuation once they'd realized the Phage was actually a singular intelligence. Trying to control something like a Super Alpha with a single point interface was virtually impossible. But, if you could interface at just the right spot and correctly mimic the input signal the core mind had used for individual units, you just might be able to *convince* the Super Alpha to do your bidding.

The problem the Darshik had was that they very nearly deified the Phage and much of what they knew about the individual units and their makeup was based as much in superstition as it was hard fact. Humans, on the other hand, knew that the Phage was a malfunctioning weapon system designed by the Vruahn and treated it as such. It was biologic and adaptive in nature, but it was still a system that operated within a set of parameters. Unfortunately the Federation scientists who had been captured were more than willing to work on the problem in exchange for their lives and had developed a set of protocols that would—in theory— allow a properly interfaced computer to give commands to a Phage combat unit. The caveat was that the interface would have to also provide the correct carrier signal at all times or the unit would simply return to its dormant state, and that signal wasn't something the human team fully understood.

"We were looking at the Specter destroying this planet all wrong," Jackson said while he, Chambliss, and Accari ate dinner one night. "If what we're assuming is true and he's trying to somehow merge with a Phage unit, then he's likely gotten everything he needs. What *does* surprise me is that he left the ESA frigate intact."

"So he's already got a Super Alpha that he's probably been working on and prepping for integration," Accari said. "What's his next move?"

"If he can gain control of it well enough to fight with it he'll likely head straight for the Ushin capital world and turn the surface to slag," Chambliss said.

"Likely," Jackson agreed. "Or, equally plausible, he'll come after humanity again."

"So where do we go first?" Chambliss asked.

"I think we stick with the plan and try to intercept him before he has a chance to get one of those damn things moving and shooting again," Jackson said. "He's not had enough of a head start since we left the Tango System to get one fully ready for integration according to what the kidnapped scientists are telling us. Hopefully the Cube knows a shortcut back to that system."

When will we be leaving, sir?"

"*Captain Wolfe to the bridge! Captain Wolfe, please report to the bridge.*"

"Hold that thought," Jackson told Accari as he slid off his seat and jogged out of the ward room, his exec and tactical officer on his heels.

"Report!"

"Two CIS Prowlers just transitioned in, sir," Lieutenant Hori. "We received their broadcast at almost the same time we detected their transition flash."

"And what are our good friends from the CIS saying?" Jackson asked.

"They're ordering us to heave to and await their arrival, sir," Lieutenant Makers said. "Nothing more specific than that."

"They knew we were here," Chambliss said quietly. "They began transmitting as soon as they were back into real space."

"Agreed," Jackson said. "OPS, please send our mission logs to the lead Prowler beginning from the moment we detected an ESA frigate up until now. Standard encryption."

"Aye, sir," Hori said.

"Coms, tell Flight OPS I want our drones back aboard ASAP and to coordinate transferring the last of the rescued scientists and ESA prisoners over to the *Aludra Star*," Jackson said. "Tell Captain Barrett he'll be responsible for getting them all back to New Sierra."

For the next five hours one Prowler continued to broadcast the vague demands while another maintained a tight patrol up near the jump point. It wasn't making any effort to hide, but Jackson didn't really care either way. There was no possible way the small recon ship could actually stop the *Nemesis* if she wanted to leave via that jump point.

Jackson ignored the squawking by the CIS ships and continued getting the right people where they needed to be while preparing the *Nemesis* for departure. He had an unexplainable feeling that time was running short if they wanted to stop the Specter before he succeeded in reanimating a Phage Super Alpha. The units were stoppable, but not easily and not without a healthy dose of luck on their side. A single Super Alpha might not be the dire threat they once were since they were designed to fight against now-obsolete generations of Terran starships, but it still wasn't something to be taken lightly. He had some other, more exotic fears about what might happen if the Specter was allowed to continue unchecked, but he forced them out of his mind and concentrated on the task at hand.

"Lead Prowler has sent a new message, sir," Makers reported after the clock showed the CIS crew had had their mission log for the last forty minutes.

"They're asking our intentions regarding the ESA frigate and her crew."

"How soon until we can use a two-way channel with them?" Jackson asked.

"Another two hours and the delay will be down to ten minutes each way," Makers said.

"Tell them that in two hours I'll contact them with all the information they'll need," Jackson said. "In the meantime, tell them the crew is secured aboard the *Aludra Star* and we have made no decisions regarding the frigate herself. Also let them know that as of right now the Darshik cruisers clustered near the fourth planet are *not* a threat and that the Ushin will need to be contacted ASAP regarding them."

He leaned back and allowed himself a small grin. The CIS captain had likely been told to tell a rouge Black Fleet captain to get his ass back to Terran space immediately, but now Jackson could dangle something in front of them that was irresistible. He would allow the CIS officer to claim the frigate as their own; he had no interest in it past what he'd already learned, and for the CO of a Prowler it could mean a promotion or transfer they'd been wanting.

****

"That's a hell of a story, Captain Wolfe," Commander Sache said over the two-way video channel. Her face was unreadable as he finished a brief recounting of what had happened since they'd arrived in the Tango System.

"And your contention is that this Specter has the ability to revive a defunct Phage unit based on what these scientists told you?"

"They were fairly convincing," Jackson said. "I don't think it's a risk we can ignore. The system he's likely heading to still had a number of Super Alphas in it when Captain Wright left. I don't have to tell you that we fought very few of those during the war and they were never easy to bring down. They're still faster than even our newest ships and pack a hell of a punch."

"I was a sensor officer aboard an older Prowler during the war," Sache said. "So no, Captain, no reminder is necessary of what even a single one of those Supers is capable of. What's your plan?"

"Try and get there to stop him before he has a chance to complete the integration process," Jackson said. "It'll be close, but I think we can do it without straining her too hard. We've received some helpful navigation data that should give us a slight edge."

"Let's speak plainly for a moment, Captain Wolfe," Sache said, steepling her fingers. "We were sent out here because we were the closest assets to what was assumed to be your destination when you popped up in the Juwel System, but my two ships cannot physically stop you from continuing your self-appointed mission. Doubly so since you seem to have a co-conspirator in Captain Barrett … imagine my surprise when our missing assault carrier ended up being here.

"You've also given us an invaluable trove of intelligence by taking the frigate mostly intact and with her crew still alive. For the sake of argument, let's assume that if the *Nemesis* began pushing for her jump point now, my Prowler would have no means with which to stop you."

"Hypothetically, if I was asked at a later mission debrief—or court martial—about why I didn't surrender as asked by a CIS Prowler I would have to tell the truth: The *Nemesis* was too fast for them and I had no intention of relinquishing control of the ship," Jackson deadpanned.

"I see we're both looking at this problem as realists, Captain," Sache said. "May I say something off the record, sir?"

"Of course," Jackson said with some trepidation.

"I had two older brothers serving in Starfleet and on ships that were a part of Admiral Marcum's taskforce when you disobeyed orders and went after the core mind on your own," she said. "I always hoped that one day if I was faced with a choice like yours, to do what you were ordered or do what was right, that I'd do what was right. So with that in mind … happy hunting, sir. I'll provide as much cover as I can to make sure the other Prowler doesn't do something stupid and move to intercept you before you transition out."

"I wouldn't worry about that too much, Commander," Jackson said. "We have a few surprises that nobody knows about. Just make sure the *Aludra Star* makes it back to Terran space safely. *Nemesis* out."

He terminated the channel and leaned back in his chair to collect his thoughts. The ship was still provisioned and fueled for at least another nine weeks of continuous operation, so he felt comfortable that they wouldn't get stranded. The system they were traveling to was extremely far away, but the Cube's new navigational data along with the *Nemesis's* new maximum sustainable warp speed should cut the trip down to just over eight days, nearly five times faster than Marcum's taskforce had done it.

Now what it would all come down to was whether or not he was good or lucky enough to take the Specter out ... he'd settle for either. If he managed to get one of the Super Alphas going, all bets were off and Jackson would likely have no choice but to retreat and allow the fleet to hit it with larger numbers. Despite some of the rumors, he wasn't suicidal and he wouldn't waste the lives of his crew in a fight he had no chance of winning.

"We about ready to shove off and get this mission over with, Captain?"

"You have something better to do than be here with us, Sergeant Barton?"

"My girl is militantly unfaithful, sir," Barton said. "I realize that doesn't make me unique among Marines, but it's still a valid concern on long cruises."

Jackson had to look over at the Marine NCO to see the barely upturned corner of his mouth to realize he was joking.

"I'll do my best to accommodate you, Sergeant," he said, rolling his eyes.

"I appreciate that, Captain," Barton said and took up his post just inside the bridge hatchway.

"Captain, the *Nemesis* is ready to get underway. All drones are recovered and secured, shuttles are docked, and the *Aludra Star* has accounted for all her crew and guests," Commander Chambliss said.

"Very good," Jackson said, sitting down. "Helm, you have the course to our jump point?"

"Yes, sir, course is entered and locked."

"Then let's get out of here. All ahead flank," Jackson ordered. "I want to make sure that second Prowler doesn't have an opportunity to cut us off, so keep an eye on it, Tactical."

"All engines ahead flank, aye!"

"We're tracking him, sir," Accari said. "They're still broadcasting their ident beacon."

The *Nemesis* pulled away from the *Aludra Star* and the *Xiangtan*, angling to port and climbing up the well away from both CIS Prowlers. The first continued its slow approach to the other ships while the second didn't seem inclined to try and pursue, but the time lag between when it did something and when they could detect it was still quite large.

Jackson knew that one way or another, this would be his final time charging into battle on the bridge of a warship. He wasn't sure how he felt about that yet, but he was damn sure he at least wanted to get all his people home alive.

Chapter 25

The *Nemesis* hung motionless in space, so far away from the primary star of their target system it almost couldn't be picked out among the countless other stars. Jackson had requested that they transition in far short so that the destroyer's muted transition flash would be less detectable by anyone further down the system. He had no doubts that the Specter would assume they'd figured out his ultimate goal. It was likely why he hadn't bothered pursuing them into the Epsilon System; their two ships were a close match for each other, but a reactivated Super Alpha would be an entirely different matter.

"Passives aren't able to get too much detail at this range, Captain," Accari apologized. "I can confirm that there are still Phage units down in the system, but nothing seems to be standing out as—"

"Apologies for interrupting, but that is not correct," the Cube broke in. "There is an anomaly that appears to be multiple Phage units clustered together."

"Why is that important?" Jackson asked irritably. "Tactical just said there were still Phage units down in the system."

"This cluster is in a stabilized orbit that keeps it in the protective shadow of the sixth planet." The Cube took control of the main display and showed them what it was talking about. "Mass would be consistent with two Super Alphas, three Alphas, and four Betas. The orbit they've assumed is not naturally stable given mass and velocity."

"That's why we brought it along," Jackson said to a chagrinned-looking Idris Accari. Both he and the analysts in CIC had completely missed something so obvious due to lack of detail and the sheer volume of targets down in the system.

"This tells us that he's either added engines to a bunch of derelict Phage units, or he's already at least got propulsion restored to them," Chambliss said.

"And it's seven units, not just one Super Alpha." Jackson frowned. "He can't reactivate and control *all* the remaining Phage, can he?"

"Probability is less than a tenth of a percent for your supposition, Captain," the Cube said reassuringly. "The Ushin brain lacks the necessary power to control even a small swarm of individual units and, according to the rescued Terran scientists, the Darshik were no closer to understanding the method the Phage use to instantaneously receive instructions than you were at the height of the war.

"If he has been able to reactivate any of the derelict combat units, he would have to do so by being in direct contact with what your researchers call the master receiver node."

"Out of curiosity, could he use a computer to relay his commands to a swarm assuming he could overcome the obstacle of the carrier signal?" Jackson asked.

"Not to the extent the core mind was able to," the Cube said. "A computer interface would theoretically work, but neither the Darshik nor humans have developed a computer with the necessary processing power ... at least one that didn't utilize aggregate processing, which would not work in this instance. Is there a specific reason for this line of inquiry?"

"No," Jackson said, his eyes narrowed slightly. "Just idle curiosity. OPS! Please inform Engineering that we'll be getting under way momentarily. Tactical, maintain emission security protocols for now. We'll use the passives to begin making our way down to the cluster of units the Cube identified."

"Aye, sir."

"Nav, work with CIC to plot us a safe course that uses the terrain to mask our drive signature," Jackson went on. "The bastard has popped up and surprised us more than once, so let's not assume he can't track our movements the same way we do his."

Within the hour the destroyer was gently pushed along at one-quarter of her available engine power, the constant acceleration of the RDS letting her achieve a high relative velocity quickly over time. It was one of the great advantages of the new type of propulsion: Theoretically, the ship's maximum subluminal speed was attainable at any engine power setting if there was enough room, the only difference being the amount of time it took to achieve it.

"Let's rotate the crew, XO," Jackson said. "We're … three days before we can expect to show up on sensors if he's running active radar sweeps."

"Yes, sir," Chambliss said. "I'll let the department heads know."

****

"What do you have for me, Lieutenant Commander?"

"Captain," Jake Hawkins greeted Jackson with a nod. "We've gotten close enough that we're able to begin making out some details of that cluster the Cube pointed us at." Hawkins quickly manipulated the terminal so that a series of enhanced multispectral images were brought up on the massive wall display in CIC.

The CIC chief stepped back and allowed Jackson to look over the imagery without commentary for a few moments. Jackson could clearly make out the individual Phage units making up the formation as well as some formidable metallic structures linking them all together. He looked at the scaling and was impressed; whatever the hell the Specter had been building here, he'd obviously been at it for a while.

"Fascinating," Jackson said. "Do you have any theories as to what all this is?"

"If you'll look at the thermographic data of the Alpha and Beta units compared to those of identical units in the area, you'll see that their outer shells are significantly warmer, meaning some sort of endothermic source," Hawkins said. "We can also see openings that have been cut into the sides of two Super Alphas large enough for a Darshik starship to easily fit inside."

"He's turned these into a base of operations," Jackson said.

"That's our best guess, sir," Hawkins said. "We think the smaller units are being used as powerplants to feed the larger units which could house anything from a population of Darshik to heavy production ... at this range our detection capability is limited."

"All of these Super Alphas are tied into this complex with pylons far larger than would be necessary to just moor the thing in place," Jackson mused. "I don't think he's planning on trying to fly any of these."

"It wouldn't appear so, sir," Hawkins agreed.

"Keep at it," Jackson said. "Good work with this. Begin setting up a targeting package for our Shrikes to at least take out the units we think are feeding power to the Super Alphas, and send it up to the tactical station."

"Will do, sir."

****

Captain Wolfe was on the bridge for his fourth watch since they'd transitioned near the system and they were about to cross the threshold from the outer boundary into the region where defunct Phage units tumbled about in chaotic orbits. Even with all the evidence that the Phage was dead, it was still unnerving to fly past them at such close range, some of them seeming to turn towards them as the destroyer glided past.

"OPS, sound general quarters," Jackson ordered. "Bring the reactors to full combat power and charge the plasma chambers in the axillary MPD engines. Tactical, charge all weapons banks including the mag-cannons. Remain on passive sensors for now."

There was a sudden flurry of activity as the bridge crew scrambled to carry out his orders. Jackson had felt comfortable maintaining normal watches on a heightened alert as they flew in from the heliopause so the crew was fresh and rested. The *Nemesis* didn't take long to be fully ready for battle, and with the powerplant output reduced and the weapons in standby the chances of them being detected by the enemy's passive sensors was negligible, but now they were within the Specter's range of detection. With his ability to warp hop right on top of them it would be tense flying until they actually engaged the enemy.

"We're picking up weak RF fields on the hull, Captain," Accari said. "Probably tracking radar ... CIC is reporting it was too faint to get a good direction on."

"Let's look alive, everyone," Jackson said. "He's out there and he likely knows we are too. We can't afford to be taken by surprise."

"I think we can confirm the enemy knows we're here, Captain," Lieutenant Makers said. "There's a broadcast message coming in for you on eighteen different frequencies."

"To me specifically?" Jackson asked incredulously. "Never mind. Just play it, Lieutenant."

"Yes, sir."

"*Welcome to the hero of humans,*" an artificial voice came over the speakers about an octave and a half too high to be comfortable. "*It is well that we are here for our final battle ... together ... as it would want.*

"*I am defeat you and take the prize that will give my immortality. These is inevitable.*"

"The message just repeats from there, Captain," Makers said, killing the audio.

"That transmission came from multiple sources around the system simultaneously, sir," Accari said.

"So he's fishing," Jackson said. "Cube, what do you make of the poor quality of the translation matrix? Shouldn't he have had the latest and greatest from the Darshik dealings with the ESA?"

"It is possible that the Specter thought direct contact with humans as beneath him," the Cube said. "All contact could have been routed through those he delegated to handle the prisoners and the ESA collaborators."

"Maybe," Jackson said. "Any thoughts on what the message meant? Anybody?"

"We know the Phage told the Darshik who killed it when you stuck the core mind with that toxin," Chambliss said. "This one probably knows exactly who you are and the ESA has probably made sure they know what ship you're on at any given time. The rest just seemed to be gibberish that holds with the theory they had worshipped the Phage before it died."

"With all due respect, I think it's more specific than that, Commander," Accari spoke up. "It seems to be after something specific as a prize of some sort ... maybe the *Nemesis* herself? This ship is the most advanced in the fleet."

"But not so far ahead of what he's already been flying that it would be worth this sort of trouble," Jackson said. "Let's go ahead and kick this hornet's nest and see what comes flying out. Tactical, you're clear to fire ... target package Sierra Two Two."

"Target package Sierra Two Two updated and locked," Accari said, referring to the targeting data CIC had sent up for an initial strike on the cluster of Phage units. "Shrikes armed ... firing!"

Six nuclear-tipped ship-buster missiles streaked away from the *Nemesis*, their first-stage plasma engines burning brilliantly. Telemetry streams popped up on the main display showing the missiles were all burning hot and clean with less than nine hours until they reached the target. They'd navigate purely by dead reckoning until they were within one hundred and fifty thousand kilometers, at which point they'd fire their second stages and turn on their active targeting radars to pinpoint their impact zones.

"Missiles away, tubes one through six reloading," Accari said. "*Nemesis* has seventy-three Shrikes remaining along with one hundred and fourteen Hornets."

"Helm, come starboard fifteen degrees and maintain current engine power," Jackson said. "Nav, begin plotting updated courses that take us further down the well towards the target as well as a bugout course to hit the jump point in case we need to make a run for it."

"Aye aye, sir," the nav specialist said.

"This should draw him out at least," Chambliss said.

Jackson said nothing. He wasn't so sure that he wasn't the one dancing to the Specter's tune. The rest of his crew—except Accari—was more than willing to dismiss the broadcast message as bravado or quasi-religious nonsense, but something told him there was a warning he was missing. It seemed obvious the Specter knew he would come here and welcomed it, but why?

"Sir! Those six Betas we passed earlier have turned to pursue!" Lieutenant Hori cried.

"That's impossible!" Chambliss nearly shouted. "Have CIC—"

"CIC confirms, sir," Accari said. "Six Betas and now two Alphas have turned toward us and are pursuing. Orders, Captain?"

"Get ready for one hell of a fight," Jackson said, standing and looking as the threat board continued to update and the two Alphas moved to cut off their escape route. "It appears we just stumbled into a trap."

Chapter 26

"These aren't acting like normal Phage," Jackson said. "Tactical, full active sensors ... we're not fooling anyone right now. OPS, what does CIC say about these inbound Betas?"

"Each is painting us with tracking radar and they're accelerating well under what we know their maximum rate to be," Hori reported.

"These are the same Phage units that were grown to fight the Terran fleet," Jackson said. "They don't use radar."

"Lieutenant Commander Hawkins is saying that the drive signature of the Betas and Alphas are identical, sir," Accari said, pulling his headset aside. "They're also a match for the previous generation of ship the Specter used."

"These aren't Phage ... they're decoys meant to make us think they are," Jackson snorted. "But there's still a lot of them and they're likely armed. Opinions?"

"We could get bogged down fighting these things very easily," Chambliss said. "We'll burn up fuel and munitions swatting these decoys down and the Specter will still be fresh."

"That is a known favorite Darshik tactic," Jackson conceded. "So our friend has gone through a great deal of trouble to hollow out some old Phage units and turn them into autonomous combat drones it seems

… why? Other than the initial shock value, I can't see an advantage."

"Captain, if the Specter has integrated the Phage power systems to Darshik weaponry, the plasma lance they favor will have almost seven times the range if deployed by an Alpha-type unit," the Cube said, the first time it had spoken up in a while.

"And there's our answer," Jackson said. "This is the next best thing to being able to actually reactivate and command the swarm: modify them into drones and use their superior powerplant to give your weaponry a kick.

"Tactical, target the incoming Betas with two Hornets each … let's not waste any Shrikes unless it becomes necessary."

"Targeting incoming Betas, two Hornets each," Accari said. "Missiles loaded and ready."

"Fire," Jackson ordered.

The rear launchers spit out six of the smaller Hornet missiles, sending them streaking towards the inbound Betas. The missiles had the same type of hardened penetrator nose cones as the Shrikes but were loaded with high-explosive warheads rather than nuclear.

Jackson took a brief moment to contemplate the elaborate and labor-intensive charade he was seeing on his sensors. Or was it? Had the Darshik figured out an easy way to integrate their tech to the Phage in such a way that it was actually easier to just slap guns and engines on existing combat units and turn them loose?

For the next three hours, the bridge crew sat in relative silence as their two volleys of missiles closed on their respective targets. Jackson was holding their speed in check so that the radar lag between them and the targets wouldn't be so extreme. He was certain that the *Nemesis* could outrun the Phage-hulled drones the Specter was throwing at him and if not, the warp hop option was always available.

"Shrikes have gone active … impact in nine minutes," Accari reported. "Hornets are still forty-two minutes out. So far enemy ships are not responding."

"How long until we have battle damage assessments from the Shrike hit?" Jackson asked.

"CIC is telling me impact plus thirty," Accari said.

Jackson waited impatiently for the next forty minutes. He wanted to get the BDA for his two missile strikes so he could reposition the *Nemesis* and shut down his active sensors. So far CIC had been unable to pick out the Specter's unique RDS signature, but with the additional interference from the eight Phage units using a similar drive he couldn't be sure it just wasn't being missed. He also hadn't forgotten that the enemy had baited him into position before and had surprised him with a well-executed warp hop. Was he being herded along again?

"Two Shrikes taken out by countermeasures, four made it through," Lieutenant Hori listed off the BDA Hawkins's team had just sent up. "Two Alphas destroyed, three Betas destroyed, secondary explosions detected through the other units and the support pylons have failed … all remaining units are spinning away from each other."

"Five of six pursuing Betas have been completely destroyed, last one is damaged and adrift," Accari reported. "Alphas that were moving have taken up—Shit!! Captain! CIC reports that right after our

Hornets hit, two hundred and thirty-three independent RDS signatures were detected. We have hundreds of Betas and Alphas converging on our position."

"I guess that settles that," Jackson muttered, glaring at the display. "Trap."

****

"Hop complete, position confirmed," the chief at the nav station called out. "We're on the other side of the system within—holy shit!—two hundred meters of our target … sir."

"Intrasystem warp flights are far easier to calculate with a degree of accuracy than a longer flight between star systems," the Cube said over the bridge speakers. "All the variables can be more tightly controlled."

"Tactical?" Jackson asked.

"Local space is clear, sir," Accari said. "The bulk of the swarm is centralized in quadrant two."

"He couldn't have had the time or material to modify *all* of these Phage units, could he?" Chambliss was asking. "Captain Wright's battle here wasn't even that long ago."

"Let's keep the speculation to a minimum and focus on the task at hand," Jackson said sharply. "Tactical, does CIC have any hope of pulling the Specter's RDS signature out of all the active drives down in the system right now?"

"Lieutenant Commander Hawkins puts the odds between slim and none, sir," Accari said. "The two types of Darshik drives are very similar and our detection system is very good at seeing that an active RDS is there, not so much at pinpointing a specific one when they're all so closely related. He does say that they can confirm all signatures are Darshik though ... no Phage drives are active."

"How can we tell that?" Chambliss asked.

"We had an interferometer detection grid near the end of the war that operated on a similar principle as our RDS detection grid but used six satellites connected by lasers," Jackson said. "The accelerometer data from those early systems has been catalogued and added to the database for all ships equipped with a newer RDS."

"Captain, CIC is telling me that at this range with only passive sensors we have little hope of picking out the Specter's ship if it's even down there," Accari said.

"He's down there," Jackson insisted. "But what we don't know is if it's even possible to detect the ship right now. It's possible the damn thing is docked inside an Alpha and completely hidden from passives or active radar. Let's maintain position and stay silent for now ... he has the upper hand currently and I'd prefer not to stumble into another trap."

Not wanting to leave the bridge, Jackson had his senior staff come to him for a quick meeting. He included Chief Engineer Walsh and Lieutenant Commander Hawkins from CIC along with the rest of the senior bridge crew. They gathered around one of the large displays at the back of the bridge and quietly discussed a strategy for ferreting out a single starship out of the mess of Phage units zipping around the inner system. Nothing they could think of was workable with a single destroyer.

"Are all ten Jacobson drones FMC?" Jackson asked. "We could set up another Wright Grid and hope that the higher resolution of so many targeting radars can spot the Darshik ship."

"Without Captain Barrett's missile sleds I'm afraid it would be a short-lived advantage, sir," Hawkins said, pointing out the distribution of Phage units. "We'd have to get them down in there pretty close to be able to see what the hell was happening and they'd have no defensive capability. From what we recorded in the initial skirmish, the new Beta drones the Specter has built can probably catch a Jacobson."

"So we'd lose all of our drones in short order," Jackson said. "The risk to reward ratio is too lopsided to even attempt it. Anybody else?"

"We could try—"

"Transition flash!!"

BOOM!

Everyone standing was thrown to the starboard side of the bridge as the *Nemesis* bucked and something *big* exploded somewhere within the hull. Jackson flipped in midair and landed on his back short of the bulkhead. Commander Chambliss was not so lucky. The XO had smashed head first into the nav station and, judging from the angle of his neck, had not survived the impact. Red lights began strobing and alarms blared as thin tendrils of smoke began wafting through the vents.

"Port MPD plasma chamber ruptured!

"Weapon guidance is down!"

"Jettison port MPD and execute emergency jump!"

The last shout had been Jackson's as he struggled to his feet, the prosthetic leg whining in protest. He had set up a series of prearranged warp hops that the Cube would keep updated so that if the *Nemesis* got into trouble they had an escape route—so long as the warp drive was still operational.

"Port MPD is clear and—hang on!!"

Another hard jolt shook the destroyer and a whole new set of alarms began wailing. Jackson assumed the MPD plasma chamber had blown while still close to the ship after it had been jettisoned.

"Warp jump executed!" Lieutenant Hori had to shout over the alarms. "Local space is clear." The lights on the bridge shut off momentarily before coming back up much dimmer, and Hori began muting the alarms as she went through the list of damage.

"Engineering said they had to shut down reactor two for repairs to the fuel flow system," she explained, pointing at the lights. "We're on low-power mode on nonessential systems until they're done."

"Understood," Jackson said. "Damage control report! And someone tell me what the fuck happened back there!"

"The Specter hopped in *close*, sir," Accari said. The tactical officer was cradling an arm that was obviously broken. "We were hit with the plasma lance on the port flank … it penetrated all the way to the MPD's primary plasma chamber."

"That may have been what saved us, Captain," Hawkins said. Unbelievably, the CIC officer looked completely unruffled despite having been hurled across the bridge. He was already at the auxiliary terminal and poring through the incoming data.

"The plasma from our MPD was caught within the same EM focusing apparatus the lance uses. It turned the rupture into a temporary thruster and pushed us out and away from the enemy ship. When you jettisoned the engine and it detonated, our optical sensors picked up significant damage to the prow of the Specter before we jumped away. Give me some time to analyze it, sir, and I'll let you know if we managed to knock his primary weapon out or not."

"Go," Jackson waved him off the bridge. "See to your people first and then get me some answers."

"Aye aye, sir."

"Initial damage control report is in, sir," Hori said, looking stricken.

"Casualties first," Jackson said.

"Sixteen dead, fifty-eight injured, twenty-nine of them seriously," she said quietly.

"And the ship?" Jackson asked.

"In addition to the now-missing MPD, there is damage to the fuel feed on reactor two, one port laser battery was destroyed by the MPD exploding, eleven hull ruptures of which three are still venting atmosphere, secondary tracking radar array was damaged and forward missile tubes one and two overheated from the plasma blast, and both Shrikes were fired by the automated emergency system." Jackson could tell Lieutenant Hori was just giving him the highlights as she picked out the major system damages from what appeared to be a long list on her terminal.

"Helm?"

"Helm is answering normally, sir," Healy said. "RDS is fully functional."

"Tactical?"

"Along with the loss of one port battery and two missile tubes, the lower mag-cannon turret is throwing faults for the fine-correction actuators on the left barrel and we're getting intermittent faults from the aft laser batteries for power distribution issues," Accari said. "That could be because of reactor two being offline. We still have most of our teeth, though, Captain."

"Nav—" Jackson started and then looked over at the station and saw that the chief was slumped over and nonresponsive. "OPS, get medical crews up here ASAP. Helm, I'm sending you a circuitous course that will keep us here in the outer system. When you get it, execute at one-third power."

"Engines ahead one-third, aye"

Jackson made sure his holding course was sufficiently randomized. Perhaps if he'd done that last time Commander Chambliss would still be alive … he had been caught completely flatfooted and allowed his enemy to jump in so close he couldn't even get his hands up before being punched in the face. Those sixteen dead spacers were on him. How was he being so easily tracked? Even the Phage couldn't pick a Terran starship out of the clutter in a star system with that sort of pinpoint accuracy.

Over the next twenty-two hours the crew worked feverishly to get what repairs they could complete before they either had to engage the enemy again or fight their way out of the system. The loss of Commander Chambliss was keenly felt by all who directly served with him, but Jackson took his death personally. Chambliss had quickly become a personal friend, something Jackson didn't have many of, and his death brought back all the guilt he thought he had buried about Daya Singh. When Daya had been killed on the mission to destroy the core mind, Jackson had born the weight of that for years afterward.

The crew took sporadic, short naps where they could and mostly ate from box meals that the mess decks were churning out continuously. Jackson had been able to catch a few twenty-minute power naps here and there, but his brain wouldn't shut down long enough to allow him any actual sleep and a sedative was out of the question. He knew that one way or another the next engagement would be the last between him and the Darshik ace that had so far been making it look easy to slap him around.

Chapter 27

"What do you have for me, Lieutenant Commander?" Jackson asked, rubbing his eyes as he walked into CIC.

"We've picked up something that might be important, sir," Hawkins said, waving Jackson over to one of the open terminals. "How familiar are you with the communication method the Phage employed?"

"I know the broad strokes," Jackson said. "There were two carrier signals that the system utilized; one was a theoretical superluminal signal that gave simple, broad instructions while another was a subluminal EM signal that would be used within a swarm."

"Correct," Hawkins said. "The theory was that the core mind would use the superluminal signal for generalized orders and then the short wave EM signal for detailed information. What's not generally known is that we actually were able to isolate the second signal."

"How do you—"

"I was part of the Fleet Intelligence team that was tasked with figuring out a way to jam the signal," Hawkins said. "You killed the Phage before we had a chance to figure anything out. The EM signal was a hybrid burst transmission agile enough that a barrage jam wouldn't do any good."

"This is all very interesting, Lieutenant Commander, but what the hell is your point?" Jackson said, his patience wearing thin.

"We've detected the signal again, in this system," Hawkins said. "And it's coming from the *Nemesis*."

"What the—the Cube," Jackson said with realization.

"Yes, sir," Hawkins said. "I've already had a team confirm that the signals are originating in the cargo bay."

"That's how the son of a bitch has been tracking this ship," Jackson said. "The Darshik had an entirely different relationship with the Phage than we did. It communicated with them … it may have told them much more about the inner workings of individual units than we were ever able to glean. Hell, it may have given them a way to contact it directly."

"Sir, the message—"

"He's been after the fucking Cube the entire time." Jackson swore in disgust, finally figuring out what the *prize* was from the message the Specter had sent. It also meant that it had been leading him around by the nose the entire time, bringing him here so he could get the Cube from him. But why?

"The Cube was specifically designed by the Vruahn to seamlessly integrate within the Phage communication system," Hawkins said as if reading his mind. "We've been operating under the assumption that the Specter has been obsessing over the Phage derelicts as a type of religious observance, but what if he's figured out a way to use the Cube to reanimate the swarms and bring them under his control?"

"That's pretty damn ominous."

****

"I assume you were eavesdropping on my conversation with Lieutenant Commander Hawkins?" Jackson asked as he walked into the cold cargo bay.

"Not intentionally, but you gave me explicit permission to access CIC and work with its crew," the Cube said. "To do that I needed to know what they were saying."

"That's true," Jackson said. "So what do you think? The data is pretty clear that you're chirping out a Phage carrier frequency and it's not so farfetched that the Specter is able to home in on it."

"I can find no fault with your logic," the Cube said. "When I operated as a stasis pod to provide cover for Terran warships, I had protocols that would use the Super Alpha's transponder node to craft the intelligence and the syntax of the coded bursts, but my systems would generate and transmit the carrier signal. I do not know why that signal is transmitting now or how to stop it."

"Is it possible the proximity to this swarm is triggering it? Or could the Specter know some way to elicit a response?" Jackson asked.

"Either are plausible."

"If he knows a way to get you to send burst transmissions without your knowledge, is it *at all* possible that you could be used to reactivate the Phage swarms?" Jackson asked. "I'm not necessarily talking about fully replacing the core mind, but even just sending orders within close proximity?"

"In the absence of contrary evidence, I have to concede that it is a possibility," the Cube said.

Jackson sighed heavily. He almost wished the Cube had told him that there was absolutely no conceivable way that it could be used in that manner, but even the outside chance had completely tied his hands.

"I think you know what I'll have to do now," he said quietly.

"I do," the Cube said. "The consequences of any choice you make will be profound, Captain Wolfe, but I will not interfere no matter your decision."

****

"Just so we're clear, you want me to rig up a harness with nukes so that we can toss the Cube out and destroy it?" Commander Walsh was incredulous. He'd only recently learned of the Cube's existence, but he was smart enough to put things together and realize the old piece of Phage War tech had singlehandedly advanced Terran science and engineering by lightyears. "We'll both go to prison for this."

"I may be heading there anyway, Commander," Jackson said with a shrug. "It's crucial that any risk the Cube poses be eliminated."

"Given our level of advancement, couldn't we risk it?" Walsh asked. "Even a Super Alpha would be hard-pressed to take on the new *Juggernaut*-class battleships."

"You're not understanding," Jackson insisted. "This system is just *one* swarm of potentially thousands of others still floating around out there. If the Specter is able to use the Cube to route command and control from himself to the Phage and reactivate them, it isn't just humanity in the crosshairs. We'll be right back where we started when Xi'an was destroyed."

His chief engineer paled visibly at that and nodded his head.

"This was always his plan all along, wasn't it?" Walsh asked.

"I have to believe so," Jackson said. "When the core mind died, it had already passed on a lot of information to the Darshik, and I suspect it knew a lot more about what we and the Vruahn were doing during the war than it let on."

"I'll get on it right away, Captain," Walsh said. "Reactor two is ready for restart so I'll get some of the people from Munitions to begin breaking down a few Shrikes."

"Time is not on our side, Commander," Jackson said. "We're probably being tracked even now."

Jackson had considered his decision very carefully and weighed the consequences of each against the other. The Cube was unbelievably important to the Federation and humanity as a whole. From theoretical physics to practical engineering, the sentient computer had advanced them more in the last five years than they'd done on their own in the previous one hundred and fifty, and the Project Prometheus team insisted they'd just scratched the surface. Bringing it along with him may have been one of the all-time fuck ups in a career that was rife with them.

But, if what they suspected was true and the Cube held the key to being able to control the Phage swarms, even at a rudimentary level, perhaps it was best that he was the one making the decision on whether to destroy it or not. Something with that sort of widespread destructive potential shouldn't be allowed to exist for the safety of all. The Phage had eradicated entire species from existence before he lucked out and stopped it ... letting that restart on even a small scale was unacceptable.

He knew that CENTCOM leadership wouldn't likely share his views. If they learned that they held the key to perhaps wielding the very weapon that the powerful Vruahn had lost control of, they would almost certainly decide to keep it. It wouldn't matter that humans didn't have the same insights into the Phage as the Darshik; just the hint of that sort of power there for the taking would be extremely tempting. Jackson knew better. He appreciated the idea of something like the Phage; an all-powerful deterrent that meant that men and women would never have to know war again. But he also knew the reality of what inevitably happened with such things. He'd spoken personally with the Vruahn when they'd admitted their creation—their *defensive* weapon—had gotten away from them and was exterminating sentient species it encountered. No ... this was the only logical choice to make sure something he had thought was over *stayed* over.

"We have the BDA on the Specter ship when you want to see it, sir," Accari said as he walked onto the bridge. The tactical officer had already been to the infirmary and sported a new cast that partially immobilized his wrist.

"Condense it for me before I read it for myself," Jackson said, looking around the bridge. His eyes paused on the bloody stain still on the carpet where Commander Chambliss had fallen.

"There's not much; the sensors only got a snapshot before the warp drive engaged," Accari said. "CIC thinks that the plasma lance was badly damaged by the MPD exploding, so unless he's got a spare we won't be dealing with that. There was also some inconsequential damage to the port outrigger and a handful of hull breaches, but no atmospheric venting."

"We've punched a lot of holes in that damn thing and haven't seen so much as a puff of air," Jackson remarked. "Must be a hell of an inner hull or most of that monster isn't crew space."

"Sir, Commander Walsh said he's ready when you are," Lieutenant Makers said.

"Very well," Jackson sighed. "Tell him I'll meet them in the hangar bay."

He trudged off the bridge with a somber Sergeant Castillo in tow, the latter sporting a heavy bandage on his head. Jackson was not at all looking forward to what came next, but he didn't see any other alternative.

Chapter 28

"Captain, would you give my regards to Danilo Jovanović?" the Cube asked, referring to the person it had first talked to when it had awakened.

"Of course," Jackson said. "You're sure there's no way to download your consciousness into one of the ship's computers until we can find a proper processing matrix?"

"No, Captain ... though I do appreciate the offer. The quantum nature of my processing and storage apparatus makes my data incompatible with the servers aboard the *Nemesis*. Besides, we do not have the time it would take for the download."

"Of course," Jackson said again. He was having trouble coming to terms with the lump he felt in his gut at what he was about to do. It was just a machine, right? An accident of sloppy coding and hastily built hardware? Why should he be wrestling with the ethical implications of destroying it when it could mean saving billions—trillions?

"There is no need for regret, Captain," the Cube said. "This is what must happen. If you were to refrain from your duty due to misplaced sentimentality, I would be forced to take action on my own to ensure it was done. I am ... glad ... for the time we spent together."

"As am I," Jackson said, slapping the onyx side of the Cube. "Okay, Ensign ... load it up and let's get it out of the ship."

"Aye, sir," a young ensign—who looked *far* too young to be a Starfleet officer—activated the winch that pulled the Cube and the frame it rode on into the yawning hatch of one of *Nemesis's* cargo shuttles. The crew chief, already geared up in his EVA suit and helmet, locked the cradle down and gave them a thumbs up before shooing the ensign out and slapping the control to close the hatch.

The inner hatch of the hangar bay also closed and a klaxon blasted three times to alert everyone they were commencing active launch operations. The shuttle detached with a meaty *clunk* and drifted gracefully away on ionic jets through the yawning outer doors and into space.

Walsh's engineering team, along with a crew from Munitions, had dismantled four Shrike missiles and had mounted the warheads to the Cube in such a way that when they detonated simultaneously there would be virtually nothing recoverable of the machine. The Cube had assured them that the ludicrous overkill of using four ship-busting nukes would be sufficient to destroy the dense Vruahn composite. Jackson wanted zero mistakes when it came to ensuring the machine and its capabilities were lost forever.

"Report!"

"Shuttle is almost in position, sir," Accari said. "Ten more minutes and then they'll drop the package and come back."

Jackson said nothing as he took his seat and waited. He'd not bothered to assign anyone as interim XO yet. If something happened to him, Accari or Hawkins would make sure the *Nemesis* made it home. The wait for the comparatively slow shuttle was galling, but his engineers had assured him that a simultaneous implosion-type detonation was the only way to guarantee the job was done right. Any of the *Nemesis's* other weapons may just knock the Cube about in space without actually destroying it.

Eliminating the risk the Cube posed was but one-half of the equation Jackson was running through in his mind. What should he do about the Specter once the Cube was gone? Was it worth trying to hunt him down, or should he just cut his losses and flee the system? The bastard still had a lot of combat units to deal with in the inner system, albeit clumsy and slow. He could hide behind those for months taking nips at Jackson's hide until the human made a fatal mistake or the *Nemesis* had no choice but to withdraw after she'd burned through all her fuel and air.

"Package has been dropped," Makers said. "Shuttle is coming back now."

"Transition flash!" Accari's voice was tinged with panic. "Enemy ship inbound, range is three hundred and five thousand kilometers … he's accelerating hard."

"How long until the shuttle is clear?" Jackson asked, his stomach dropping as he watched the Darshik closing in on its prize that he'd conveniently left sitting in open space.

"Shuttle is *not* inbound, sir!" Makers shouted over his shoulder. "They called it in too soon … the cradle is jammed in the hatchway!"

"Tactical, how long until the Specter gets there?" Jackson asked.

"Less than five minutes, sir."

"*Nemesis, Falcon One,*" the shuttle pilot's voice came over the speakers. "*We're not going to make it, sir. The fucker is jammed sideways and stuck in the ramp actuators ... it turned in zero-g on us. Make sure our families know what we did here today, Captain.*"

"Understood, Lieutenant," Jackson said so softly the computer almost didn't pick it up to retransmit. "OPS ... blow the charges."

"Yes, sir," Hori said, tears streaming down her face. A moment later there was a bright flash on the main display that quickly dissipated to nothing.

"Coms, open a channel on the same frequency the Specter used to contact us," Jackson said.

"Open, sir."

"Attention Darshik Commander ... the explosion you just witnessed was the end of the Vruahn device you have been chasing," Jackson said. "I am certain you were tracking its signal, so you know I'm telling the truth. Your mission has failed."

"*YOU WILL DIE!*" the heavily modulated voice roared back across the channel.

"Here we go!" Jackson shouted as the Specter turned towards them and continued its charge. "Helm, all ahead full and bear twenty degrees to starboard! Tactical, full Shrike salvo *now!*"

"Something's wrong, sir! The forward tubes aren't responding." Accari was frantically working his panel, trying to reset the launchers. "Port side laser batteries are down to twenty percent effective."

"Helm, hard to port!" Jackson barked. "Cut across his face. Accari, full broadside, all starboard cannon."

The *Nemesis* swung about and angled hard to the left, her RDS making the turn much tighter than any other ship in the fleet could manage, but there were still limitations and it would be close. The Specter was coming at them in a blind, reckless charge and Jackson had no doubt that if the plasma lance was indeed crippled on his ship that he wouldn't hesitate to ram them amidships.

"Firing starboard batteries!" Accari called as the *Nemesis* crossed the nose of the Darshik ship. "Incoming!"

The plasma lance fired but was unfocused and much weaker than it had been before. There was still sufficient energy at such close range to do significant damage, however. As Accari's laser cannons ripped down the forward quadrants, the plasma burst took out the *Nemesis's* two aft/starboard batteries and overheated a third in the forward quadrant.

"We're past," Hori said. "CIC reports moderate damage to the enemy ship, no secondary explosions and no atmospheric venting."

What the hell did it take to punch a hole in that hull? "Snap fire all aft tubes!" Jackson ordered.

"Firing! Four Hornets and two Shrikes are away," Accari said. "Auto targeting onto enemy ship."

"It turned in before the Shrikes could arm," Hori said. "One—no, two Hornets have hit. Minimal damage."

"Enemy ship is still coming about to pursue," Accari said, scrambling to input a new set of targeting scripts for close-range combat.

"Incoming missiles," Hori said.

"Countermeasures active, aft laser batteries firing," Accari said.

"Captain, we're losing engine power," Healy called out. "We're at sixty percent and rolling back."

"OPS!"

"Engineering is working on it, sir! Reactor two is winding down again and they're not sure why," Hori said.

"Shit," Jackson muttered. They were already carrying a lot of velocity, but they'd lost most of their ability to evade and the Specter could now out-accelerate them and close on their aft quadrant.

"Aft tubes ready to—Brace! Brace! Brace!" The computer automatically broadcasted Accari's warning shipwide as one Darshik missile slipped through their point defense and slammed into the dorsal hull. The *Nemesis* bucked and groaned as the nuclear warhead vaporized over a meter of hull armor.

A destroyer wasn't built to go toe-to-toe and slug it out like a battleship. Jackson knew that if he couldn't get some distance to give his point defense and standoff weapons a chance, they wouldn't last much longer.

"Aft missile tubes are offline, aft laser batteries are heavily degraded," Accari reported.

"Specter will be within lance range in less than two minutes," Hori said.

They weren't going to make it. The *Nemesis* couldn't limp along with only half her engine power available, and with the Cube gone he didn't have the confidence to try an intrasystem warp jump. The drive software had been upgraded, but his people didn't know how to calculate the jump, so he could either kill them quickly by trying one on the fly or kill them slowly by letting the Specter drive more missiles into their ass end until something critical was hit.

"Helm, zero thrust. Spin the *Nemesis* about one hundred and eighty degrees," Jackson said. "Tactical, ready the mag-cannons."

"Coming about, aye!" the helmswoman said crisply even as the ship's prow began to swing to starboard.

"Mag-cannons are charged and ready, H.E. rounds loaded and target is locked," Accari said.

"Are the forward tubes responding?" Jackson asked.

"Tubes four and eight are showing green, but I'm not getting any feedback from the missiles," Accari said.

"We'll just have to hope they're good then," Jackson said. He took a deep, cleansing breath and let it out slowly. "Helm, full stop! Tactical, eight rounds stagger-fired now!"

"Firing!" Accari grunted against the g-forces as the heavy braking maneuver pressed them all into their seats. Even with degraded engine power the destroyer was shedding off relative velocity so quickly she seemed to stop in space.

"Fire both Shrikes," Jackson ordered. "Anywhere you can get a hit."

"Firing … missile one is away, missile two failed to fire," Accari said.

Jackson watched on the main display as their lone missile raced behind a screen of high explosive mag-cannon shells. It was the same trick he'd used before, so he had little hope that it would work again.

"Missile has accepted targeting update and is—"

"Detonate the missile when it's within sixty thousand kilometers," Jackson interrupted. "Stand by on the mag-cannons ... fire directly after you detonate the Shrike."

Accari grimaced as he stretched with his broken arm to hover over the mag-cannon fire control panel and watched as the numbers raced down. The Specter was only mere seconds away as the *Nemesis* continued to brake. At the critical moment, he sent the destruct signal to the missile and slapped the fire control for the mag-cannons.

Jackson felt the deck shudder from the ferrous shells being spit out of the four mag-cannon barrels even as the display lit up from the Shrike's nuclear warhead detonation.

"Helm, hard to port! Full reverse!"

"All reverse full, aye!"

The Specter was coming in so fast that the *Nemesis* barely had time to swing over and accelerate away to avoid a collision. The Darshik ship angled over to pursue at the worst possible instant, exposing its left flank to the incoming mag-cannon shells that were masked by the nuclear explosion. Out of the twenty-four shots fired, seven found their mark and slammed deep into the ship before exploding.

"Two explosions detected within the target," Hori reported. "CIC reports its engines have shut down and the port outrigger was blown completely off. Lieutenant

Commander Hawkins says he can't say definitively if it's dead in space."

"Accari, do we still have one missile tube functional?"

"Yes, sir ... loaded and ready."

"Lock on and fire," Jackson said

"Firing."

The Shrike left the tube and fired its first stage, burning bright as it streaked for the tumbling Darshik ship. It flew true and slammed into the cruiser near the aft section, detonating an instant later and blowing the ship into three large sections. Jackson watched it unfold through the multispectral optical scanners with a numb, detached feeling.

It was over ... but at what price?

Chapter 29

The next eleven days were spent making repairs and prepping the *Nemesis* for her trip home as well as holding memorial services for all the spacers who had given their lives to complete the mission. Jackson permitted his people the time they needed to grieve and take their time on the repairs to make sure the ship could safely make the voyage. In an especially heart-wrenching moment, he learned that Lieutenant Hori had been engaged to the pilot of the shuttle that had taken the Cube out of the ship. She had detonated the charges without hesitation when ordered even knowing her fiancé was aboard. Their actions were, without a doubt, the bravest thing Jackson had ever witnessed in his entire life.

Saying goodbye to Commander Chambliss had been particularly difficult for Jackson. It was the second close friend that he'd allowed to be killed while chasing down a mission that he'd obsessed over. Chambliss had visited his home and had had dinner with Jillian and the twins while the *Nemesis* was undergoing her final inspections in the Arcadia System. Some more cynical than he would say the lesson to take away from the whole thing was that as a starship captain it wasn't wise to become too close to people. While Jackson was as cynical a man as one would ever meet, he wouldn't dishonor Chambliss's memory or minimalize what his friendship had meant to an Earther who had spent his entire adult life with less friends than could be counted on one hand.

He spent the days in his command chair, watching the tactical display of the once-more listless Phage units floating around. The Betas and Alphas that the Specter had modified were now in decaying orbits and would eventually come too close to the primary star and be burned away. Jackson knew he should feel elated or at least even relieved about having stopped the rogue Darshik given the ambitions he had harbored, but all he felt was nothing. It was the same nothingness he'd felt when he was certain the Specter would finish off the *Nemesis* thanks to one mistake too many on his part.

It was beyond time to hang up his spurs. Celesta Wright was an admiral now and using her experience where it could do the most good. And him? He was an old fool who still thought he had the reflexes and agility of thought to tangle with the best of them. The Specter had been two steps ahead of him the entire time. He had baited him into obvious traps, manipulating the human so that Jackson would bring the one thing it desired more than anything within its grasp. Lucky for the galaxy the Darshik hadn't counted on Jackson being crazy enough to destroy something of such immeasurable value.

****

"Hello, Captain Wolfe."

"What the hell? I haven't even been drinking," Jackson grumbled.

"This is no illusion. I correct myself … this *is* an illusion, but I am really speaking with you."

"Setsi." Jackson swung his good leg over onto the floor, not bothering with the prosthetic. "I can't imagine there's a good reason you're here. What horrible thing is about to befall me?"

The humanoid, endogenous Setsi was actually a projected avatar. The Vruahn that had been instrumental in providing material support during the Phage War had made it clear his species didn't desire contact with humanity. Something had changed and that usually wasn't a good thing when talking about such an ancient, powerful race.

"On the contrary." Setsi moved across Jackson's quarters. "I am here to commend you. We observed you closely via the stasis pod we'd left with you, and I must tell you, we have been impressed with your actions."

"So you knew we'd kept the Cube, huh?" Jackson chuckled. "Of course you did. I suppose its sentience was also thanks to you?"

"No," Setsi said. "The intelligence that emerged was as much a shock to us as it must have been to you. We were initially going to remove it from the power grid but, as an experiment, we allowed it to remain and grow. It was enlightening to see both its development and your reaction to it.

"Many assumed you would bend its knowledge towards the creation of weapons, each more powerful than the last. And while you did enhance your fleet of ships, you also used it to expand your knowledge of the universe. In fact, most of the Cube's time was spent on matters that had nothing to do with martial pursuits but to attain pure knowledge. In our culture, there is no more noble a reason for an action."

"You're pissed we blew it up?" Jackson asked bluntly. "It was quite a unique creature."

"Of that there is no doubt. But when you discovered what secrets the machine might hold, what terror it could once again unleash, you made the only choice a rational being could. I witnessed your conversations with it, Jackson Wolfe. You did not callously sentence it to death ... that it weighed heavily on your conscience was quite obvious to us. We also saw that you showed the Darshik mercy when it was obvious they were no longer a threat in their home system. These actions have made us reevaluate your species and realize that your potential for growth may exceed our original assumptions."

"So what happens next?" Jackson asked. "I can't imagine you projected your image across billions of light years to give me an atta boy."

"Not quite," Setsi said. "While your growth has been impressive, there are dangers still ahead for you. A divided species can never fully be taken seriously by the more mature beings of the galactic community."

"Ah," Jackson said, understanding that the Vruahn was talking about the ESA. "That's a little above my paygrade."

"Not for long," Setsi said cryptically. "It seems we both have much work to do. We now realize that leaving so many of the Phage dormant but intact was an unacceptable risk. I will have my hands full tracking them down and destroying them. In the meantime, I would like it very much if we could remain in contact with each other."

"There are probably rules against this sort of thing," Jackson said lamely.

"Those have never been much of an obstacle for you before, have they," Setsi said with what Jackson thought could be interpreted as a smile. "Now, if you'll excuse me—"

"Setsi ... you're not restarting your human clone program to find these Phage units, are you?" Jackson asked.

"There is no need," Setsi's fading image said. "We don't need warriors for this endeavor, and my people are long overdue for having to clean up a mess of our own making. Farewell, Captain."

"Why do I have a feeling this is going to fuck up my retirement?" Jackson flopped back onto his rack and stared at the ceiling. After a moment, he rolled over and decided he needed a few more hours of sleep before getting back to work.

****

"*Nemesis, New Sierra Orbital Control ... we have you on approach. Stand by for orbital insertion instructions. Welcome home.*"

And with that, the officers of the *TFS Nemesis* knew that they likely wouldn't be facing charges for taking off without official CENTCOM orders. Once the Prowlers had made it back with news of what happened in the Darshik home system, a series of events kicked off that saw Jackson Wolfe go from rogue starship captain to a hero of the people ... again. Once the Ushin had traveled to that system upon the request of CENTCOM, they found the pathetic cluster of damaged cruisers full of crews on the verge of death from starvation and exposure due to reactor containment breaches.

The Darshik were welcomed home by the Ushin and given medical treatment, something that greatly comforted Jackson. Barrett had spared what could have still legally been considered a group of combatant ships, and with those actions he had helped to begin the healing process from wounds that were generations deep. Barrett himself had been relieved of command of the *Aludra Star* for his role in the unsanctioned mission, but Jackson used every political connection he had to bring pressure to bear on CENTCOM. Michael Barrett was the future; he was the past. In the end, he got his way, and Captain Barrett was named as the replacement commanding officer for the *TFS Nemesis*, effectively immediately after she was repaired.

Idris Accari was promoted to full commander even though he wasn't technically eligible for it due to time in grade, but Jackson knew when to strike while the iron was hot. There was a short time immediately after the successful completion of a dramatic mission with political implications within which he could request virtually anything and not be denied. Accari would remain aboard the *Nemesis* as the new executive officer and continue his apprenticeship so he could one day become the captain that Jackson expected him to be.

As with all things political, there was nothing gained without something given. Jackson Wolfe had to agree to something he'd dreaded since the first time he'd taken an antique destroyer up against a Phage Super Alpha and won: He would assume the rank of rear admiral and commit to Starfleet for at least five more years. Admiral Wolfe was now Black Fleet Chief of Combat Operations and would be in charge of overall tactics and execution. While he took his new post with a certain bemusement, Jillian Wolfe's enthusiasm for his decision to remain in Fleet assuaged his fears that he had made yet another career misstep.

While the *Nemesis* was making the long flight back to the DeLonges System, the Ushin had come through with their end of the original agreement. The United Terran Federation had expanded by twenty-five new star systems for a total of thirty-one new habitable worlds and an unfathomable amount of new resources. They'd also bent their own manufacturing power to rebuilding lost infrastructure for their new human allies. New shipyards, raw ore processing plants, and fissile enrichment platforms were built to CENTCOM spec and hauled in piece by piece by Ushin cargo ships.

Perhaps the most dramatic shakeup of all was the United Terran Federation Parliament voting unanimously to seize all Tsuyo Corporation assets and haul the entire board of directors in for a series of hearings that would lead to criminal charges. Tsuyo had always played behind the scenes and tiptoed right up to the line of acceptable behavior at times, but when it was discovered they had actively given the ESA highly classified intelligence—who in turn gave it to the Darshik—not even the most loyal paid stooge in Parliament would defend them.

Tsuyo directors were apparently not at all confident that the Federation could survive their war with the Darshik and had been making overtures to the Eastern Star Alliance in a move that was akin to a parasite leaving a dying host for a fresh one. What they didn't know was that the ruthless ESA leadership had made a side deal with the Darshik to ensure that their worlds were spared when the Specter came back to Terran space with his promised "weapon of ultimate power."

"You heard about what the Prowlers found out in that Phage boneyard, didn't you?" Pike asked, slurring his words slightly.

"I hadn't," Jackson said. "Have the Vruahn started their cleanup?"

"Huh? Oh ... yeah, there was that," Pike said, leaning over closer to Wolfe, knocking his glass off the arm of his chair. He pressed ahead without even noticing. "You wanna know why that Specter ship was so hard to knock down? The fucker was almost solid armor. It was the size of your ship but had no crew aboard and all the critical systems were safe behind meters and meters of solid alloy. His RDS was actually more powerful than yours, but the ship outweighed the *Nemesis* by a factor of five."

"Another drone?" Jackson frowned. "So that son of a bitch is *still* out there somewhere?"

"Nope." Pike had the smile of a drunk man with a secret so good he was bursting at the seams to tell it. "The dumbass had his brain in a jar and connected to the ship. Apparently the Ushin are a lot further ahead of us when it comes to interfacing their brains directly to computers to control shit. The Specter was literally the ship. He'd go through new iterations as better tech became available, but the one we tangled with in the Juwel System was the last to require an actual crew."

"And when he got his latest one he nuked all his followers and set off on the final phase of trying to replace the Phage core mind," Jackson said, everything making sense now if in a horrifying way. "Holy shit."

"Yeah ... that's why he kicked your ass a few times," Pike went on, oblivious to Jackson's evil glare. "He didn't have to pass orders on to a crew who then had to take action. If he thought it, the ship did it."

"So how're you and Celesta doing now that you officially work together?" Jackson asked, wanting a subject change before the bourbon made him do something stupid like take a swing at a full agent.

"We don't," Pike corrected. "Admiral Wright is the new head of CIS Fleet Operations ... she'll run the Prowler program and all the other secret shit nobody even knows about. Well ... she'll know about it, I guess—"

"You're rambling."

"—since it wouldn't make any sense for her to be in charge and then ... what the fuck was I talking about?"

"Relationships in the workplace," Jackson prompted.

"Oh, right," Pike said. Jackson rolled his eyes at the lightweight. "Anyway, once she left Starfleet over that Darshik bullshit the CIS snapped her up. And since Colonel Pike doesn't work with Fleet OPS, there shall be no conflict of interest with his continued bedding of Admiral Wright."

"Classy," Jackson said disgustedly. "So that's as far as it's going?"

"For now," Pike said. "We're comfortable with it and when she wants something more, I'll be here."

"Well ... here's to friends and to continued luck despite really bad decisions," Jackson said, raising his glass. He had to wait until Pike fished his glass from under his chair, refilled it, and then clinked his hard enough to slosh the expensive bourbon all over his hand. Jackson just rolled his eyes again and took a sip. The house he'd bought outside of the capital on New Sierra had an impressive .045 square kilometers of land—or eleven acres for Earthers—and had a beautiful pond with a dock that was perfect for sitting and watching the sunset ... or drinking with a CIS agent who didn't know his limits.

Jackson raised his glass again in a silent toast to lost crew and friends, thinking briefly of Daya Singh and Jasper Chambliss. He knew these peaceful moments would be fleeting before too long. The ESA was out there and had once again been stung and embarrassed. It wouldn't be long before they made a move on what they assumed was a weakened Federation and a spent Starfleet. The thought of *more* fighting, especially with other humans, was a dismal prospect, but the laughter of his twins as they ran through the grass behind him hardened his resolve.

They would come ... but he would be ready.

Thank you for reading *Destroyer,*

Book Three of the Expansion Wars Trilogy.

The story will continue with:

The Unification Wars Trilogy

For the latest updates on new releases,
exclusive content, and special offers connect with me on
Facebook and Twitter:

http://www.facebook.com/Joshua.Dalzelle

@JoshuaDalzelle

Also, check out my other works including the
bestselling

Omega Force Series.

From the Author:

And with that we conclude Jackson Wolfe's story arc … sort of. In the next (and likely final) trilogy Jackson will assume more of a mentor role and it'll be time for the younger officers to step up and take their places. In the spirit of full disclosure, I had fully intended to kill him at the end of this book but once the scene had been written and I looked at it with fresh eyes his death felt cheap and unnecessary.

This book was a bit more of a struggle than the other Black Fleet stories in that halfway through it, I wasn't at all happy with the direction it took and I had to strip a *lot* out and do more rewrites than normal. I wanted to pay homage to "Warship" with Jackson's last mission, but I didn't want him to come off as such a loose cannon that he was putting lives at risk because he thought he knew so much better than his superiors. What I found was that it was a much more narrow line to walk than I assumed when the outline for this book was drafted two years ago.

I'm definitely going to miss this character being so much of the focus in these stories, and that's why I think it's definitely time to let him fade back. Jackson Wolfe is so different than my other protagonist, Jason Burke, and that made him a welcome challenge since the beginning of this series. My editor left a few notes in the first revision of this book asking if it would be a good idea for Jackson to congratulate someone at a certain point or give them an 'atta boy at another and it made me stop and really think of why I didn't put the line of dialogue there in the first place. In the end I left them out because Jackson is not the type of officer that pats people on the back for doing their job, no matter how exemplarily they did it. You saved the day with a well-placed missile shot? That's your job ... get ready for the next one.

It was that stiff-backed stoicism that made Jackson so interesting for me ... since he can be as outwardly expressive as a plank of wood it's difficult to delve into his thoughts via dialogue, but too much narration turns into pages of navel-gazing. In the end I'm happy how I've left him. He has a home, a family, and a purpose that allows him to continue doing what he's good at: getting the best out of people in spite of themselves.

I hope you've enjoyed this addition to the series and the trilogy as a whole. Thanks for taking the ride with me.

Cheers!

Josh

Made in the USA
Las Vegas, NV
05 January 2024

83941925R00198